Life Rewritten

andrea johnston

Cover design by Jada D'Lee of Jada D'Lee Designs
www.jadadleedesigns.com
Editing by Kristina Circelli of Red Road Editing
www.kristinacircelli.com/red-road-editing
Interior design by Stacey Blake of Champagne Formats
http://champagneformats.com

ISBN: 978-0-9966309-1-7
First Edition

Dedication

For anyone who believes in a
Happily Ever After
and for those that need help believing.

Chapter One

"I'M SORRY, WHAT?"

I had to have heard him wrong, right? There is no way this guy is serious. And yet, by the look on his face, I'm pretty sure he is.

This is the worst date ever.

"I *said* I would love to take you back to your house and pleasure your feet," he says with more than a hint of disdain.

Well, hell. I *had* heard him correctly. He said *pleasure* and *feet*. Together. On purpose. Oh, I'm going to pleasure my feet all right, by sticking my stiletto up his ass. This guy is nuts if he thinks I'm taking him back to my house so he can get his rocks off by messing with my feet. I get it; I am wearing some pretty hot shoes. I thought they were ridiculous at first, but my sister, Charlotte, insisted they were a must have for my new life. I still don't know why I need a new life, but I listened, and if I'm completely honest, I love them. Peep-toe, leopard-print, five-inch stilettos that make me feel like I can hold my own in this crazy world. They give me the power I need for moments like this.

"You know, Phillip, I don't think I'm really there."

I'm not likely to ever actually be there. Sadly for Phillip, I lack a poker face and imagine my eyes have fluttered a minimum of ten times while I purse my lips and inhale through my nose and out through my mouth.

Looking across the table, I am greeted with a furrowed brow and a look I can't quite put my finger on, but I know it isn't welcoming. Shit. I'd hoped to at least leave this date with a friend.

I should be putting together a reasonable and mature statement to put this expression-filled standstill to an end. I am, instead, plotting the demise of my best friend, Anna. Before this date I spoke to her on the phone and was privy to one of her rah-rah cheerleader speeches. *"Oh Victoria, this will be great. He's really good looking and by the way he's looking into the camera I bet he talks dirty!"* Anna is more of the "dirty cheerleader" as you can tell.

That cheerleader moment aside, both Anna and Charlotte are always there for me before one of these first dates. Each of them offers me support, motivation, and just enough straight talk to calm my nerves. While that *may* sound like a pep talk, it isn't. I don't need a pep talk, but considering that until thirteen months ago I hadn't dated in close to twenty years, I need something.

After my husband, Patrick, passed away three years ago, dating was not something I considered. Heck, my social calendar for the months after he passed away consisted of an exchange of thank yous with the pizza delivery boy. But dating? Not even close to something I contemplated. I was a newly single mom to a teenage boy simply trying to figure out how to just be me without being a we.

About six months after I said my goodbye to the man I loved and vowed to spend my life with I came across an envelope. I recognized the horrific and somewhat scary-looking penmanship immediately. It was a letter from Patrick. I stared at that envelope, not wanting to read its contents, for days. I carried it with me from room to room like some sort of security blanket. Well, a taunting security blanket. There were nights I would wake up and swear the damn thing was just staring at me. I know in reality envelopes don't stare but this was a staring envelope, trust me. Then, on a rainy and gloomy day, I swallowed my nervousness and fear and opened the taunting envelope. And there, in that same scary-looking penmanship, were the words and love giving me the nudge I needed to start living my life again.

As the weeks and then months went by, I began finding more and more of those same envelopes strategically placed throughout the house. Some of the contents were long letters full of memories and plans while others were simply reminders and random thoughts that would make me smile: *Don't forget you need to have someone clean the rain gutters at least twice a year. Why does that bird always dive bomb Gerard's head when he's trimming the rear hedges? Don't forget – U R 2 Legit 2 Quit.*

Through those letters, Patrick was guiding me to this next phase of my life. He managed to hide each one in just the right place for just the right moment. Of course, after the second envelope appeared Anna wanted to rip the house apart and find all of them. I refused. This was how he wanted me to find them and I would let him lead the way.

Just about a year after Patrick passed I found *the letter.* The letter I knew was coming but made me queasy thinking about. The letter that would be different than the others. It was the letter where my husband, my heart and soul, encouraged me to let go and move on. Through a series of perfect words he told me the day would come that I would be ready to date and maybe even fall in love again. I remember snorting in disbelief and horror – *fall in love?* Never one to mince words, he insisted that regardless of what I thought was appropriate or how much time had passed I was required to put myself out there. I *had* to take the leap. This was not a maybe situation. I knew he was right.

So here we are . . . I'm online dating. It's really awful. Maybe awful is too strong of a word. It's weird, it's stressful, and it's *hard*. Dating is almost like a really long job interview. Except instead of a power suit and a great up-do you're squeezed into some Spanx and trying not to order food that will stick to your teeth.

My best friend is single. My sister is single. I've heard horror story after horror story over the years about dating. But, it isn't until you're in the trenches, until you live it, that you really see the full picture. Don't get me wrong, I've met some great guys. I've also met some that are . . . we'll just say they can be interesting. My son, Justin, thinks interesting is good. I tried explaining that listening to a man ramble on and on about his eleven cats, their varying food preferences, and array of kitty playgrounds isn't interesting. In fact, it is a little frightening. He just laughed. I did not. I'm also not exaggerating. *Eleven.*

I suppose a savvier gal would consider that a little insight into what is out there. I am apparently clueless because after cat-boy was "Let's do it" guy. His real name is Chuck and he's from Texas. Now, I have been known to find an accent attractive. And Chuck's accent carried just enough drawl that it made me think of horseback riding at sunset. That was, until I realized no matter what question I posed, "Let's do it" was the answer. *"Hey Chuck, did you want more chips?"* *"Hey, let's do it." "If you'll excuse me I'm going to use the ladies room."* You guessed it, *"Let's do it."* No, let's not. I made it through that meal only because there was promise of cake - I was all about that.

Tonight's date with Phillip started out no different than the rest. Promising profile, funny in text messages, and normal(ish) on the phone. I say "ish" because in retrospect I should have questioned his "quirks." The first few times we talked I thought the long pauses were sweet, assuming they were because he was shy. By long pause I mean, I could have put the phone down, thrown a load of laundry in the washer, and made a cup of tea before he was on to the next sentence. Add to that his desire to talk ad nauseum about whether walking and running are good for one's feet, I should have run . . . literally.

Other than Anna's opinion that he may be "dirty," Charlotte was the one who encouraged me to accept the invitation for dinner. *She* was the one who insisted he was probably just nervous. I listened to her, but made sure I still had my escape plan in place. Anna calls it "the morning walk of no shame" because she's always pulling for a sleepover and says at forty we shouldn't have shame. Charlotte refuses to acknowledge there is any sort of plan to get out of a date because she truly believes every date is an opportunity for a new friend. I don't disagree. I am neither shameful nor do I disagree that each date is an opportunity to make a new friend. It just seems like, *maybe*, Phillip isn't friend material.

At this point, I just want to meet someone who isn't interested in a harem of cats or, in the case of this bozo, my feet. Feet. Am I that much of a prude? I'm not naive enough to think fetishes aren't out there, but come on, maybe that little tidbit should be listed under *Special Interests* section on the dating profile. Sure, my shoes are sexy and I did just get a pedicure but they are my feet and not exactly what I would consider my pleasure point. That little spot below my ear. Right before you hit the actual neck. You know what spot I'm talking about. *That* is my pleasure point. I would even go out on a limb to say that is most women's pleasure point, or at the very least *one of a woman's pleasure points.*

"Victoria? Did you hear me?" Cue the scratching record sound.

"I'm sorry, Phillip, what was that?"

"I *said* perhaps next time." Well this has escalated quickly. He's gone from a hint of disdain to flat-out annoyance. Just stay calm. Do not engage. Do not raise an eyebrow or blink excessively. This guy isn't worth it.

"You know, I'm kind of feeling a little off and maybe I should just call it a night. Dinner was lovely but I think I'll pass on the dessert." That was perfect. Easy escape in 3, 2. . .

"Well, that's too bad. I really felt we had a connection. No matter, I'll just ask the waiter to split the check and we can get out of here." Yep, he did. He just said we're going to split the check. Suddenly it's like sixth grade and Tommy Jackson invited me for ice cream and then balked at the idea of paying fifteen cents for a cone. That's fine by me as long as it gets me out of here and away from this guy. This is where the escape plan comes into play. On the advice of my amazing son I always carry just enough cash should this exact situation arise. Thankfully, I don't have to sit through the awkwardness of waiting for change and the valet was instructed to keep my car nearby. You know, just in case. In one fluid motion I stand, drop the cash on the table, say goodnight, and walk out without a look back.

I manage to make it out to the valet line with ease and without a scene. While I wait for my car to be brought around, I take a moment to really appreciate my surroundings. Abbott Falls, Washington - population 13,697 - is your typical small town nestled in the mountains of the Pacific Northwest. Abbott Falls is my idea of perfection - greenery and nature as far as you can see, minutes from amazing hiking among natural waterfalls and streams yet only forty-five minutes from the city. It has made my venture out into the dating world possible. I can live in my own private and simple world and dress myself up for a date in the city without a second thought.

I take the opportunity to glance over my shoulder toward the restaurant entrance and see that Phillip has already found my replacement. I know he's moved on when I take a quick peek at the young woman's shoes and I notice her perfectly pedicured toes. Good luck, doll. I let out a little giggle at the hilarity of this night as I catch out of the corner of my eye, a young couple who are really hitting it off. By hitting it off I mean either she's really bad at giving mouth to mouth or she's about to eat his face. Good for them. I'm ready for that. Well, not the face eating but the connection and intimacy.

I miss it. I miss a partner. I'm putting myself out there. I'm attempting and truthfully failing at online dating. Phillip and his *"special interest"* was officially one date too many in my thirteen-month journey into this somewhat crazy and obviously not for me world. I think it's time to call it a loss and hang up the keyboard. Something tells me that both Charlotte and Anna are going to be ready to commit me for this idea but they'll have to deal with it.

Ah there she is, my sweet baby. The last gift I received from Patrick before his death - a beautiful blue convertible with the best sound system money could buy. Of course Justin hates that I choose to listen to the greatness that is Kool & the Gang or Earth, Wind & Fire at the highest volume I can stand. He can't understand my love of that "old crap" instead of something "cool." Whatever, it makes me happy and that is what I need; well, and maybe some rocky road and a little time with *Friends*.

After a quick thank you and one final glance at the happy couple, I hop in my baby and head for home. I don't even bother to put the top up even though it's a bit chilly. Spring is quickly approaching and while winters can be quite cold, we are being blessed with a glimpse into spring. I cannot wait for spring, it is one of my favorite times of the year and the thought of the warmer weather puts a smile on my face and I being to sing along without a care in the world while I kick it into fifth gear. My thoughts turn to Phillip. Was I too picky? Am I too picky? Anna is always telling me how I should embrace the unknown. I've explained that dating is unknown for me and I can't embrace it any more than I already do. I mean, I let my eighteen-year-old son create my profile for the dating site and I never turn down a date that meets the "Son Checklist."

Once I decided, or reluctantly agreed, to start online dating I had the most ridiculous profile. Of course, I didn't think it was ridiculous at the time, but the reality is it was awful. The photos I chose to portray me were nothing short of boring and unflattering. In many ways, I was seeing who I had become – a lonely woman without the motivation to do much but pull on a pair of yoga pants and put her hair in a messy bun. Reality check in the realest form – pictures. Of course those same photos were accurate yet in this instance accurate was code for not flattering. Then there were the words. *I'm a 40-something widow with a son in college. I love spending time with my friends and my dog."* Anna said I might as well have said, *"Hey I'm an old desperate lady looking for a buddy,"* and Charlotte could only shake her head and pat my shoulder reminding me that I wasn't even forty yet. This is when Justin nicely nudged me out of the way and composed the following:

First the obvious - I'm single! This is my bold move for the year and I'm looking for someone to join in the adventure! I can't promise you a home cooked meal - cooking isn't my thing - but I can promise we'll laugh while we eat take-out.

After setting me straight with what seems to be a much better start to a profile, Justin was gone and the girls and I were left to put the finishing touches on the profile. As with any girl's night, there was plenty of laughing - at my expense. Charlotte pulled out her phone and found a picture she had taken of me on a hike. She insisted, and Anna agreed, it was the perfect profile picture. It wasn't (isn't) a picture I would have chosen but apparently it shows my assets - my smile, my legs, and my love of where I live.

Since his father's death, Justin has become quite protective of me. Not in the 'sit on the porch with a shotgun' way, but he wants to see who I am considering for a date and have a vote. When I took the first weary steps into dating, he created the "Son Checklist" and even all these months later, we follow the parameters of that list. Normally, I would be on the same page as the rest of the world and not bring my son into my dating life but we're creating our own normal and new reality, with our own rules. Plus, there's a *check list* - that is always a good thing.

Like any mom with a college-age son, I have bribed Justin with food and clean clothes. While he would rather be off with his buddies any night of the week doing things I'll pretend I don't know he's doing, he must allow me at least one night per week to be his mom. I have implemented a steadfast rule of a *minimum* of one dinner per week in exchange for granting him input into my dating life. Basically, Justin shows up on my doorstep with bags of dirty laundry, I feed him, he argues with me about how much time I think he should spend studying and I lecture him on the benefits of sorting his whites from his colors. In essence, it is your basic mother/son bonding night. Well, except where he pulls out the *check list* and we log into my account on the dating website.

When Justin first showed Anna, Charlotte, and myself the list I was equal parts proud, embarrassed and confused.

1) You can't be bald. Unless it's natural, then fine. But if you do it on purpose that's weird.

2) No young dudes. You have to be older than mom but not too old or just a little younger but not too young.

3) Must have a dog. NO EXCEPTIONS.

Now, in his defense, Justin was in high school and I don't think male pattern baldness was then, nor is it now, on his radar. I had to agree with him on item two; I am not looking to be someone's Mrs. Robinson nor do I want to be someone's young play thing. The dog requirement made me smile. Of course, where I read the list as a sign of unconditional love and permission from my son, Anna and Charlotte saw it as a challenge.

A major point of contention between my three favorite people was the age gap for dating. While I had my own personal preferences, I decided it was best to not participate in the heated debate of whether I should date a man seven to ten years younger than me or only two to four years older. Justin held his ground and in the end claimed the victory of age range and a truce was met – no more than four years younger or ten years older. Thank goodness for a stubborn child.

As I pull off of the main highway and onto the road that leads me home I am reminded of the day we found this house. Married just a short time and not yet parents, our friends and family couldn't understand our desire to leave the city and head for a quieter and simpler life. Of course, once people started visiting they understood the draw to Abbott Falls and stopped questioning our decision. Now, our decision to purchase a fixer upper is a different story. Neither Patrick nor I ever claimed to be very handy but with Patrick's career as an accountant allowing him to move anywhere, we opted to not only become home owners but home renovators *and* business own-ers.

As I pull into our drive and make my way to my parking spot, I take the moment to savor just how very blessed I am to have this home and the property it lies on. Then I'm hit almost immediately following that with too damn big this all is. How in the hell have I never noticed that?

Entering the house, I put my post-date routine into action – shoes off, slippers on, a text to Anna and Charlotte: **I'm home - 10am recap with coffee :)** and a pint of rocky road in my hand.

As I make my way up the stairs to my room, I vow to start a plan for this new life I'm venturing into. I'll never forget the past but it's time I put my best foot forward and find my new happiness.

Chapter Two

COFFEE. IS THERE anything better? The smell. The color. *The caffeine!* I'm a firm believer in the concept that nothing starts a day off like a freshly brewed cup of coffee.

After a night like last night I need this more than ever. I went home and snuggled in for some TV and rocky road with no problem. Sadly sleep was not on my side and I spent most of the night tossing and turning and I woke feeling unsettled. I don't like unsettled. I like structure. And plans. Plans are good. Lists are better.

Thankfully I have Irish Coffee, a quirky coffee house in town that has easily become my second home. I come here daily not just because coffee tastes better here but because the pastries are to die for and the company is welcoming and more like family.

The first time I found myself here, it was dreary morning just a few weeks after Patrick's funeral. Sleep was a spiteful bitch that fought me in ways I had never experienced. I remember waking up and look around our home and needing out. I needed to breathe and sometimes being in that house, breathing was difficult.

Eventually, I found myself standing in front of a set of doors with a beautifully etched four-leaf clover. As I opened those doors the scents wrapped around me like a comforting hug and I suddenly felt overcome with peace. I knew I would be welcome here.

Of course, I knew there was a possibility that someone would give me *the look,* the "I'm so sorry you lost your husband but I don't really know what to say so I'm just going to offer you a sad and sympathetic smile" look. And years later, I'm still coming here almost daily and the looks have lessened. I've learned that they'll never really stop but the moments are far and few between.

The moment I enter the doors today, I instantly relax and realize how desperate I am for some caffeine, a pastry, and one of those feelings of a hug.

"Good morning, Victoria, what can I get for you today?"

What a loaded question. Sleep, a way to drop ten pounds without diet or exercise, a date that doesn't end with me running from a restaurant, you know, the usual.

"Hey Sara, I'm not sure. What's good today?"

"You tell me, I know you had a date last night," Sara says with that perfect smile of young innocence. Oh how I hope she never has to deal with these schmucks in the middle-age dating world.

"The date was . . . interesting but uneventful."

"Well, that's unfortunate. How about just the special and this yummy banana bread?" she says as she's already placing the items on a tray.

Oh banana bread, now she is speaking my language. It has fruit, I'm already making good decisions today. I haven't been able to figure out what makes this bread so amazing but the owner of Irish Coffee is also the pastry chef. Baker? Genius is what he is. Plus, he isn't too hard on the eyes.

Dillon Laughlin is a phenomenal baker and by the amount of customers here this morning, an equally excellent business man. He is also a little like our own town mystery man. I've been coming to this shop, his shop, for a few years now and have barely spoken three words to the man. I'm having trouble deciding if he's a jerk or just simply lacks social skills. Regardless, this mystery man? Movie-star handsome. No, not movie star. It's beyond movie star. Let's just say, if every professional male model, leading man, and rock star molded into one man, it still wouldn't hold a candle to Dillon. And he bakes. *Bakes.*

"Sara, it's like you speak my language. Oh and of course, the girls are coming so if you could throw their usual together too," I reply and head to my table.

"My table" sounds a little pretentious but the little sign sitting next to the flowers confirms it is in fact, reserved for me. Most mornings I sit here, ponder life, read a little, and people watch. I love to people watch and try to figure out each person's story. I suppose that little habit of mine is contributed to my love of reading.

I especially love people watching with my girls. Both Anna and Charlotte tease me about how put out they are to have to drive close to an hour for coffee. Of course, when Dillon is stocking the pastry displays they suddenly don't mind the drive.

Speak of the devils, just as I take my first sip of my coffee, a dark roast with a splash of cream and one sugar, Anna and Charlotte make an entrance as only they know how – demanding attention.

Anna Crawford and I met in the sixth grade and have been best friends ever since. A good three inches taller than me with legs for days, she is a force to be reckoned with. That saying "as different as night and day" has never been truer than with Anna and I. Of course, where we are alike is in all the ways that matter. From the outside looking in, nobody would ever pair us as best friends. My soul sister has beautiful and naturally perfect wavy blonde hair with big hazel eyes, she is all legs and earned that amazing body of hers with discipline (that I lack) and motivation (that I ignore). Always dressed to impress and ready to take on the world, she exudes confidence. This serves her well in the courtroom and has helped her become a very successful litigator. While successful in the courtroom, her brash attitude and lack of filter can often put people off but that is what I love most about her, Anna is unapologetic for being her.

Then there's Charlotte Williams, my sweet baby sister. She hates when I call her that. We're ten years apart in age and when we were growing up that seemed like one hundred years. Now that we're older and both single the years don't seem as far between. Like me, Charlotte has dark hair and eyes but that is where the similarities stop. Char Char is a spirited aka perky five feet tall with short hair and a body she earns daily with her job as a personal trainer and yoga instructor. Growing up Charlotte always asked me when she was going to be tall and have "bewbelies" like me. While I tried to be a supportive big sister and tell her that any day she would be tall and her girls would grow, she never did and neither did they. Every so often I am reminded of this broken promise and my failure as a big sister.

"Okay, Vic, this better be good because there was a smiley face on that text," Charlotte says as she flops down in her chair and proceeds to stuff a lemon poppy seed muffin in her face.

Anna snickers at Charlotte's comment and probably her sudden lack of table skills. Taking a sip of her tea, Anna and I make eye contact I can tell by her expression just how unimpressed she is. I don't think she's expecting the date recap I am about to provide.

"He offered to pleasure me."

Charlotte stops mid chew looking like a cross between a chipmunk and toddler with frosting all over face; Anna begins to choke and her eyes widen the size of saucers; and Charlotte proceeds to smack our friend on the back so hard I'll be surprised if she doesn't leave a mark. I continue to smile like I've won the Lottery. Catching Anna off-guard is something I love to do.

Once she manages to regain her composure Anna speaks. "I'm

sorry, what? But it's ten AM. You said –"

"Let me be a little more specific. He offered to take me home. So that he could pleasure . . . my *FEET*!" I barely squeak out the word feet because I'm already laughing hysterically, both at the memory and at the expression on both of their faces. Charlotte is appalled. Anna is, I'm not sure, but I think annoyed.

She says, "And? Come on, Victoria! You cannot be that stuffy. They're just feet. Maybe you would have liked it."

That, of course, is Anna for you.

I manage a little composure before I respond. "Anna, please. You know me better than that. But it gets worse."

I pick up my cup and glance at Charlotte. I can see her mind going, she's thinking. Her head is tilted to the right then the left, she's blinking excessively – a habit we share – and then leans in as she begins to whisper, "Please don't say he offered pleasuring som*ething else*. I don't think I can hear that."

"Thankfully no, he was/is apparently only interested in my feet. In fact, once I told him no he told me we'd be splitting the check. Can you believe that? What an ass. I tossed some money on the table and ran like my ass was on fire."

For the next few minutes we all laugh and declare we must offer my pedicurist much bigger tips for her quality work. Once the laughter dies down, I take a deep breath and prepare to admit defeat.

"Girls, I think it's time to hang up my dating shoes for a while. Put the keyboard away and give up the online gig."

All of a sudden they are both so serious. They look at each other, then me. *Uh-oh, this cannot be good.* There are times my insecurities get the best of me and I worry that during their drives they talk about me and if I still need fixing. I know they worry. There was a time they had reason to worry but I'm really okay.

"Just say it. I know you two spent the hour drive talking about me." That may have been a little snarkier than I'd like and I probably should apologize.

"Oh get over yourself. We don't spend the hour talking about you. Honestly, we probably should to save my sanity. No, instead I have to listen to Charlotte go on and on about that fish, Fido, and some guy she's crushing on."

"Whatever, so what if I talk about Fido and Tate. At least I *talk*. You don't talk about anything. You just hum. Who hums? You just drive in silence, it's scary. It's like you're plotting something. It's just weird."

I don't know about the radio silence in the car but I can confirm that this conversation is weird. I don't think I've seen these two bicker like this since Anna and I were in high school. Something is obviously amiss with both of them. I sit here for a few moments just watching them. It's a little like a tennis match - back and forth, left to right. I catch tidbits here and there about Trader Joe's, silence being golden, and organic fish food.

"Okaaay, I'm not sure what is going on here but good to know I am not your topic of conversation. I've decided to give up dating. I can't do anymore first dates and honestly I'm beginning to wonder if it's even worth it at this point."

"I agree. Dating seemed like the natural step, but maybe we jumped the gun so to speak. How about a hobby?"

I look at Anna partially intrigued but mostly confused. A hobby. Not a bad idea.

"Like knitting or pottery?" Both of those hobbies are supposed to be therapeutic, right? I could do that. Maybe I should consider going back to school. I did love school and used to dream of being a teacher or a guidance counselor.

"YES! You could drive into the city and take one of my classes or we could set you up for a few training sessions a week! It would be so fun!" While I get that Charlotte loves working out and finds it peaceful and relaxing, it is not my thing. Of course watching her sit here clapping and hopping in her seat like a toddler getting a scoop of ice cream is sweet to watch. Ice cream. I should pick up more on the way home.

"Really, Charlotte, your sister is not going to become a gym rat. Have you met her? Yes, a hobby. I'm not sure knitting and/or pottery is your thing but there has to be some sort of activity that interests you and would get you out and about meeting people. Maybe that's what you need more than dating, socializing."

After spending the morning and part of the afternoon with the girls I made a quick stop for some necessities – ice cream and wine – and head home. I vowed to spend some time this weekend researching activities and made Charlotte promise to call me later so I can hear all about this Tate guy. Anna rolled her eyes and the mention of Tate but I know when we're chatting online later she'll want an update. She plays tough but she loves Charlotte as much as I do.

It's such a lovely day and I feel like spending some time with my current book boyfriend. Yes, book boyfriend. The current object of my affection is the ultimate fantasy man – intelligent, great sense of humor, handsome, kind, sexy, slightly alpha but in a good way not a creepy way, and most of all he worships the heroine. See, ultimate and *fantasy*.

I grab my e-reader and make my way to my own personal oasis in the backyard. This spot, nestled in the corner of the patio, sur-rounded by trees, plants, and flowers was a gift from Patrick and Jus-tin for Mother's Day. Cozy and comforted, I snuggle into my chaise, put my favorite lightweight blanket over my feet, and watch Tilly, our eight-year-old German Shepherd, chase a bird around the yard.

I smile at the memory of Patrick struggling to put this chaise together. He was so certain the manufacturer left parts out of the packaging. It wasn't until Justin asked why he was sitting on some of the parts that he finally admitted that maybe he wasn't as handy as he thought he was. I love those memories and I love this spot. I think everyone deserves a place they can escape to. For some, that may be a spot like this and for others it may be a comfy chair in front of a fire. Regardless of the location, a place of your own with nothing but quiet and a good book is good for the soul. If I have learned anything in these last few years, it is to enjoy the moments and take the time to appreciate what I have.

After a few hours of reading I grab Tilly and we head in the house for dinner and maybe a movie - just the two of us. Sometimes the thought of it just being us in this big house scares me and makes me sad. Charlotte called as promised and filled me in on Tate. Well, what she knows about Tate, which is basically his work schedule. I fulfilled my older sister duty and listened and offered the occasional "oh" in response to her excitement. I love hearing Charlotte excited about something; there have been too many times that she's been far from happy. A few updates to Anna and I was ready to call it a day.

As I settle in to bed I realize that I need to pick a hobby, because I'd rather scratch my eyes out than browse another set of online dating profiles.

Chapter Three

I T HAS BEEN six weeks since my date with Phillip and his prop-
osition. After that night of "fun" and my decision to take a break
from online dating, I ventured out into the world of hobbies.
When I say venture I mean take them on with a vengeance. Unfortunately for everyone in my life, specifically Justin, it's been less exciting and perhaps slightly more frightening.

Although Anna had vehemently objected to the idea of knitting
as a hobby, I figured it made the most sense. Ladies of all ages knit;
it can't be hard, right? Wrong. Oh, at first I was completely confident in my venture. I read no less than three how-to books, watched
some online videos, and went to a class. I made Charlotte, Justin, and
Anna each a personal gift. When I presented Charlotte with a color-
ful cap she smiled, Justin smiled, and Anna rolled her eyes.

"Oh Vic, it's really pretty . . ..umm . . ." Charlotte mumbled. Maybe the pattern is a little wild for her, but I thought that was the best
part.

"What is it, Char? Be honest."

"Well, it's just that. . .um. Okay fine, look, if I was a toddler this wouldn't fit on my head. I love it for sure but, umm, I think I'm going to use it as a coffee cup koozie." Fabulous, a beret style cap turned koozie.

"Wow, Mom, thanks. I love my . . . scarf?" Justin questioned as he held it up like it was a contagious disease.

"Oh for goodness sake. It's a pair of mittens. Why did I think I could knit!" I cried and we all had broken out in laughter. Anna gladly took her scarf that was supposed to be a blanket and I agreed to never pick up a set of knitting needles again.

Then I had the brilliant idea that sports may be the answer. I really shouldn't be allowed to come up with ideas. Turns out tennis is hard - literally, the tennis balls hurt when they hit you in the face.

Don't even get me started on bowling. Bowling leagues are no joke. I thought, *Bowling is fun and there's music and a team. Perfect!* I was wrong. A bowling league is serious business. I thought I could just sign up, get a cute shirt, and use one of the balls that you use on any other Saturday night. I lasted fifteen minutes before I was put in my place.

"Look here, missy," Stella, the league queen, err leader, said to me. "This isn't some little housewife party. We aim to make the Alley Cats the number one all women's bowling league in the region." Okay ,well, yay you, Stella.

"I'm excited to be part of the Alley Cats and will do what I can to help get us to number one!" I had cheered. Stella wasn't buying it.

"Well, dear, you can help by quitting. I saw you in warm-up. It's not happening. We can't have a sixty-two bringing us down. You'll have to go." And with that I was dumped by the Alley Cats bowling league.

When I decided to turn to expanding my culinary skills, I was confident I had finally found my hobby. I make a mean grilled cheese so I assumed I could master the skill of chicken masala. Turns out, they are not the same. Justin was a good sport and succumbed to my efforts, as awful - and charred - as they were.

Of course, my sister was less than impressed with my decision to not strictly focus on exercise. I have been going to the gym more and actually taking classes. She keeps insisting that because I never stay for the entire class and usually am late, it doesn't count. I say it does, we've agreed to disagree.

Anna is still confused as to why I was so opposed to a little foot action, but she is trying to be supportive. She even considered calling Phillip. She has made me promise to commit to something. Obviously this is a non-issue, I'm nothing if not a commitment kind of gal. I mean, I joined a gym with a three-year contract. If that doesn't scream commitment I don't know what does.

Like his mom, Justin is all about commitment too. He promised me when he moved out this semester to live with roommates closer to campus that we would still have dinner together at least once a week. Never one to disappoint, Justin never comes home empty-handed. Yes, there is a sack of laundry that only a mom can help him with - his words, not mine - but he also comes armed with cake. Tonight he's here with a layered triple-chocolate cake and his determination to get me to connect with my true passion.

"Mom, I just don't get why you put yourself through all of this," he says with a chocolate-covered face that reminds me of him on his third birthday. So sweet, messy, and perfect.

"What don't you get, Justin? I promised to commit to something and for the life of me I cannot think of anything to do. I've tried it all. Working out. Online classes. I even tried knitting for goodness sake." Thankfully Justin speaks 'Mom stuffs her face with chocolate' language fluently because I said all of this while shoveling cake in my mouth.

"It just seems obvious to me, that's all. I don't think you have to change who you are. I know Auntie Charlotte and Anna want you to try new things, but that's not you, Mom. I mean, yeah when you got rid of the brown bomber and got the convertible that was change, but that was a thing. I don't want you to change who you are. You're my mom and I love you and your cake face."

It's okay, I cried too. What mom wouldn't? My eighteen-year-old son is just so profound and kind. Of course, he follows up his moment of awesome with the loudest belch ever known to mankind. Still, profound.

"All right, smarty-pants, tell me the obvious," I reply with all sincerity.

"Books," he says with the same confidence I saw in his father. Of course, the look of confusion on my face was the polar opposite of his expression. This was evident when he started laughing hysterically.

"Books? What, I should get more books? Come on, Justin, I have an entire closet full of books. Plus, now that I have my e-reader I have another couple hundred staring at me every time I power it up. I think your plan needs a little work," I state matter-of-factly. And there it is, the part of me that I wish he hadn't inherited - the eye roll. It's not just any eye roll, it's an expressive *"oh please"* eye roll and my son is the master.

"I guess I have to really explain this to you. Mom, you love to read. You love escaping into those books, or whatever. I mean, I don't get why you would read on purpose, but it's part of who you are. I remember when I was a kid and you used to have a book with you everywhere you went. Sometimes it was embarrassing, but it made you smile. Dad and I knew what to get you for every Christmas and birthday because as long as it was a book you were happy. So there's your answer. Books and reading. That is what makes you happy. Well, and apparently cake because I think you just ate this entire cake," he says as he literally licks the plate.

I did not eat the entire cake. Obviously, Justin helped since his face looks like he landed face first in a pile of frosting.

Could it really be that simple? Reading? I mean, I do love to read. I love spending my days with a cup of tea, sitting in my nook with Tilly at my feet and a book in my hands. Of course, being a dog, Tilly is more interested in chasing squirrels or her tail, but the whole time I'm sitting there is like pure heaven. I am outside of myself and drawn into a story. I am always in awe of the authors of these books and how they can live a normal life while creating such greatness. I just don't see how that equals my new commitment. I'm already committed to reading, it's my love.

Once Justin has realized there is no more cake and that sitting around watching old episodes of *Friends* with his mom isn't exactly the highlight of his college life, he heads back to his own apartment. I'm left alone with my thoughts which even on a good day can be a frightening way to be. If only I could see life like an eighteen-year-old, simple. What do I love? I love to read, I love books in any form. Heck, I love cake and coffee. I *really* love my home. I love that it is nestled in the mountains and there is nothing but stillness around me. Yes I am lonely at times and wish I had more people around, but I wouldn't trade this for the world. I wonder if there are other people like me out there. People who have good lives but are just missing a little something extra.

As I turn off the lights and make my way up the stairs to my bedroom, I stop and really look at my home. It is beautiful. Patrick made sure we were taken care of when he was alive and continues to do so in his death.

I met Patrick Bennett the first day of Economics, freshman year of college. I'd love to say it was love at first sight, but really it was annoyance at first sight. I was running late. I had to get across campus and the gods were against me at that moment. The skies opened and it rained harder than anything I had ever experienced.

Running into the building, I slipped and landed flat on my ass.

I've never claimed to be graceful or even coordinated for that matter, but when I heard a deep laugh coming from behind me I hopped up prepared to spar. Looking back, I kind of love that the same laugh that pissed me off at the moment became my favorite sound in the world. It's the laugh of the man I planned to spend my life with and the laugh of my son. After shooting the man, who by the way was very handsome with a dimple that caught my attention even through my frustration and embarrassment, the dirtiest look I could gather, I strolled right into class - and he followed.

I remember mumbling under my breath that I just couldn't catch a break and distinctly heard "Oh don't worry, I'll catch you," as I took my seat. My first reaction was that the guy laughing was in my class. Oh no, it was worse - he was the teacher's assistant. Great. Needless to say, I wasn't exactly thrilled to have to deal with him on a regular basis. After months of him flirting and me ignoring his efforts, I relented and agreed to one date. I didn't spend a day of my life without that laughing guy in it for the next twenty years.

Patrick Bennett was kind, loving, funny, and my best friend. Not a day passed that he didn't tell me he loved me. He made me feel special and cared for every moment I was with him and even the moments we were apart. His kisses were like coming home and I was blessed every moment I was allowed to love him.

Then came the day four years ago when the doctor told us those moments were coming to an end. At first it seemed like a sick joke, because Patrick was only forty-one and healthy as an ox. He was an avid runner who religiously met with his doctor every year to keep my mind at ease. I knew that he'd always be here with me, until the day the doctor asked that I come with him to an appointment. I had myself convinced I needed to be there to talk about normal things like cholesterol and eating habits. I was wrong.

We took on the battle against cancer like we did everything else - together. For a solid year we faced that horrible disease head-on and with a drive I didn't even know we had. Throughout that year, we tried to give Justin the most normal life possible for a teenager watching his father fight for his life. It was hard, it was lonely, and it was sad. Unfortunately for us, the universe had a different plan and a year after his diagnosis, we buried Patrick under a willow tree and said goodbye.

It's hard to look back at that time and believe I made it through. I don't think I could have gotten to where I am without Charlotte and Anna. There were others, but those two were my rocks. I only wish now, looking back, that I could have been there to see it all happen. Anna at lacrosse with Justin, dressed to the nines in her Ann Taylor suit trying to understand why the players don't use hands. Charlotte trying to help Justin with homework by way of Google. But, I wasn't there. I was lost in my sadness and loneliness.

It was dark, but I made it out. Eventually, I learned to live again. To laugh and smile. I learned to appreciate every day for what it is - a blessing. And Justin, he learned that life is precious and to always live each moment to the fullest. I always knew he would grow into an amazing man but I believe seeing his father fight like he did has filled Justin with an amazing strength he doesn't even know he has.

I'm brought back to the present when I see my bed. About a year and a half after Patrick passed, Anna insisted I get a new bed. I was so hurt and angry. It was the bed I shared with Patrick and where I could still feel him. She explained to me that it was also the bed I sleep in alone. She reminded me that I would never bring another man to the bed I shared with Patrick. Now, I can laugh at the memory of her telling me this and me smacking her with my towel like she was on fire. Another man? In my bed? Please, that would never happen. But now, all these months later? I want that opportunity. I want something more. Maybe Justin is right and my answer is there, in my books. My happy place.

Chapter Four

"ANNA, DO YOU hear this crap? My sister has lost her effing mind."

Crickets. There's nothing. This scares me. Charlotte must notice it too because now she's staring at Anna. In the almost thirty years I've known Anna, this is a first. She appears speechless.

"I heard her, Charlotte, relax. And what's with 'crap' and 'effing'? Why are you talking like there are small children around? And you," she points her finger at me like my Gram used to do when she was making a point, "it's about damn time you get your shit together."

Okay, not exactly the response I was expecting. About damn time? She's acting like she had this thought all along. Like . . . wait a minute.

"Anna, when was the last time you talked to Justin?" I ask when really I already know the answer.

"Oh Vic, you know I talk to my godson every week and you shouldn't be surprised to hear that you are our favorite topic of discussion. Now, since you've finally managed to come up with an idea that makes sense, I would like to hear what you are planning."

Anna is nothing if not straight to the point. I love that about her. She is honest and fearless but would never say something to be hurtful. True, sometimes her words hurt, but after about ten minutes you realize she speaks from the heart.

Clearing my throat like I'm about to take the stage at a major convention, I repeat myself for the third time, "I am going to turn the house into a retreat for book lovers and maybe authors. I want to have a place where women, and I guess men, can go and just relax and decompress through books. I want to turn Patrick's office into an actual library where people can borrow books during their stay. I'll finally finish the property and add little nooks where people can go to be alone with their stories and just relax."

Ultimately, I'd love to have authors as guests for these retreats and offer options that are more like a bed and breakfast. I am keeping those ideas to myself right now; it's all a little overwhelming. Of course Anna is sitting there with her usual smart-ass smirk and Charlotte is pouting because to her, the idea of just hanging out reading is the most ridiculous idea ever, but both are just staring at me.

"What? Is there something on my face? You are both freaking me out. This is a bad idea. I shouldn't do it. I mean, I can just volunteer at the library or something. This is silly, what was I thinking." It's like I can't stop.

Finally my sister closes her mouth and looks at me with complete seriousness. That in itself should freak me out, but for some reason I find it comforting. And then she starts laughing. What in the actual hell? And then Anna joins her and it isn't long before I'm laughing too. Kevin, the barista on duty, stops and asks us if we're okay and that only makes the situation funnier.

After what seems like an eternity we manage to get it together enough for my sister to give it the green light. "Well, Vic, I still don't get why a person would want to read for fun but whatever floats your boat. I'm in. Of course, if you open this little book thing up to men I'm going to have to actually pick up a book. I hear men that read are really honest and kind and that is really sexy. So yeah if there are men, I'm there. Oh, who am I kidding, I'm there anyway." I look to Anna, who has lifted her glass to signal a toast; I guess she's in too. What we're in for I really don't know, but I think this could be pretty cool.

The girls leave me with my thoughts and my table at Irish Coffee to come up with a plan. Remember that "I love structure and lists" crap I said earlier? Well, creating that structure gives me hives. Not real hives, but on the inside hives. I imagine my insides look like a strawberry. Come up with a plan. Sounds easy enough.

While my home is, in all seriousness, far too large for just me, it is an ideal spot for something like this business I'm planning. Being married to an accountant with great investment instincts will afford me the opportunity to really make a go of this. While I was aware we were living a comfortable life, I wasn't fully aware of just how comfortable until after Patrick passed. I was quite surprised when I met with a colleague of Patrick's after his death; between investments, the sale of the business, and life insurance policies, neither Justin nor I will ever have to struggle.

Our home sits on a large piece of property and while it has taken us most of the twelve years we've been there, the upgrades are finally complete. I live in a beautiful town with a magnificent backdrop. I love to read and know there are others like me. Sadly I also know that isn't enough. That is a dream, not a plan.

Before I can tackle the first draft of a business plan, I decide I need a pick me up. A pick me up in the form of a refill of coffee and perhaps a scone. Or éclair. Maybe a cupcake. Definitely a cupcake.

Before I make it to the counter, I notice Dillon coming through the doors of the kitchen with a tray of freshly baked goods. Like the next gal, I can truly appreciate a tray of freshly baked treats. I also can appreciate the man carrying them. Sweet Moses. Maybe I should switch to iced coffee, it seems to have warmed up a little in here. Is it even possible for a man to make an apron look sexy? Is that a dimple? It's really hot in here, they should check the air conditioning.

I'm deep in these thoughts when I hear Sara talking. "Are you okay, Victoria?" she asks me with a slight giggle. Great, I've been caught checking out more than the brownies and scones. There is no doubt that my chest is red and that redness is making its way to my cheeks. Thankfully the reason for the blushing has returned to the kitchen.

"Oh," I clear my throat a little with an awkward smile directed at Sara. "I'm fine. I think I'm going to be here for a little while and need a pick me up. I'll take whatever was just placed in the case and a refill."

Sara smiles at me as she fills my cup and places what appears to be a piece of chocolate heaven on my plate – a cupcake that I can guarantee is going to require an extra mile added to my evening walk. Sara begins removing her apron and offers me a smile.

"I'm getting ready to head out for the day. I guess I'll see you tomorrow," she says.

"Actually, Sara, do you have a minute before you leave?" I ask and she nods and heads around the counter toward me. As we approach my table, she shakes out her ponytail and pulls out her phone. That is something I'm adding to my list – no technology outside of e-readers at the retreats. I've come to appreciate the moments that I unplug, step away from technology, and simply relax.

"What's up?" Sara asks me as I sit down and she begins tapping at her phone. When she looks up I motion for her to take the seat across from me. Sara pulls out the chair and looks from me to my notebook to my e-reader and back to me. She has a hint of confusion and perhaps a little bit of fear in her eyes. I can't help but offer her a sincere smile, one that I have used many times with Justin to put him at ease. It seems to work with Sara just as well. Although, I can still see an obvious question brewing in her head. Ha! I said brewing . . . never mind.

"Well, I'm thinking of starting a business. I'd be dealing with the public and wondered if you could give me a little insight." I'm almost intimidated by how seriously she looks at me.

I clear my throat. "Don't worry, I'm not opening a coffee house or anything." I see her shoulders relax. "I'm thinking of something like a daily retreat for book enthusiasts."

Sara looks at me for what feels like forever and then with a smile says, "Okay. I'm not sure how I can help you but shoot."

"Well, as I said I'm thinking of starting a business. Unfortunately, I've become somewhat of a creature of habit and tend to only see the same people in town. I was curious if you see a lot of people here at Irish Coffee reading and just kind of escaping."

Honestly, what I really want to know is if people would buy into this plan I have. "Also, what about tourists? I know that the town is working hard to increase tourism but I wasn't sure if we have any sort of influx like some of the seaside towns."

"So, uhhmm, you want people – strangers – to come to your house to *read books*?" Sara asks me with wide eyes and an obvious dislike of reading for pleasure. I can't help but laugh a little, the glory of youth. When you think reading is boring and only for school.

"Well, yes. It would be more of an escape from everyday life with very limited technology," I say as I motion toward her phone, my phone, and yes, my e-reader.

"Truly, I want to offer people an opportunity to get away and regroup in a peaceful setting. I think reading is relaxing and it always makes me feel less stressed so I thought why not." Sara is looking at me like it's either the craziest or best idea ever. I can't tell.

"Hmmm . . . it's not something I'd be into, but then again I'm only eighteen. My mom and my aunts would love it. They are always reading those paperbacks where the guy has long hair and the lady is always in his arms half asleep. I think I know what they are reading but if I'm honest I don't think I *want* to know." She scrunches her nose like she's smelling old milk as she says the last part. I guess if I was her age and imagining my mom and aunts reading about sex I'd look like that too.

"Well, that's something then. Your mom and aunts live locally, right?" Sara nods and smiles like she just had the most wonderful idea. It is not lost on me that I am sitting here talking about something that may very well be life changing for me with an eighteen year old girl.

"I guess I should talk to people a little older than you, no offense. Sadly, I don't really have many friends in town anymore." This is the truth. I used to have a slew of girlfriends; well, other moms anyway. We were never without a birthday party or dinner party invitation until we battled cancer. Our life took a different turn and I kind of lost contact with everyone. Once the kids grew up it seemed like we all just found other interests.

"Why not ask Dillon? He'd know more about the tourists and all of that. I'm sure he's putting together another tray of goodies for the display," Sara tells me and I confirm that I was indeed caught looking at him earlier. Lovely. "I'll just go get him for you," Sara says, standing up quickly.

"Oh, uh, no that's okay. I wouldn't want to bug him. Besides, he's not really the friendliest guy. I've been coming here for years and all he says is 'Ello or Mornin.' Not even 'hello.'" I hear the nervousness in my voice, which is just weird. Thinking of talking to Dillon makes me nervous, and that is completely embarrassing.

Sara starts laughing and literally snorts. What the hell did I say? Oh no! Did I say he makes me nervous out loud? I do that sometimes. I think it and boom it's out of my mouth before I can even filter. It's a curse no matter what Anna says. A. Curse. "Sara, seriously what did I say? You are kind of freaking me out here."

"Oh, Victoria, he says 'Ello' cause of his accent. He's originally from Ireland and even though his accent is hardly noticeable and is practically gone, sometimes it just comes out. You should hear him when whatever he's baking doesn't come out perfect. It's a little hard to understand. He's totally friendly but really, he doesn't talk much to anyone because he's shy. I like to tease him and threaten to fix him up with one of my aunts but he gets so embarrassed I couldn't do it. Those ladies would eat him alive."

He's Irish? Like Pierce Brosnan Irish? Holyshitballs. Dillon just went from attractive to swoon-worthy in one conversation. Did I say how much I love an accent? And how Pierce Brosnan was and is the best 007 ever? Wait, where did she go? Crap crap CRAP!

"Victoria, I was telling Dillon how you are planning to start your own business. He's like super smart with business stuff so he could totally help you. I've got to go so I'll see you tomorrow!" She's shouting this through the shop as she leaves.

Thankfully by now I'm the only one left, except Hank, who's sitting at the counter and couldn't care less what is happening. Why does 'my age' on Dillon look brooding and sexy and on me it looks 'mom'?

"Ello, Victoria. Sara said you wanted to ask me something?" Dillon is quite possibly the most beautiful human being I've ever seen in person. No, I'm not comparing him to the dates from Hell or even to Patrick. Patrick was handsome and any woman who met him would agree. But Dillon? Dillon is a whole new level of sexy-handsome.

"Oh, it's okay. I'm sure you're busy. You know, running a business and baking or whatever you know, doing stuff." Yes, Victoria, keep talking. Please, I don't think you've made a complete ass of yourself just yet. "I'm just going to go. So, uh, thanks anyway," I say as he pulls out the chair across from me and sits down.

"No, really it's okay. I have time. I know what it's like to just start a business from scratch. I'd love to help you avoid the mistakes I made. What kind of business is it? Sara was talking so fast I heard 'business, books, house, I don't get it,' and then we were standing here. So tell me what you're doing."

I am mesmerized. It should be against all possibilities for any man to have that blue of eyes. These aren't your run-of-the-mill blue, they are more like the ocean and the sky swirled together to make a pool of perfect. Something about the way they sit in contrast to his long dark lashes, which by the way women everywhere would kill for, just calls for you to look at them. And the hair? It's like velvet; I want to just pet it. That would most likely be frowned upon but I can't help it. Then I notice the slightest crescent-shaped scar to the side of his left eye and it takes all my restraint to not reach across and touch it. Again, likely frowned upon. If I take ten more seconds to focus on his lips I may actually combust. I'm acting like some love struck teenager not a grown woman attempting to convince others, and myself, I can start a business.

I manage to muster enough self-control to quickly relay my idea to him, including the parts I've kept to myself. He seems interested and nods appropriately.

"Well, that's some plan," he chuckles. "I think it sounds great. Ambitious, but great. If you like, I would love to help you get started. I'm sure there is a lot to think of and while I may not know a lot about retreats, I can offer an ear for brainstorming."

An ear. Even his ears are sexy – they don't even have the slightest point. Not like these little Elvin ears I'm sporting. Stop, he's still talking.

". . .baked goods to help you along. I've seen you here while you read and I imagine brownies and muffins would go a long way with a house full of book enthusiasts." That smile again, one that could sell toothpaste without even trying. Can he tell I'm distracted by his uber sexiness? Deep breaths, Victoria, deep breaths.

"I know, it does seem overly ambitious, but it's just that I need something for me. My husband passed away three years ago and my son is off to college. I feel like I'm just trudging along and need something to anchor me. Dating seems to be a bust and as much as I would like to be the next Serena Williams, sports don't seem to be my forte." If that isn't an understatement.

"Maybe nothing will come of all of this but I just feel like this could work. I love to read, the written word . . . it is so powerful. Nothing compares relaxing with a good book and the knowledge that nothing and nobody will interrupt you. There have to be others out there that agree. Does that sound silly?" I want his approval. I need justification from someone other than Anna, Charlotte, and Justin. I didn't realize that until now.

"Victoria, first, I am sorry for your loss. I remember when your husband passed; it was quite sad. I am the last person to comment on dating; I let my cousin, Alana, talk me into the dating websites once and that was enough. I've never been able to look at hot wax the same - don't ask." I can't help but smile and wonder . . . hot wax?

"My hobby has turned into my passion and allows me to live a life I love. That being said, if you believe in it then you will be successful." Why couldn't the online dating site pair me up with Dillon or someone Dillon-y. It's a word, or at the very least, should be.

"How about this, take some time to make a plan. List everything out and don't hold back. Then, if you like, I'll join you for one of your morning cups of coffee and check it out. Would that work for you?" Is he kidding? Like I could drink coffee while looking at the pettable hair. Oh, he's still talking.

"I'll be honest, I don't have many friends in Abbott Falls and while I have a great staff, I could use a little more adult conversation. So if you're willing, I'd be honored to help."

Oh no, the honor would be all mine. "Sorry? Did you say something?" Dillon asks.

Crap. Filter, Victoria. I pull it together enough for us to agree that I'll take a few weeks and prepare a preliminary plan. Dillon isn't the man I thought he was and is definitely a lot more fun to look at than Phillip the foot guy. I know for a fact there is no dye job and, if I'm being honest, I bet he gives a great foot massage.

Chapter Five

OVER THE NEXT few weeks I am beyond busy. Between my weekly dinner with Justin, my continued efforts to advance my culinary skills and maybe be the next Top Chef, exercising, having my girl time, and creating a business plan, I barely have time to do the one thing that started all of this - take time for me and read. It does not go unnoticed when I have Anna and Charlotte over for dinner one night.

"Vic, I was talking to one of the trainers at work the other day. She was telling me about some book she read; apparently she finds reading as life changing as you do." Charlotte and I have something else in common besides hair and eye color - sarcasm. "I didn't bother telling her about the retreat since she's never taken a day off in her life, but I promised I'd get some book recommendations from you."

"I haven't been reading."

I sample the sauce I have simmering. It's a simple marinara and, apparently, not even I can mess that up. Now the pasta is a different story. I cannot cook a noodle properly to save my life. I defer that task to Anna. I look up to see both the girls looking at me mid sip and considering their love of wine that says a lot.

"What? It's not a big deal, I'm working on my business plan and I'm supposed to meet with Dillon next week to go over the details."

"Dillon, huh?" Anna smiles while she winks at me. Anna is a winker, did I already say that? Sometimes the winking gets her in trouble. She doesn't see the big deal, but when a certain judge pointed out that he was married and wouldn't take kindly to her open flirting in his courtroom, she kind of got the point. "Please do tell us about Dillon and this 'plan.'"

I know where she's going with this but good gravy, it's not like he's interested in anything more than friendship. Honestly, friendship may be pushing his intentions.

We spend the next few hours going over my business plan, including the part where I turn my home into a bed and breakfast. That's what flowing wine does, gives me loose lips.

Over the course of the evening I heard "Why do you want people in your home? What if they have malaria or something?" more than once. I kindly explained to my sister that I was pretty sure nobody coming for a day-long retreat to read was going to spread malaria.

Anna, on the other hand, was more concerned about logistics, "I just don't see where you will put these people; just because you have five spare rooms doesn't mean you should open up your house to strangers? What about bathrooms? Who in the hell is going to clean up after these people?" All valid questions, but coming from Anna, a woman who lives in a one-bedroom condo in a high rise with a full-time cleaning service, I don't see where the concern is coming from.

Both ladies were on the receiving end of quite a few eye rolls and shrugs from me. If I've learned anything over the years it is to let them both have their say and just nod. Charlotte maintains her position that I should add some sort of exercise option to the retreats and Anna thinks I should encourage singles weekends. As much as I try to defend the idea that no, not everyone wants to exercise to relax and that I am not going to be responsible for hooking people up, they both insist they are right.

While I don't like revisiting my attempts at dating, I have to admit after some wine the events themselves are hilarious. Charlotte's favorite date story is Ted Sweat. Literally. His name is Sweat and he was like a damn fountain. We chatted online and via text for about two weeks before I agreed to meet him for a day date. I wasn't completely sold on him but figured he was nice and I could, at the very least, gain a new friend. What I wasn't prepared for was the sweat shower he gave everyone in his path. Ted is a car salesman, excuse me, high-end car salesman. He insisted for our date that we meet at the dealership so he could take me on a drive in style. I thought it sounded fun and gave him points for originality. And then I got to the lot. The first thing I noticed was how damn hot it was and that I hoped whatever car he chose had air-conditioning. When I saw Ted pulling out a cherry-red Ferrari I about shit myself. This was going to be awesome. Not exactly handsome, there was still something about Ted that I wanted to get to know. Sadly, after thirty minutes into our drive he still looked like he was standing outside in the heat and I was concerned.

Ted also talked to the Ferrari and caressed it. Yes, caressed. That's the only way to describe what he was doing to the dash as he would mumble, "Oh you like that, don't you?" It was interesting to say the least. We drove for about an hour when he pulled into a parking lot . . . of Sizzler. Ted called it *The* Sizzler but I just can't. I'm not opposed to Sizzler but when your date is driving you around in a Ferrari you kind of expect at least Chili's. Ted was still sweating and now his shirt was soaked as we headed inside, but I was still hopeful and well, I didn't have much choice at this point. It wasn't until he ordered our meal and tried to negotiate the use of his expired coupon that I noticed the sweat was flying. Everywhere. I couldn't handle it. I ran to the restroom, feigned illness, and asked to end the date. Ted was very kind and promised to call me later to reschedule. We did talk a few days later and to my surprise he actually mentioned the sweating. We decided that romance wasn't in the cards for us and there were no more bodily fluid-flying dates for Ted and me.

As I recount the date with Ted, all three of us are in hysterics and we laugh until our sides hurt. After a perfect night of wine, laughing, and more wine the girls and I snuggle up in my bed for the night.

Morning comes way too early and the reason for my headache is evident when I stumble to the kitchen - five empty wine bottles. Whoops. I spot a note from Anna that they had to leave early because "your brat sister thinks exercise is important even with a hangover" and that she'll talk to me later. I'd have to agree that my sister is a brat and she might also be insane to even think of exercise today. I'll have to thank Anna for getting her out of the house before she had a chance to include me in this asinine plan of fitness.

I've decided today is a day that I must relax. No business plan and no attempts at a new hobby. Today is just for me and I am going to spend it with a good book. After a quick shower, about a gallon of water, and some aspirin I'm in my favorite nook ready to spend quality time lost in the words and emotions on the page. After a little bit of me time and some of my favorite coffee from Irish Coffee, I'm feeling human again. I realize while I'm sitting there that this cup of coffee doesn't taste nearly as good as when I have it at the shop. Whether it is the coffee itself or the recent company each morning, I'm not sure.

As I near the end of my book, I find myself envisioning Dillon as the hero, Sebastian Longworth III. Something about that name and the way he is described reminded me so much of Dillon. Each time we've met over coffee and talked about my business plan, he has seemed so confident, kind, and truly interested in what I'm doing. Sebastian Longworth *the third,* the suffix is important for this guy, let me tell you is brooding and from the way the author describes him, unbelievably handsome. I digress, that's how it always is in these books, a perfect leading man when we all know no such man exists.

Anna has teased me for years about my unconditional love for contemporary romance novels. I can hear her now as I sit here: *"Victoria, you cannot be serious. Another one of your 'this man is so perfect and dreamy he can do know wrong. I bet he can build a house, run an empire, and likely birth children he's so damn perfect. It's all lies, why do you torment yourself?"* Did I mention Anna can be a little cynical?

I fully admit I am buying into fiction and not ashamed by it at all. These characters have to be inspired by someone real, right? Besides, this author has something like seventeen books released so whoever is inspiring Sebastian should just keep on inspiring

While I was lucky enough to be treated like a queen by Patrick, nothing compares to the level of worship in these books. The hero treasures the heroine like a precious metal, never once putting himself first. Well, unless he's turned on the smoldering alpha male part of his personality – that's a completely different story. I suppose that is why it's fiction and why I love getting lost in it.

Although I promised not to work today, I make a mental note to add this author as my #1 retreat special guest. Now if I can only figure out how to make that happen. As if some best-selling author is going to want to come to my home and do a private reading and signing. I just have to stay positive and come up with a plan, or a list. A list would be good.

Chapter Six

DILLON LAUGHLIN IS more than just a pretty face. He has managed to give me enough guidance to become a legitimate business owner. It became official when I framed the business license for "Pages and Quiet - A Book Lovers Retreat" and hung it on my wall. Maybe choosing the name after a night of chocolate martinis and using a Boggle game as inspiration wasn't the best plan, but Justin gave the name his stamp of approval so there you have it. P&Q's first event is scheduled and I have six ladies booked for a one-day retreat. Yes, five of the ladies are Sara's mother and aunts escaping their households that seem to be overrun by men and little boys. The sixth is a woman who responded to my flyer at the library.

Thank goodness for lists because the one I have going for all of the things that have to be completed would give Santa's Naughty or Nice list a run for its money. Specifically, the property needs to be finished and the individual reading nooks established. Of course, I also have to somehow design a website and prepare an agenda with back-up plans as needed.

One may say that having a plan in case of a major natural disaster, say a hurricane, is a little extreme. I disagree. It could happen. So what if Abbott Falls is more likely to have a freak blizzard than hurricane? It's best to be prepared.

I am pleased to know that regardless of having so many first dates with zero romantic result, I've managed to meet men who can help me with the ever-mounting list of things I need help with to get this business off the ground. Normally, I'd feel awkward calling someone I never managed to have a second date with, but in the end I have never been rude and therefore all of my bridges are intact.

One of the first men I started talking with online was Alex. I'll be honest, it was his picture that drew me to him and it was that same picture that didn't allow for a second date. Alex and I had chatted via messenger and exchanged texts for quite a bit and exchanged pictures. I sent him one of me at a Mother's Day picnic when I was looking pretty damn fabulous. He sent me a picture of him at a Halloween party, which I loved. He was dressed 70's disco style and we know from my taste in music - I loved it.

I loved it until Alex showed up for our lunch date and I realized it wasn't a Halloween party, it was him . . . in the 70s, 1979 to be exact but still. Apparently, Alex hasn't quite figured out that you shouldn't send a potential date your thirty-year-old picture and be surprised when she spits out her iced tea upon your arrival. Gone was the cool Leif Garrett-inspired hair and I was looking at a not-so-cool Donald Trump-inspired hair *piece*.

The clothes? When I thought they were a costume, it was cute. Now? With the additional seventy-five pounds or so squeezed into the polyester, not so much. I know I know, I'm no Heidi Klum, but come on . . . it was a *leisure suit!* Once we got past his less-than-honest approach, we found we actually had quite a bit in common, but I decided friends was the only way to end things.

We don't talk often, but when I needed a landscape company to help with the reading nooks, Alex was my go-to guy. He gave me a kick-ass deal and the result was beautiful. Using my original nook as inspiration, he created little havens for eight other readers. Some areas are surrounded by water features and others by greenery. All have a chaise, side table, and a sense of peace.

With the first retreat quickly approaching, I've leaned on Anna, Charlotte, and Justin to give me support. Today it's just Anna and me going through my to-do list and what-if checklists.

"Victoria Bennett. Stop. You need to relax," Anna snaps as I start spouting off my to-do list again. "I will not spend my day off watching you go crazy. I see enough of that shit during the week. Have you ever been to a courthouse and just sat and watched? It is really fascinating - people are nuts."

Anna has been complaining about her work so much lately I feel like I should be concerned. When we were growing up we both wanted to be teachers, specifically she wanted to work with high school kids at risk. After watching her parents struggle financially and concluding it was because they were both underpaid teachers, she decided to go to law school and have a career that would always pay her well. I worried then, like I do now, that she sacrificed happiness for security. I never say that to her because she'd probably kick me and I'm partial to avoiding that at all costs.

I can't bite my tongue completely. "Anna, are you okay? Is work okay?" I ask as I sit down next to her.

"I'm fine. This isn't about me, we're here to get your business going. So please, let's not do this, okay?" I hear the words, though mostly I see the hurt in her eyes. Something is wrong, but I know Anna and if she's not ready, she's not ready.

Trying to lighten the mood, I whisper, "If you need a little smutty read, I have those books set aside." There it is, that eye roll and smile.

"Oh honey, trust me *that* is the least of my problems."

That serious moment behind us, we continue to work on P&Q business. Anna insists we act out some sort of improv scene with her playing the role of guest. Channeling her inner diva, my dear friend is using some sort of strange accent that is hilarious and kind of awesome. After a few more hours, she's mumbling something about sushi and breakfast as she tosses me an air kiss and is headed home.

My phone signals a text from Charlotte.

My phone says clear skies and no rain for Sat!

Charlotte knows that I'm worried about the weather for the retreat. I want the guests, all six of them, to enjoy the reading nooks and they can't if the weather turns to crap. She's been sending me weather updates multiple times a day all week. At first, I wondered if she was mocking my "quirks" about the weather but then I realized I don't care and I'm grateful for the updates.

Thank goodness! What are you up to? Big date?

No date. I did talk to Tate today :)

Oh Charlotte. She is still obsessing over the Trader Joe's guy. I love my sister but at some point I think I'm officially going to worry. Or maybe I'll just laugh. I assume the first and hope for the latter.

Talk talk or about work.

Talk. I invited him to coffee. He said YES! We're going on Friday

Yay! Can't wait to hear all about it.

After a few more minutes of texting and my little sister boosting my ego, I decide to take Tilly for a quick walk. Alone with my thoughts can be hit or miss for me. Sometimes I just make lists in my head and other times I think of Patrick. I think he would be proud of me. This makes me smile, as I realize I'm no longer dwelling or second guessing myself. I am excited.

Chapter Seven

AS THE WEEK progresses, I confirm Charlotte, Anna, and Justin will be here bright and early to help me set up. It's likely they are on "Let's see how long it takes for Victoria to lose her shit" watch but I'll take the help. Besides, what I need from there, in addition to support is someone to pour me a cocktail when I need it.

By Saturday, I've scrubbed and polished everything possible. The reading nooks have been set up, re-set, and okay, set a third time. I made my Costco run and have the salad and sandwiches chilled and ready to go. Sara is bringing me pastries from Irish Coffee so all I have to do is wait . . . six hours for everyone to get here.

I may be a little excited and perhaps overly caffeinated.

By 10:00 the troops have arrived and my caffeine high has started to lessen. I take a minute to pull Charlotte aside.

"Char, how was coffee with Tate?" I ask excitedly. I have my fingers crossed that she'll have a positive reaction.

"It was good, he's really nice." This is encouraging, and I go to say as much but she cuts me off.

"And gay," she sighs. Oh, Charlotte.

"Hun, I'm sorry. I know you really liked him." I lean in for a hug and she's . . . laughing. "Char, are you okay?"

"Vic, I feel so silly. What was I thinking? When he told me and I was surprised he started laughing. I started laughing. It was hysterical. He invited his husband to meet us and they are freaking fantastic. We're going out to a club tonight," she says with a big smile, linking arms with me as I just shake my head.

Everyone manages to keep me distracted and on task for a solid thirty minutes. With how I've been feeling, that is quite the success for them. When the doorbell rings I'm a little taken aback. It is far too early for the guests and if they are already arriving, what am I going to feed them? Lunch at 10:30 in the morning? I guess, but I could go for those baked goods and Sara isn't here and . . . just answer the door. Relax. I head to the door feeling as nervous as I did the day I took my driver's license test. It's like a swarm of butterflies has taken up residence in my stomach while a dragon flaps its wings next to them. Basically, I want to throw up.

What lies before me is a shock. All six-foot something of him, swirly blue eyes, and dressed like a gift from the hunk heavens . . . Dillon.

"Mornin," he says with that toothpaste-commercial smile. Oh boy.

"Hi. Uh, what are you doing here? What's all that?" I say, pointing at the bags of what appear to be groceries he is holding. Groceries? Has word gotten back to him that I am not exactly Rachael Ray in the kitchen? We've been spending afternoons together working on my plan and I suppose becoming friends, yet none of this has come up. We don't really get too personal, just talking about movies, my love of books, baking, and our town.

"Goodies for your guests. Well, not quite, but the ingredients to create them," he replies with a simple shrug and a move into the house.

I step aside and hear Justin chuckle and whisper, "Close your mouth, Mom, it's just groceries." Justin gives Dillon the "what's up" nod as he's heading to the kitchen.

"Ello, ladies. Beautiful mornin', isn't it?" Dillon says as he starts emptying his bags. He wasn't kidding, he even brought his own measuring cups. Just because I choose to eat culinary treats created by others doesn't mean I don't have the means to create my own. I have measuring cups, for goodness sake. Of course mine are from Target and hot pink, but that is neither here nor there.

Anna kicks my shin while I hear Charlotte giggle. Apparently I'm still standing there with my mouth open. Classy. "Hello, Dillon, it *is* a lovely morning. Isn't it, *Victoria*?" Anna asks as I give her the evil eye and pull up a chair. Not one to be deterred by my so-called evil eye, Anna continues, "So, Dillon, what brings you by?"

"Well, I knew Sara was supposed to bring the treats for today and to be honest I couldn't see her here. She has referred to reading as 'so, like weird and scary.' Plus, I feel compelled to see this first day through. Plus, I wanted to be here to help Victoria with Pages and Quiet if she needed it."

He says all of this without a single misstep as he moves with ease about my kitchen. I'm sure my kitchen appreciates his presence. Dillon begins pouring ingredients into a bowl, never once pausing to squat down and check his measurements. Show off.

"What better way to get people to relax than the smell of freshly baked muffins? Don't you agree, ladies?"

Oh sweet baby jeebus. He's going to bake. In my kitchen. He could only be sexier if he mopped the floors after. Get it together, girl, he's just a guy. Barely a friend and definitely not interested in a forty-year-old single mom with a fondness for spending her nights with a pint of ice cream and book.

"Well, don't let us stop you. We'll just be right over here watching the show," Anna coyly replies.

A show is putting it mildly. The three of us sit there like we are watching the creation of a new civilization. He's a master with a whisk. How is he not getting stuff all over him? I have to shower, spray down the kitchen, and still don't get everything clean after I make some break 'n bake cookies. And is it normal to find forearms sexy? There's a hint of a tattoo above his shirt sleeve. And Charlotte has already whispered how he must obviously work out to have that chest. I'm ignoring her assessment. I couldn't care less if he's just blessed, I could watch this show all day.

"Victoria?" I hear my name but I'm so focused on those arms it takes yet another kick to the shin before I look up, thoroughly embarrassed when I realize Dillon has been talking to me.

"Sorry. I just spaced out for a sec. What was that?" Please don't ask me anything that requires me to leave the room. I don't want to miss any of this.

"I was asking if you wanted to come over here and help me. That way you'll be honest with your guests when you say you made muffins." Swoon. I'm swooning. And apparently, so is Charlotte because she lets out the sigh I am holding in. Suddenly I hear hysterical laughter coming from the doorway. Justin. He's lucky I love him.

"Justin, really? Is it really that funny?" I ask as I stand and face him with the best Mom face I can manage.

"Mom, it really is. I don't think Dillon has any idea what he's asking and I think I'll go outside and play with Tilly just to keep her safe," he says as he grabs an apple and heads out the back door.

"Don't mind him, come over here and help me. Nothing will feel sweeter than proving him wrong," Dillon says with a big grin.

I want nothing more for Dillon to be right. I grab my apron off the hook and tie it as I make my way to his side. He looks at my apron and lets out a chuckle as he shakes his head. I look down and can instantly feel the blush creep up my neck to my cheeks. "Wine Not" is displayed directly across my chest. I love this apron and really, "wine not".

Over the next thirty minutes Dillon patiently tries to help me melt chocolate. I don't care what anyone says, anyone can catch a pot of chocolate on fire. Dillon ushers us out of the kitchen so he can finish just as the first guests arrive.

I open the door to a smiling face and a big hug. Leah, Sara's mom, is a hugger. She is also just as sweet as Sara and can't stop gushing at how exciting it is to know she gets to sit and read uninterrupted today. Leah goes on to explain to me that Sara is not only her only daughter but the eldest of four. She has three boys all under the age of thirteen. It's agreed, she needs this day more than anyone. I ask Justin to show her around and tell her I'll be out to check on her later.

Suddenly my home is filled with the laughter of Leah's sisters. While most have brought their own books I offer them use of the newly established library if they like. Last to arrive is the woman from the public library, Elaine.

Also a widow, Elaine is about sixty years old and though I'm not the tallest gal in the world, I'm pushing Amazon woman status with Elaine. She greets me with the warmest hug and a slight hint of tears in her eyes. This tugs at my heart as she thanks me profusely for opening my home to the town. I always thought I was doing this to find my happiness; it never occurred to me that it would make a difference to others.

As expected, my team has called it a day and by 2:30 it's just the ladies in their nooks, me in my office, and Dillon in the doorway.

"Oh my goodness, you scared me!" I shout when I look up to see him. He's leaning against the doorway, arms crossed, with a gentle smile on his face. Stupid butterflies are back. This man makes me so nervous!

"Sorry." Is he being shy? "I just wanted to see how things were going. I also baked another batch of the muffins and left them cooling. I was going to head out but wanted to make sure you were okay."

"Oh." That's a hell of a response. The day seems to have been a success, a small kitchen fire withstanding. I'd love for Dillon to stay the rest of the day and see it all the way through with me.

"May I sit?" he asks. I nod and just smile. I'm apparently a puppet. "I soaked and tried to save the pot but alas I believe we'll have to call it a loss." Kill me now.

"Well, as you probably guessed, I won't really miss it," I say with a little grin.

"Tell me how you think the day is going? The ladies seem to be happy and it really is peaceful here."

"Honestly, I think it is going perfect. I made the right decision to start with a small and intimate event. I'm hoping to do a few more like this and then I'll be ready to start the longer retreats."

Talking about P&Q is easy. I can talk to him about my business and not feel nearly as nervous as when we are just having a simple conversation. In all of those first dates, I never once felt this nervous. Truly, not even Patrick made me this off-balance. I'm sure as much as I enjoy having him here, he's equally as ready to get out of here.

"Dillon, I can't thank you enough for all the help you've given me. I really appreciate it. You've become somewhat of a mentor for me and truly a good friend. I'd love to pay you back somehow." I whisper the last part and look up to see him smiling at me like he has as secret.

"Coffee."

"What? You want me to make a pot of coffee?" He's chuckling now and I feel dumb. "Oh, of course not. I need to *pay you* for the coffee and treats. Let me just find my checkbook." I start rummaging through the desk drawer for my checkbook and am likely six different shades of embarrassed.

"*Victoria*," he says my name like a purr. What in the hell? "Stop. I don't want your money, I want to have coffee with you. And not at Irish Coffee either. Let's go into the city and have a proper date."

"To . . . to . . . to*gether*?" I squeak out.

Again, the chuckle. Damn his sexiness. "Yes, Victoria. Together. A proper date. You did say you were dating, right? It's time I get out there and what better way than with a friend. Say you'll go. If it makes you feel better, we'll consider it payment for today's treats."

"Okay? Sounds fun." A date. He wants to take me on a date. I'm pretty sure I may combust. We stand up and I walk him to the door.

"Thank you again, Dillon. I really do appreciate all that you've done for me and P&Q. And, I'm looking forward to coffee." I appreciate him and I am beyond looking forward to coffee. I may not be breathing right now at the idea, but who really needs to breathe.

"Coffee date, Victoria. And you are welcome. It really was my pleasure and honestly the most fun I've had in a long time. I've got a busy week but I'll be in touch, okay?" he says as he gets to the end of the porch.

"Okay. Oh and Dillon? Can we not call it a date. That sounds like pressure and I'd rather just enjoy the time with a friend," I say with a sincere smile.

"We'll call it whatever you want. But, Victoria?" he pauses. "It is a date." And just like that he turns and walks down the steps toward his truck.

Oh. My. Word. I'm going on a *date* date with Dillon. My dreams are going to rock tonight! Assuming these aren't actual butterflies in my stomach.

Chapter Eight

NORMALLY WHEN I have a new date I would immediately call or text Anna and Charlotte. For my date with Dillon, I didn't. At first I was just so confused about the entire idea then that quickly turned to my fear that they'd make it into a bigger deal than it really is. Plus, there's a part of me that likes having my own friend I don't have to share. I suppose this is all part of the finding my happiness and moving forward. I'm making it happen.

It's time for me to stand on my own two feet. I have spent the years since Patrick passed depending so much on the support of others and in my role as Justin's mom. Somehow along the way I lost Victoria. For goodness sake, it took the entire village to create my online dating profile. I don't even pick a date outfit without Anna and Charlotte helping and I couldn't make it out the door before each date without their pep talks. I've let them all take care of me. I've relied on their shoulders to cry and lean on. I'm realizing, never did I make any of it happen on my own. That is about to change.

It has been just shy of a week since the mini retreat and the response has been great. While I've had high hopes of this being successful, the truth of it is that I'm scared out of my mind. One of the things Dillon and I discussed during our mentoring meetings what my need to start small and build a business. I can see where I was, perhaps, a little overzealous with my initial plans for a bed-and-breakfast-style retreat. Small and intimate is much more my style anyway. Of course, I still plan on working to have authors at some of the retreats. I love the idea of supporting and promoting local and indie authors.

I've attempted to reach out to my favorite author, D.L. Cardwell, to appear as the first featured author of P&Q. I may be scaling back the big picture for my business but a girl has priorities and the chance to fangirl over my favorite author? I'm all in. I've submitted a formal request to her publicist and while it's taking everything I have not to send another, okay a third, I'm being cool and patient while I wait for a response. I will say this though, whoever is in charge of D.L. Cardwell and her personal appearances should give pointers to the government because she's locked up tighter than Fort Knox.

I'm still committed to my mornings at Irish Coffee but have yet to see Dillon since he left my house. I ever so casually asked Sara where he was the other day. That was a slightly awkward conversation.

"So, Sara, I haven't seen Dillon this week. Is he sick?"

"No, he's not sick. I figured you knew he was out of town considering you are *friends* and all." I wasn't sure what she was implying with the way she said friends but I chose to ignore her smirk and insinuations. Insinuations by an eighteen-year-old are just uncomfortable.

After further casual questioning, I discovered that Dillon flew out early this week to the East Coast for business. Sara said he is scheduled to be back in town sometime over the next few days.

At first, I was bummed because I was looking forward to finalizing our date plans. Then, I was relieved. I was relieved because this lack of communication is going to force me to be chill. Relaxed. Not crazy. Basically, not be me until he calls or I see him. Then my phone dings with a text . . . from Dillon.

Hey there. So I was thinking our coffee date this Tuesday? Let me know

Eep. At this point the fact that he types out all the words is like foreplay. I mean awesome. Not foreplay. We are friends. If I get another text from someone that replaces vowels with numbers I may scream. Now to reply just right. I can't seem too eager and I can't seem too laid back. Maybe I should just tell Anna about all of this. She'd have the perfect response. But no. I can't. Here goes nothing.

Sounds great. 10:00?

Perfect :)

Happy face! Now I have like three days to drop twenty pounds and stop being a crazy person. Or I could just take this for what it is. Friends going to the city to have coffee. Easy peasy, lemon squeezy. Who the hell am I kidding? After the first dates from hell I'm going out for coffee with probably the hottest guy - Irish guy - on the West Coast.

A quick check of my email just adds to this already crazy day. An actual response from D.L. Cardwell's publicist. Well, it's probably a generic response from her "people" but whatever, it's a response saying she'd be *thrilled* to discuss "the possibility of D.L. attending your event."

Thrilled! Shut. The. Front. Door. She wants to come. Here. This is bananas. Why is the room spinning? Shit on a stick, I'm having a panic attack. Calm down, Victoria, you can do this. It's what you want. You are making things happen. I shoot off a quick reply and spend the rest of the day on cloud nine.

The next few days fly by. I'm really finding my groove with P&Q. Heck, I even managed to create a website. Well, by *I created* I actually mean a website was created.

Dan was online date number . . . I don't recall what number he was but after all was said and done, he became a friend and bonus - he's a website designer. While there was never a romantic future for Dan and me, mostly because I couldn't get past the excessive snif-fling and the fact that he lived with his mother, we've become good friends.

I'm not being judgmental, really I'm not. It's just the mom thing wasn't "oh what an awesome son, he lives with his mom to help her out." No, it's more "oh he's forty-five and never moved out of the house." I tell no lies. He never moved out. I was surprised to say the least and told him as much.

"So, even college? You never moved out of your parents' house?" I am still perplexed as I recall the conversation. The date had been going well and I was actually learning to tolerate the sniffles.

"No. I stayed local. Never really saw the point of leaving home just for the sake of leaving. Plus, once my dad passed, it was my re-sponsibility to stay and help my mother." Sniffle, sniffle.

"I'm sorry about your father, when did he pass?" I assumed it wasn't too long ago and I know from losing Patrick it is an awful thing to go through.

"1981," he replied while he took a big drink of his Arnold Palm-er. He didn't seemed phased by the fact that he was a kid when he lost his father.

"Well, I'm very sorry for your loss. You're quite successful though, right? A web designer? And you never wanted to get a place of your own?" I was so confused.

"Nah, like I said I never really saw the point. I converted a few of the guest rooms into an office and work from home. My mom is a phenomenal cook and knows exactly how I prefer my socks folded. Besides all of that, she is my best friend and I enjoy spending time with her." And, I'm out.

I smile at the memory and had my fingers crossed when I called Dan for some help designing the website for P&Q. He's still living with his mother, however, he did purchase a vacation home in Mexico. His intent is to head south at least three times a year for some rest and relaxation. Sure he plans to take his mother with him. Nevertheless, I am proud of his strides.

With a little guidance from Dan, I managed to create a fun and a little quirky website. I'm pretty proud of myself and the feedback has been great.

As I lean on the counter in my kitchen looking out the window, I feel Patrick. Every so often I feel his presence and know that he's pushing me along and is proud. Not presence like a spirit or ghost, but like part of my soul. Almost from the moment I (reluctantly) agreed to date him, he supported me unconditionally. He always encouraged me to take the time to do what makes me happy and refused to allow me to feel selfish for it. I may have lost that a little since his death, but ever as patient in his death as he was in life, he's been here guiding me to this point. I know he is happy to see me getting happy again. I only hope he's okay with whatever friendship I have with Dillon.

Oh crap, Dillon. Our date is tomorrow. Again I'm questioning my decision to keep this a secret. Since I'm on my own for the pre-date pep talk, I need to start that now.

Most importantly, it's a friend date, not *date* date. It's only coffee for shit's sake, relax. What do you wear on a friend date for coffee? I need to be dressed in a way that says, "We're friends, it's just coffee, this is no big deal even though you are the hottest guy to ever walk the earth." Easy enough, right?

This calls for the two things that only make sense when making a decision like this - rocky road and *Friends*. Before I can even get the first scoop in the dish I hear my phone.

Looking forward to our date. Plan on walking a bit. :)

Looking forward to it? I'm not giggling or anything, no worries. Okay, maybe I'm giggling. And smiling profusely. Definitely smiling.

Walking?

Yes, walking. You didn't think we'd just sit and drink coffee did you?

Well, yeah, kind of.

Haha. Guess not. Ok, so no stilettos. Got it. See you at 10 :)

Night

Goodnight

Walking. Damnit. So now I need to add "totally casual" to the list of what my outfit says.

I was so distracted by Dillon's text I didn't even sit down and watch *Friends*. Let's not get carried away though, I still had my rocky road.

Since the only other person that knows about this not really a date, date is Tilly, I put on a fashion show just for her to choose what I'm going to wear. Not only can you not rely on the weather here in the Pacific Northwest, you also cannot rely on the opinion of your German Shepherd for fashion advice. I realized after forty-five minutes of scouring the closet that I needed to not only stop stressing about this, but I also needed Anna. I shoot her off a quick text to call me - 911!

"Do I need to pack a bag?!"

"What? No. Sorry, it's not an emergency like that, it's . . . I have to tell you something but you can't freak out like you do. Promise?"

"No. I do not promise, but I'll try. What is it? You've decided to give the foot thing a try after all?" she snickers. Really? I thought we had moved past that.

"Shut it. I . . . Well, I have a non-date with Dillon tomorrow and I don't know what to wear."

"What in the hell is a non-date? And, thank God. I didn't think you'd go for it but that man is sex on a stick." I swear she purred when she said sex.

"Really, Anna? Sex on a stick? Okay, I'll give you sexy. It's a non-date because I'm not dating. We're going into the city for coffee and just as *friends*. But he does make me nervous and I want to still look nice. He said we will be walking so I'm trying to look casual yet still look good and prepared for walking. I need you! Help me."

I can hear her pour a glass of wine. Why didn't I think of wine? That would have helped this process along tremendously.

"Whatever, it's a date. I like him. More importantly Justin likes him and Patrick would too. I'm happy for you. Now, quit being a ninny and suck it up. You're hot and could wear a gunny sack and it wouldn't matter. However, I do want to see you get laid so let's sex it up a bit." And there she is, ladies and gents, my best friend and her lack of a filter.

After twenty minutes of defending my wardrobe and my reluctance to admit I actually need to do some shopping, we settle on the "these make my ass look fantastic" jeans, a lilac short-sleeved V-neck, and a lightweight cardigan. Keeping walking in mind I choose my favorite old-school Chucks. Casual, sporty, and relaxed - at least I hope. I hang up, promising to call her tomorrow and give her a play-by-play report, and snuggle into my bed and spend a little time with the new D.L. Cardwell book I just started. As usual there is a perfect man for the beautiful, if slightly broken, heroine. It is fiction, after all.

Chapter Nine

MORNING COMES QUICKLY and the nerves kick in almost immediately. Thankfully I have enough work to do that I don't have time to dwell. As I sit at my desk I am reminded of Dillon standing in the doorway looking all kinds of dreamy and being sincere and kind. a few weeks ago. He really is a good guy and I am truly grateful for his friendship. After a quick set of responses to inquiries on the website and confirmation of a few reservations, it's time to start pacing while I wait for him to get here.

At 10:00 sharp the doorbell rings and I have to remind myself to breathe and smile. It's only Dillon. I open the door and am jabbering away before I even look up.

"Hey there, I'll be just be. . ." holy shit. I guess like my "these make my ass look fantastic" jeans, he has a "this makes me look like a sexy piece of man candy" shirt. "Umm, yeah, a sec. So come on in. No kidding, sex on a stick." No that didn't sound completely ridiculous, Victoria. Not at all. You also don't sound like you just swallowed one of Tilly's squeak toys. I grab my purse off the side table and turn back around to that smile. He's hysterically laughing. Oh shit.

"Sex on a stick? Do tell," he says almost mockingly.

"What? I didn't say that. I, uh, said shit on a stick. It's a thing. Anyway, all set. Ready to go?" I can't help but blush profusely and give him a weak smile as I ask. Note to self: talk to your brain about using a filter and kill Anna.

"First, good mornin'. I haven't heard that expression before but duly noted. And yes, if you are ready, let's go. But . . . I have to say, you look very lovely and I'm really freaking nervous," he says as he moves aside and I step out the door.

"You're nervous? Why would you be nervous, Dillon? It's coffee with a friend, right? To thank you for your help. No pressure," I remind him while I'm secretly relieved he's nervous too.

"Right. Finding your happiness, not a date, and certainly no pressure." He's smiling again. Damn him and that smile. "It's just that . . . I like you, Victoria. You make me laugh and I don't want to just lock myself away anymore. No matter what, I appreciate your friendship and am glad to know you. Now, shall we? I don't take many days off and I want to make the most of it. I hope you are ready!" he says as he opens the truck door for me.

The drive into the city is beautiful and the conversation just flows. We talk about music and I tell him how much Justin mocks my choices. Dillon gets the greatness that is Earth, Wind & Fire and just happens to have it playing for half the drive. We talk a little about Irish Coffee and P&Q. Mostly, we just talk about nothing and everything. I tell him all about life growing up with a little sister and he tells me about his three brothers. I cannot imagine three more men running around this world looking like Dillon. We avoided the big topics - Patrick, cancer, and being a widow.

As we approach the city I realize how much I miss it when my phone dings. A quick check tells me it's Anna.

Don't be nervous today. Enjoy yourself!!!!

I take a quick glance at Dillon, who is humming along to *September*, and smile.

I'll try. Having a good day?

No. I need a break in a major way.

You? I don't believe it.

Yes me. Smartass. How about dinner and a sleepover this weekend. I need out of here and I need wine.

Friday? I'll get the wine, you bring Channing and the guys :)

Deal.

"Charlotte or Anna checking on you?" Dillon asks.

I smile and giggle. Giggling should not be my go-to reaction at my age but this man seems to bring out the tween in me. "Anna. Not really checking on me, just checking in. Now are you going to tell me why there will be walking today?"

"Nah. I think I'll let that imagination of yours run wild." That damn smirk. And forearms; if he's handling that steering wheel like he would handle . . . well, you know. Damn, I sound like a horny housewife. It has been a long time and, well, Dillon is Dillon. I'd have to be dead to not notice just how damn attractive he is.

The rest of the drive is relaxed and as he looks for parking I am reminded of all the benefits of living in the city. I love my quiet town, but the excitement and energy the city exudes is addictive. We park and head over to a cafe Dillon insists has the best lattes and the most amazing freshly baked bread. Once we are seated and place our orders I actually feel relaxed. He's so easy to be around and there are no expectations.

"This is really nice, Dillon. I forgot how much I enjoy the city sometimes."

"How often do you get back?"

"It's starting to feel like it's not often enough. Patrick and I lived here until Justin was about two years old. I loved it but never doubted our move," I say with a little hiccup in my voice. That's how it is sometimes when I think about the past. I push the thought away and offer a smile that I can feel doesn't quite reach full capacity.

"I'd love to hear more about Patrick. It seems like you had a wonderful life. Care to tell me about it? I understand if it's too personal." The sincerity in his voice as he says this is almost too much. He truly means it. We are on a non-date and he wants to hear about my husband.

"Really? You want to talk about Patrick? That's really amazing," I say, and mean it.

"Victoria, we are friends. Of course I want to know about him. He is a part of you and that's never going to change. From the little I know of Justin, I assume he was a good guy and you were a great couple." He smiles and I know that he is sincere. He really does want to know.

I give him the Reader's Digest version of our relationship and marriage. We laugh a lot and I'm just now noticing I haven't cried. I'm talking about Patrick and haven't cried. Talking to Dillon just seems natural. We manage to make it through our meal and he wasn't lying when he said the bread was amazing. Once the plates are cleared and our lattes are in front of us, I continue.

"Then, we got his diagnosis. It was a shock to say the least," I solemnly admit.

"How long did you fight?" he asks. The look of concern is evident and he asked as if he understands I fought just as hard.

"Ten months and twenty-three days," I say while looking away, sensing the first tear. Suddenly I feel his hand over mine and a wave of relief washes over me. I look at him, and although the topic is about my husband and it is so serious, I feel peaceful looking at him; I trust him. "It was hard, but as much as I miss him, I am grateful he is no longer suffering." He squeezes my hand while I keep going. "Dillon, I appreciate you caring enough to ask. More than you know. But, can we table this topic? I want to have fun today. Like you said, you don't get many days off so let's push the serious stuff off for another time, okay?"

"Whatever the lady wishes." He winks and motions for the waiter. Once he pays the bill he stands and offers me his hand, which I accept.

"Are you ready to put those Chucks to use?" he asks with a mischievous smirk as he releases my hand.

"Finally! The great mystery shall be revealed. You, sir, better make it worth it or you're going to owe me dinner too!" I jokingly say while I smack his arm playfully.

Once again, he grabs my hand. Dillon really has a thing for my hand, not that I'm complaining. He looks me in the eye without a hint of humor, "I hoped to buy you dinner."

And here I stand. On the sidewalk, speechless with my newly released hand feeling slightly lonely. Damn, this guy is good. We walk for blocks and blocks before he stops in front of a storefront that looks abandoned. I should be grateful he appears to be on board with the "this isn't a date" concept since standing in front of abandoned buildings isn't really romantic.

"What do you think?" he asks me.

"About what? This boarded-up building? It's quite lovely, but I would have gone with a darker piece of wood to cover the windows," I say like a complete smart-ass. "What are we doing here?"

"I'm considering expanding Irish Coffee. I've had some interest to franchise. I'm not sure I want to move in that direction, but one of my brothers wants to partner up and open a larger shop here in the city." He's moving. Of course, the one friend I have in town and he's leaving. Fabulous, there goes my heart. Sunk like the Titanic.

"Dillon, that's fantastic. Really, you deserve it. Irish Coffee is wonderful and I think you'd do great in the city. It seems to agree with you," I say with what I hope comes out as being sincere.

"Oh, I'm not moving. Liam is considering relocating back here to the West Coast and wants to take the reins on this one. He's all business and has a big plan for the company. As long as he leaves the current Irish Coffee alone I'm fine with it," he tells me. "Come on, I have three more locations I want to show you." Well that was close. I feel like I just dodged a major bullet. For some reason I don't want to lose this *friend*.

We spend the next few hours looking at storefronts for Irish Coffee #2. I can see how excited he is at the idea of his company growing, but knowing he doesn't have to handle it all on his own. Like always, our conversations just flow. I'm completely comfortable with Dillon and I think he is with me too. Around 3:00 I hit a wall. I'm exhausted from lack of sleep. Or maybe it's because dating in my forties is a lot more tiring than it was in my twenties. When I was young I could stay up all night, work all day, and still have the energy to walk what feels like fifteen miles on a date. Now? Not so much. As much as I try to avoid it, the big yawn I'm in the middle of doesn't go unnoticed.

"Tired?" Dillon asks. I just shrug, trying not to show just how exhausted I really am. "I guess I have walked you across half the city. I'm sorry. Let's head back and think about dinner," Dillon says as he once again grabs my hand. Only this time he doesn't let go and I realize I don't want him to. I was right, the way he handled the steering wheel . . . just like he would handle me, err . . . a woman.

The walk back to the truck is pretty uneventful and as he holds the door while I get in, he stops and says, "Thank you." I must look confused because he clears his throat and again says, "Thank you. Thank you for making this day fun and for being a good friend. Now, since this has been the non-date portion of the day, can we officially head into the real date part?" Damn that sexy smile.

"Absolutely," I confidently reply.

As we drive in comfortable silence, I must doze off because I startle awake when he stops in front of my house. "Oh my goodness,

I can't believe I fell asleep! Dillon! You should have woken me," I say, embarrassed.

"First, I couldn't if I tried. You were dead to the world. Plus, if I want to have a proper dinner date with you I figured you needed the rest." He is around the truck and opening the door before I can open it. "I'm thinking I'll leave you for a few hours and then I'll be back to take you to dinner. Sound good?" He walks me to the door while asking.

"Sounds perfect. Say seven o'clock?" With a nod and a kiss to the cheek – kiss to the cheek! – he's gone. Suddenly my phone dings.

Don't you dare hold out on us! How was the date? ~Anna & Char

You'd think we were triplets with some sort of super connection or that while I was gone with Dillon they installed hidden cameras around the house. Without analyzing how they knew the minute I got home, I must decide just how naughty I want to be. Turns out very.

Not sure. It's not over. TTYL :)

3, 2 . . . ring.

I answer the phone laughing as I make my way to my bedroom and kick off my shoes. "What took you so long?"

"It's not over?! Is he there right now?" Charlotte whispers.

I hear Anna in the background. "Char, you don't have to whisper. He can't hear you."

I'm laughing at not only the whispering but the fact that Anna actually felt she needed to explain it to Charlotte. "Well, it's on pause. He's coming back in a few hours and we're going to dinner. Today was not a date but tonight IS!" I flop down on my bed with a huge smile on my face. I hear a slight struggle with the phone and suddenly Anna is on the line.

"Congratulations, you have broken the routine!" Say what? "You are going on a second date!" Wow, I guess I am. No, because today wasn't . . . oh get over it, Victoria, it totally was a date.

"Yeah well, I need to nap, wash off this day, and find something perfect to wear. Girls, I'll catch you tomorrow!" I say as I click off the phone. I set my alarm for a little nap and fall into a deep sleep with a huge smile on my face.

Tonight I settle on a simple floral summer dress and sandals. I realize as I'm putting on my earrings that I'm not nervous, only excited. I dab on a little perfume and head down to the office until Dillon gets here. I have quite a few reservations for retreats and an email from Dan confirming a few updates to the website and that he is ready to update with the D.L. Cardwell information whenever it is available. I guess my dream is now a reality. I can't believe it! I pay a few bills and send Justin a quick text.

Hey kiddo, just wanted to say hi. Up for some breakfast Friday?

Hey mom sounds good c u then

How much would it kill him to spell out "*see you*," this kid. There's the bell and *my date*. I answer the door, but first remind my brain to use the filter. I've reached my maximum in embarrassing moments today. Deep breath, smile. . .

"Hey." Wow, Victoria, you've got a way with words.

"Ello. Ready? It's a bit chilly, you may want a sweater," Dillon says while smiling that smile I've grown quite accustomed to. I grab a cardigan and we're off. Abbott Falls is most definitely a town by any standards. We're a small town but we are not low on restaurants; it seems that our community is made up of foodies. I'm thrilled when we pull into the parking lot of my favorite Italian bistro, Salvatore's. The owner and head chef, Stefano Alberti, prides himself on authentic home-style food. Yes, I too assumed the restaurant would be named after the owner and head chef but according to Stefano, it is the name of the son he never had. After nine daughters he and his wife, Isabella, decided to give up on having a son and opted for the restaurant.

Have you ever had a romantic fantasy? Not like dirty fantasy but romance and perfection? This date was that. I know, no man is perfect. I know that Dillon is not perfect and we've established I'm often a hot mess, but it's like none of that mattered. We had great food and great conversation. Exchanging stories of our childhood, our teen years (his were a lot more fun than mine), and how much we've changed in recent years - it was truly a wonderful evening.

On the drive back to my house we talk a little about P&Q and Irish Coffee. He really cares for the kids who work for him and I love how much he supports them in their education and passions.

"Well, I'm not surprised to hear that Sara wants to be a teacher. She is such a sweet girl," I reply after he tells me he is helping her choose a college. "You really care about those kids, don't you?"

"Of course I do. We're really like a family and I couldn't live with myself if I didn't take the time for them. I was blessed to have a supportive family and some of them don't have that," he tells me with a simple shrug.

"Well, not all employers would be so involved. I think it's great. What will you do when they all move on?" I know what it feels like, and the way he talks about these kids, they are almost like his own.

"Find the next generation, I suppose. Unless you're looking to take on a second job?" he suggests with a little chuckle and a wink. Obviously he's trying to lighten the mood. Not that the mood is dark, but come on, I burned chocolate. I started a freaking fire in my kitchen assisting him. I'm sure the twinkle in his eyes is less about having me as an employee and more about fear at the thought of me using an espresso machine.

"As amazing as working with you would be, I'm pretty sure me plus an espresso machine is a recipe for disaster! Besides, what would happen to my table? It would be so lonely." We both laugh and he agrees.

Once we arrive at my house, I don't even bother trying to open the door since I know he'll do it. We reach my front door and I realize this is the moment of truth. I'm overwhelmed by an extreme case of the nervous butterflies battling the dragon. Is he going to kiss me? How much freaking garlic was in that pasta? I should have had a mint.

"Victoria, I have had an amazing day . . . .. and evening. I'd love to see you again. I also understand we need to keep it casual and on the friend level. Would that be okay?" he asks me. I clear my throat and look into his eyes, the swirls of blue. Are they actually swirling? It's almost like the sky has met the horizon and I can't look away. Dillon Laughlin has eyes that transport you to a different place. Shake it off, sister, it's time to get real.

"Dillon, we are friends and I had a great time. I'd love to spend more time together." He releases the deep breath I didn't realize he was holding and gives me a quick smile while he grabs my hand and gives it a quick squeeze. I never realized until then that he gets it - he understands how big of a step I'm taking. I smile and squeeze back. With that simple understanding he gives me another perfect kiss to the cheek and is heading down the porch steps to his truck. He pauses and faces me with a little wave and he's gone.

I don't know how long I stood there staring at the empty street, but the sound of a pterodactyl brought me to my senses. Fine, it wasn't a pterodactyl, but it was a bat and that's equally creepy. I head inside, close the door, and . . . there may have been dancing. Maybe. Just a little. Keeping with the required routine I shoot off a text to the girls.

I'm home :) All is GREAT, no coffee recap see you Friday!
Yay sis! See u then
Gawd yes, I'm bringing Channing!
Tilly makes her way to greet me and cocks her head, I guess even my canine girlfriend can sense my giddiness. "Come on, Till,

let's hit the sack. Momma has some dreams to have."

And boy oh boy are the dreams worth it.

Chapter Ten

A S THE SUN fills my bedroom with beautiful shades of gold, I wake with a huge smile on my face. I feel a sense of normalcy. However strange that may sound, it's the only way I can describe my feelings. I hate the term "normal" because it almost infers that there is only one way to be. In this case, it's *my normal*. I feel ready to rise without fear of what the day is going to bring. I feel confident in myself. I almost feel like I could wear white today and not spill. I said almost; I'm feeling confident, not crazy.

I tackle the morning rituals and figure it's a good day for some mindless house cleaning and just taking care of day-to-day stuff. Once I make it downstairs to start the first load of laundry for the day and start of the coffee, I grab my phone off the charger and see I already have a text. I glimpse at the clock, 7:43, much earlier than anyone in my life would think to text me. Dillon. Eep.

Morning beautiful. I have to head out of town last minute but wanted to say hello and thanks again for yesterday. D.

Morning to you. I had a blast yesterday. Enjoy your trip.

I hit send before I can decide if I should say more. Nope, we're friends and that was totally friendly. I could really get used to being called beautiful by Dillon. When I read it, I hear it with an Irish brogue, even though he doesn't really have one.

Pages & Quiet is quickly becoming a business. I've had a few inquiries from book clubs asking if they can start using the facility for their meetings and have the next few weeks booked for day-long events. Easily consumed with work and my daily routine, I'm only interrupted by a delivery. After a quick review I grab my phone.

"Good morning, Anna Crawford's office," Jill, Anna's long-time assistant, answers.

"Hey, Jill, it's Victoria."

"Hi, Victoria. How are you?" After a minute of chit chat she says she'll put me through to Anna.

"To what do I owe this pleasure?" Anna mumbles. I assume she's eating at her desk. I know Jill is constantly bugging her to leave the office for meals to get a little break but she insists there is no time.

"Anna, really? Are you eating and on the phone? What if I was a client?" I ask.

"Weeellll, Jill does screen the calls first so that's a non-issue. Did you call just to lecture me on my eating habits? I get enough of that from that drill sergeant out front," she says a little more clearly. I explain that I received the contract from D.L. Cardwell's publicist and ask her if she will take a look at it.

"Of course. Do you think it can wait until Friday? I can look it over then," she replies.

"Sure, just wanted to make sure. How are you doing? If we're bringing out *Magic Mike* it is serious business." *Magic Mike* is our go-to for when we need a major break from our reality. To say we watched it a lot after Patrick passed is putting it mildly. Nothing like a cast of sexy to pass the time. Plus, I'll never hear the song *Pony* the same again. Normally, I am not the biggest Channing Tatum fan. Anna and I leave that title for Charlotte. That being said, we are women and I'm sure there's scientific proof that this movie can solve any problem even if only for two hours.

"I'm fine. It's just . . . I don't want to talk about it. Tell me about *Dillon* and your day-long date!" I can hear her settle in for what she expects to be a long story. Sorry to disappoint.

"Nuh-uh. You have to wait until Friday. I want to recap the date only once. But are you sure you're okay? You know you can tell me anything. I worry about you," I say with all my love and sincerity.

"I'm really fine. I know you are always there for me and I love you for it. I just need to handle some of this myself. When I'm ready you'll be my first call, okay?"

I smile, knowing that was really hard for Miss Independent. "Always. So I'm thinking we go big on Friday - pizza, wine, chocolate. What do you think?" The mention of pizza will pull her from her funk. As expected, she spends the next five minutes expressing her undying devotion to the pizza pie and we hang up with both of us laughing.

I shoot off a quick text to Charlotte telling her there will be carbs on Friday so she can prepare herself. See, I'm a good sister. I'm still waiting to hear about her night clubbing with Tate and his husband. Poor Char, she has almost as much luck with men as I do. It's almost like we're related.

I've been good most of the day, not really thinking of Dillon and our date. This means I have analyzed it to death. I can't make heads or tails of my feelings. If I'm honest I was a little bummed there was no kiss, but I'm equally relieved. I think we both know I'm not there yet. I need to take this slower than a tortoise in a race. That doesn't stop me from sending him a text.

Hey you. What are the chances if I call Sara I'll be able to get some of your sinful brownies?

Talk about making my day, just the person I was thinking

about.

Wow. He's quick.

Oh really? You've been thinking of me? Do tell.

Apparently I can flirt - by text and with hundreds, or maybe thousands, of miles between us.

First I was thinking how I can't wait to have our next date. Plus I just passed a little bookstore and thought how much you'd enjoy it.

You sound pretty confident there's going to be a next date ;)

Yes ma'am I am. Have you been to New York before?

Are you planning that for our next date? I say YES!

And I love a good bookstore.

Haha well I think a trip across the country is more suitable for a 4th date not 2nd :)

I guess you have a point. So tell me more about this thinking of me. . .

We carry on like this for what feels like seconds but is really twenty minutes.

Shit, I have to go into a meeting. Can I call you while I'm here?

I'd love that.

Good. Oh and Sara has a batch of those brownies ready for you.

Thank you!! Good luck in your meeting.

Thanks. Have a good night beautiful.

Bye handsome.

To say I was much more at ease with Dillon on the phone than in person would be an understatement. I found myself being more bold and flirtatious while still feeling completely comfortable. He called me a few hours after our flirtexting - is that a word? If it isn't, it should be. We laughed a lot and told each other about our day. It was just a simple conversation but when I hung up, I felt completely content and relaxed.

We talked daily, well okay multiple times a day, plus the constant texting for the rest of his trip. There was no mention of our impending date. It is as if we don't need to acknowledge that it's going to happen, we just know. I also know that at some point I'm going to have to admit to myself that I want to date Dillon. I want to see where this goes and I think he feels the same way.

When I wake up Friday morning I am unbelievably excited for a fun girl's night. I love that we still have these sleepovers because they make us feel like teenagers again. The only difference now is that Anna and I *want* Charlotte there. When we were teenagers and had our sleepovers, Charlotte was like one of those little gnats that you absently swat at and never actually catch. That was when the ten-year age difference was as big as the Grand Canyon. You know, when you're fourteen and your little four-year-old sister is demanding she be included in *everything*. Painting toe nails, facials, debating which Corey was hotter (Haim, duh), and lip syncing to our favorite songs - she was there, chanting, "Please, TorrrreeeeUH! Please! Please! Puh-hhllleeeeasseeeeee!" Oh good gravy, fine!

Now? Having a girl's night isn't complete without Charlotte. She makes me laugh and always knows when I need a distraction. When my thoughts get serious and I need someone to bring me back to the now. Of course, sometimes her intent isn't to make me laugh, it's just that she's so ridiculously funny when she's being serious. Or in love. Lust. Like? Whatever, when she's crushing.

Tonight we are going big. Major carb and junk food fest - pizza, triple-chocolate-chip ice cream, popcorn, licorice, and regular soda. No diet anything tonight! Anna called this gathering and is bringing *Magic Mike*, which means there's something stirring in her life. I am planning on badgering her until she dishes; it's not like her to keep all of whatever this is inside. Charlotte has promised to explain the whole "Tate's husband" situation. Not that it's a "situation," but she's so not affected by it I kind of wonder if I should worry. And me . . . Well, us. Dillon and I. Are we an us? No we aren't - yet.

It's like he knows when I'm thinking of him.

Just wanted to say goodnight before the girls get there.

Goodnight? It's only 4:00! Are you implying we're old?

Absolutely NOT! You can't be old because then I'm ancient. I just know you will be all girly and not have time for the likes of me later.

Well gramps I do plan on being girly tonight. There may even be a pillow fight.

Gramps?! And don't be cruel - pillow fight?!

Ha! Kidding. I would never hurt my pillows, they are too important to me! Seriously though I think all 3 of us need this. Are you back in town yet?

Not yet. Later tonight. I'll let you go and get ready. Call you over the weekend?

Absolutely. And thanks.

Thanks?

For getting that I/we still need these nights. Not all men would understand.

Well, Ms. Bennett, I am not all men.

How can one statement make me giggle? No, Dillon, you are not all men!

That is a fact.

Here goes nothing.

Can I cook you dinner Sunday?

How about WE cook dinner Sunday? 7:00?

Swoon.

Sounds perfect. Have a safe flight.

Thanks. See you Sunday.

Chapter Eleven

"ARE YOU SHITTING me right now, Victoria?!" Anna shouts as she walks in the kitchen. By shout I mean screeches. I didn't know she had that sound in her perfect body, but apparently she does.

"Umm, no?" I ask her, completely perplexed and elbow deep in pizza dough. I flip on the faucet and start washing my hands while I look at her wide-eyed, waiting for her to continue. "What in the fresh hell are you talking about?"

"I am not *making* the pizza. I want to indulge in ooey-gooey yumminess and I'm pretty sure we are not capable of that. In fact, I think we are more likely to catch the oven on fire," she giggles and starts unpacking bags upon bags of junk food.

She has a point. I did catch chocolate on fire. "Oh thank God. I was trying to be all domestic, but who am I kidding? Speed dial two on the house phone. You order while I go wash this crap off my hands. Is it supposed to be this sticky?!" I ask as I walk up the stairs to my room to take the loofah to my hands. By the time I make it back downstairs Charlotte is here and they have poured our first glasses of wine. I am instantly at peace and we are laughing in seconds at my moment of crazy to even think we should attempt baking a pizza.

One bottle of wine down, one pizza . . . okay, two pizzas . . . devoured and it's that time. Girl talk. Or, lay it all out on the line time.

"Girls, it's that time. We are thoroughly carb stuffed and a bit tipsy. Let's ease into it, shall we? Charlotte, you first," I direct my ridiculously dressed sister. Charlotte takes this sleepover concept literally. She's dressed in her little frilly nightie, hair in pigtails, and is sporting her bunny slippers. Yes, bunny. She insists they are not the same ones she got for her twelfth birthday; I'm not convinced. "Spill it. Not the wine. The dish," I instruct her.

A big sigh and she's off. Charlotte tells us that she did invite Tate to coffee and they really hit it off. Tate is originally from New Mexico and had been successful in real estate for years. When the market crashed, his lifestyle of luxury crashed too, so he decided to pack up his life and head to the coast. I was impressed and honestly I think Anna was too. Of course, she was probably just relieved to hear that the man she spent hours listening to Charlotte yap about wasn't just a pretty face.

"Did I tell you how handsome he is? It's probably why he was so successful selling real estate. Who could say no to perfection?" Charlotte went on and on about his perfect jaw and "chocolate-dipped eyes" - her words. You're probably wondering at what point Charlotte realized this wasn't a date and that Tate had a husband. Well, that would have been when they were leaving the coffee shop and she was hoping he'd ask her out again. She said that Tate thanked her for asking him to coffee and how he knew from the first time she bought a dozen bottles of Two Buck Chuck that they would be besties. No, that wasn't her clue, it was when a gorgeous Ken-doll-like man walked up, wrapped his arm around Tate's waist, and planted a kiss on his lips that she thought maybe this wasn't a date.

Ya think? Oh, poor Charlotte, I can only imagine the five million thoughts that went through her mind. Turns out Ken isn't Ken but Chad. Chad and Tate have been together for three years and married for six months. Chad was so excited to meet Charlotte that she quickly got over the entire non-date thing and the three of them have been inseparable since.

"And, Anna, before you ask, yes I told them I thought it was a date. They were totally okay with it and are now referring to me as Tate's wife." It's at this point that I realize Charlotte is really okay. She's still a bit lost but she's not sad. "Oh and Chad is introducing me to a guy in his office. Maybe I didn't get a boyfriend in Tate but I have two new friends and a date prospect. Cheers to me!" We clink glasses to that.

"Before we move on to listening to how amazing Dillon is, I have a few questions, Char," Anna sarcastically comments.

I choke on my wine, crap. I hoped we'd just move right past all of that. I wave away the concerned looks and sputter out, "I'm good."

"First, what the hell job does Chad do? Second, how old is this man that they want to set you up with? And, do you think it's hot when they kiss?"

"ANNA! Oh my. . .ANNA!" I shout and smack her repeatedly as she cackles like a damn chicken.

Standing abruptly with her hands on her hips, Charlotte simply says, "He works for a big marketing firm. Thirty-five. And after a few cocktails, sure." And with that she pivots and heads for the kitchen with a little extra sway in her strut.

"Geez, Vic, relax. I was kidding. Not about the job and age but the kissing. I didn't think she'd answer. Who knew Charlotte had a little kink in her? I'm a little impressed," Anna says.

Charlotte returns with chocolate and more wine. I'm procrastinating and talking about the weather, upcoming retreats, and really *anything* to avoid Dillon talk. Don't get me wrong, I cannot wait to be girly and talk about him . . . his eyes, his arms, his perfect ass, the way my heart flutters when he holds my hand, the way my knees shake with the idea of those amazing lips finally kissing mine . . . maybe I think about Dillon a bit. I know that whatever I say, Anna and Charlotte are going to ask about feelings. I'm scared that I will answer them and then all of this will be a new reality.

I realize procrastination is short-lived when Anna grabs my glass and tells me no more until I spill. Grabbing the glass *and* the bottle, I reply, "Nope. Age before beauty, babe. Tell us why we're here." Anna starts shaking her head so fast I'm afraid she's going to make herself sick. "I'm serious, Anna, what is going on? I'm worried. Charlotte is worried. Hell, I think even Tilly is worried. You know we love you, we want to help."

I may have pushed too far. I see her eyes shimmer with tears. Anna doesn't cry. In seventh grade when her pet parakeet died she didn't even bat an eye. She simply said with a straight face, "It's the circle of life, Vic," and just went on with the day. I, on the other hand, bawled like a baby and I hated that damn bird.

It takes about two seconds before both Charlotte and I are tearing up. We are sympathetic criers. It happens.

"You'll hate me. I hate me. I'm a damn hypocrite and apparently an addict," she says through sobs. Addict? Holy shit. I'm speechless. And apparently out of wine. I just grab the bottle and chug. Not the classiest and not really sympathetic when someone says "addict."

I get my act together enough to put down my glass and grab Anna's hands. "Okay. Umm, I'm not going to lie, I'm a little freaked, but I'm here. What do we need to do? Find a rehab? Counseling? Tell me. We could never hate you, right, Char?" Charlotte is sitting there just staring wide-eyed and nods slowly. While I'm the big sister, Anna is our glue. She keeps us grounded and together. If she's losing it we're in big trouble. I am truly prepared to do whatever she needs. I'll pour the rest of this bottle of wine out right away. I love her and will support her unconditionally

"What? Damnit. Poor choice of words. Do they have rehab for being . . . A HOME!" She's hysterical now and I have no idea what she is saying. It's just "home" over and over.

"Anna, honey, you've got to calm down. I'm confused. Can you break it down a bit? I want to help you but I don't understand. Are you not struggling with addiction?" I ask, completely bewildered. Now she's laughing. What in the actual hell is going on here? A breakdown? I think so. She's finally lost her mind. I figured I'd be the first to go but she's beaten me to the punch - overachiever.

"Okay, ladies, let's do some deep breathing. In for four, out for six. Come on, Anna, in for four . . . OUCH! What the hell, Victoria?" Whoops, I didn't mean to kick Charlotte that hard.

"Sorry. Instinct," I say and start repeating with Charlotte, "In for four. . ."

Anna finally calms down and takes a deep breath, standing up in front of us and motioning for us to sit closer together. We do and she begins pacing while she starts talking. "I'm sorry. I may be a little drunk and just lost it for a minute. I'm saying this once. I don't want to analyze it. I'm dealing with it." She stops and faces us. The look on her face, it's broken. My strong, beautiful, independent friend is broken. "I know you love me and I love you back but I really need to handle this on my own and figure out how to get my shit together. Okay? Don't nod, answer me."

"Okay," Charlotte and I say in unison.

"I haven't been honest with you for the last few years." Did she just say years? Shit on a stick. "I have been seeing someone, a man, for the past two years. I love him. He loves me. With our careers we've kept it under wraps. Nobody knows and last month I realized that I want you to meet him. I want to spend holidays together. I want him to meet my parents. I know, I never want anyone to meet my parents. He's the one. He's kind and loving and sweet and the sex is amazing. Like beyond amazing, what's beyond amazing? Phenomenal? Earth shattering? I mean, he can go for hours, it's just. . ."

I clear my throat and motion for her to move it along. I am not having sex. I have not had sex in what feels like a dozen years and is actually closer to almost four years, so I really don't need to hear about earth-shattering anything.

"Sorry, okay. Well, I told him this. I expected him to tell me he wanted the same things. He didn't. He told me that he loves what we have and that at this point in his career, he cannot 'change the plan.' Yes, he used air quotes. Bastard. He can't change his *plan*. Apparently plan is code for marriage. He's married." She took a pause for some wine, a big bite of chocolate, and what I expect is enough time for Charlotte and I to process what she's just said. *Married?!* Holy shit.

"I knew he was technically married but I thought this was an 'all about social status and for appearances sake' marriage. I know you hate me right now. Trust me, I hate myself enough for all of us."

I'm stunned. Anna was cheated on in college and swore she'd never go through that again and would never in her life be the other woman. This is one of those adult moments, the moments that come along and you have to look at what you have *believed* to be core beliefs on marriage, commitment, and fidelity and compare it to reality. The reality is that Anna is as much my sister as Charlotte and I will not judge her. That's not true, I will likely hold judgment, but not for long and not in a way that will allow me to do anything but love Anna unconditionally.

"He told me he loves me but he loves his wife and he is committed to the marriage and his family. The sonofabitch told me that since I was changing the rules he was going to have to stop seeing me. Can you believe that? He decided? I lived a secret and lie for two years and he's decided. Do you know the worst part?" Charlotte and I are kind of mute at this point, just nodding like puppets not really knowing what to say. "I can't even make a scene about it because of who he is. Bastard. Don't. I can't tell you. I just can't. I'll just say his name is Richard and he truly is a Dick."

I'm overwhelmed for my friend. My heart is breaking for her and I'd like to find Dick and kick his ass. I have a million questions and my mind is spinning, but I know Anna. She is telling us we can't ask questions. There is no room for that. She plops down on the couch, snuggled in the corner with her knees to her chest.

"Girls, I want you to know that I never intended for this to happen nor did I plan for it to last this long. I was dumb. I'm just embarrassed and that's why I never said anything. Most of all, I don't know how to stop the hurt. I love him. It's almost like the love I have for him is overpowering my common sense."

Charlotte looks at me and I nod as she smiles and says, "Anna, he's a piece of shit. You are a strong and beautiful woman. You don't owe us an apology. We love you."

And on that note, we finish the bottle of wine, throw in *Magic Mike*, and let Anna immerse herself in sexy men. I'm dumbfounded and my heart aches for her. She's kept this part of her life from me, from us, and still can't unload. I start picking up our trash while they are finishing up the movie. I hear my phone buzz with a text as I enter the kitchen. Before I can even pick up my phone I notice there is pizza dough *everywhere*. I really am talented in the kitchen. Everyone should take note at my ability to land dough on a *ceiling*.

I'm home. Didn't want to bother you but wanted to say hi and goodnight.

Sigh. I needed this. Dillon is a good man. An honest man. I may not know a lot about him but I know that much. He has such integrity, he could never be a Richard.

You could never bother me. I'm glad you made it safe.

How's girl's night? Pillow fights???? <fingers crossed>

Stop it. I told you I LOVE my pillows! Girl's night is interesting and was really necessary.

Uh oh. That doesn't sound good. You okay?
I'm good. I should get back.
Have a good night.
Night.
Don't forget our date ;-)
Wouldn't dream of it. Goodnight :-)
Night gorgeous.

I feel guilty for how happy and giddy that word - gorgeous - makes me. Anna just dropped a bomb about Dick and his dickness and here I am, giddy. I give myself a minute to be truly excited for that text and then push it down so I can be there for Anna.

As I head back into the room, the girls aren't talking. They are just sitting on the couch and pointing at the chair nearby. I sit and suddenly feel extremely nervous. Why am I nervous? I shouldn't be nervous or worried to talk to my best friend and my sister. The two people in this world I can tell anything to without judgment. The people who have held me and comforted me. My people. With a big smile and an even bigger sip of my wine, I start.

"Okay. So I just want to say that I'm nervous talking about this. I know I shouldn't be but I am. I feel like if I say all of this out loud it's real and I'm likely to screw it up. So just let me get through this, okay? Okay." Charlotte raises her hand like she's a school girl and I chuckle. "Yes, Miss Charlotte?" I say with my best school marm voice.

"Uh, I'm really glad you're going to tell us about sexy Dillon but . . . where's the dessert? I'm pretty sure you said sinful and brownies earlier." Shit. I run in the kitchen grab the sin on a plate and bring them back to the room with a bow.

"Muh ladies." Giggles ensue and I'm not saying someone snorted, but maybe it was me. I'm going to have one hell of a hangover tomorrow.

"Okay, so here we go. After the first retreat you all had left and I was in my office. I looked up and . . . don't make fun but it was like a romance novel scene. He was just there. Remember how he looked in the kitchen? All sexy and in control? Well, standing in the doorway to my office, arms crossed and smiling? It was the kitchen times ten."

At that visual we all let out a collective sigh. I continued with my story," Plus, I couldn't help but imagine he smelled like chocolate. I imagine he always smells like chocolate. Like he dips himself in chocolate . . . Stop laughing. It could happen." I throw a napkin at them both and now they are on the floor. Brats. It could happen you know, he could dip himself in chocolate. A girl can dream. "As I was saying, he was there then we were talking. I made an ass out of myself and he asked me to coffee. I declared coffee a non-date and he agreed. I didn't say anything to you guys because . . . well, honestly I don't know why. I just didn't. Then I had a wardrobe meltdown and called Anna. The day was great. He told me about his brothers and showed me some storefronts downtown that he's considering for an Irish Coffee #2."

I know I'm smiling like a complete weirdo at this point. I don't even care. I just had such a blast. "Anyway, we decided to have dinner. We talked and it was great. He brought me home and walked me to the door. He went out of town for the week and we've been flirtexting and. . ."

"Flir whating?" Anna repeats through cackles.

"Shut up. You've flirtexted. Maybe you didn't know it but you did. We've been texting and I guess flirting so there you have it, flirtexting! We've talked on the phone a few times. He called me gorgeous!!" And we're fourteen again, jumping up and down squealing like it's 1989 and we're at a New Kids concert. Don't judge our love of New Kids on the Block. "And we're going to have dinner Sunday. The end."

"Hold on there, Vic. Having dinner? Where? In town? The city?"

Charlotte is like the damn BAU on *Criminal Minds*. Only she's not Shemar Moore and it's not as much fun as watching on TV.

"Here." And with that I get up and walk in the kitchen. I hear footsteps and maybe someone bumping a table behind me.

"Excuse me? You can't say *here* and walk away, sister of mine. Are you cooking? We have a good feeling about this relationship and that doesn't seem like a good idea."

"First, it's not a relationship. We're friends and getting to know each other. Do I think he's hot and sexy and straight out of one of my books? Yes. Do I want him to kiss me and make me melt like the chocolate I imagine he smells like? Duh. But it's not a relationship. And no, I'm not cooking. Umm . . . *we're cooking*."

"Victoria Bennett. My very best friend in the world. You are swooning. You and that sexy Irishman are going to spend the evening here in your kitchen cooking together. That's like foreplay. OH MY GOD! You are having a week's worth of foreplay with your flir whatevering and cooking! I'm officially jealous. I swear if you have sex with him and see fireworks I will hate you forever. Well, at least for five minutes until you tell me every last detail."

"Do you hear yourself? I am not having sex with anyone. It's dinner. No big deal. Friends having dinner. The three of us had dinner tonight. Trust me, I am not putting out. Now can we be done with this? I'm ready for a pillow and maybe a little more sexy eye candy."

We each snuggle into my bed and the next thing I know Charlotte is snoring and Anna is sniffling in her sleep. I drift off thinking of how lucky I am to have these women in my life and of a chocolate kiss courtesy of a certain Irishman.

Chapter Twelve

WHY OH WHY is there a drum solo in my head? What is that taste in my mouth? Oh my God, I want to die. I can't open my eyes. I'm pretty sure I'm in Hell. Just open your eyes . . . slowly, one at a time . . . Why is it so bright? Quit being a ninny, just open the other eye . . . What is that smell? Oh no! It's me!

And that is how you start the morning after girl's night. Well, I assume that is how a *normal* person starts the morning. Charlotte is, of course, outside doing yoga. I get it, it's noon. Whatever. It's the morning after we polished off a lot of wine and each purged some major stuff and she's out there in sideways cat or whatever. Sometimes I want to throw things at her. I stumble into the kitchen mumbling to myself and there looking about as sexy as I feel is Anna. Oh, my sweet girl. . .

"Hey, hun. How are you feeling? Cause I feel like death," I ask slowly as the waves of nausea take over.

Taking a sip of her coffee and staring out the window, she gently smiles and sighs, "A little empty." Oh, this is killing me. Anna is the strongest woman I know and to hear her admit that is heartbreaking. I grab a cup of coffee, a large bottle of water, and sit down at the table with her.

Motioning toward Miss Namaste she asks, "Can you explain to me how your sister can get up like she didn't help us drink a vineyard's worth of wine last night?"

"She's barely thirty, give her a little time. It's bound to catch up to her and truthfully, I cannot wait to see her ass spread," I say and we both break out in giggles. "Anna, I'm really sorry you've been keeping so much of yourself from us. You know I would never judge you. I may not understand the situation, but I love you unconditionally. I cannot tell you how much of a rock you were for me after Patrick died. I want to be there for you, when you're ready." She smiles and nods. "But for now, I need grease and I am not cooking. Let's grab Exercise Barbie out there and get some breakfast."

Since Charlotte has managed to sweat out most of last night, we nominate her to drive us and I swear the smell of grease was like a beacon. Once we consumed our weight in deliciousness the girls dropped me at the house. I decided my bed did not get enough attention last night and headed for a nap. Remind me never again to drink wine like it's water.

I'm jarred awake later in the afternoon when I hear in the distance "Mom Mom Mom Mommy Mommy Mommy". I find myself cursing my decision to allow Justin to choose his own ringtone and his love of all things Stewie and *Family Guy*.

"Hello, son, to what do I owe the pleasure?"

"Mom, were you asleep? Are you sick? Why are you sleeping?" he says through laughs. The little shit. Obviously he talked to either Anna or Charlotte, traitors.

"Sounds like you already know. I'm fine just having a little nap. I'm getting up. I've got to clean this place. Are you still coming over for dinner?" I am suddenly overwhelmed with needing my baby. I need to feed him and talk to him. It amazes me how much his sweet smile and laugh can brighten my day. I know so much of it is because he reminds me of Patrick, the way his grin is as big as a house, and how I knew from the very beginning that he would complete our family.

The day I went into labor I looked at that same smile and heard that same laugh from his father. The nurses thought we were crazy because he kept telling me jokes while I was in labor. They kept saying, "Sir, you need to have her breathe, you did take classes, right?"

Finally, he told them the one thing that sent me over the edge and I think it was that set of laughter that finished my pushing session: "Yes we took classes, but I know my wife and she needs to laugh. She's not good under pressure if the situation is serious. She needs to laugh. And this whole thing is *serious*. I'm the coach. I'm calling the plays and the play is Make the Scary Pregnant Lady Laugh. Got it?!"

"Yes, Mom, I'll be there. Auntie Char said you may not be up for much so I was thinking burgers and chocolate mint shakes. Sound good?" God bless this child and the fact that he's in college and gets what I have done to myself. "Sounds perfect. I'll see you in a few hours. Thank you."

We hang up and I realize I do feel better. A quick shower and I manage to get the house picked up, and while I'm throwing my sheets in the wash I stop dead in my tracks. *Shit shit shit. Dinner with Dillon is tomorrow. Wait, he didn't text me today. Oh no. He's changing his mind. No, he's giving me space.* Time to suck it up and stop convincing myself he's already dumping me.

Hey there. Are we still on for dinner tomorrow?

Hello there Princess Wine-o. How are you feeling?

Umm . . . what now? How does he know there was wine?

Victoria? I was kidding. Yes, 7:00?

Oh shit. Did I call him? Did he call me? Well, he's calling now. "Hello?" I answer tentatively.

"Victoria, are you okay? I'm sorry, I was kidding. I didn't mean to offend you." I'm not sure anything he said was funny but I can't help myself from breaking into hysterical laughter.

"Oh thank God, you're laughing. Don't do that again." Now we're both laughing.

"I'm sorry, Dillon. I'm not offended at all but I am curious how you know about the wine."

"You told me. Girl's night equals wine night. I feel like an ass, Victoria. I'm sorry."

"Oh just stop. Truthfully, I've only been awake a few hours and I was scared I may have called you last night. I'm the one that is embarrassed and hope you won't hold it against me." Now I'm shy *and* embarrassed. Get it together, sister. He's laughing, that's a good thing, right?

"Never. So dinner tomorrow, I was thinking maybe we could grill something and enjoy that beautiful retreat space of yours. Sound good?" I'm sorry, what? Is he talking? I'm still hearing his laugh, which should not be such a turn-on.

"Um, what? Oh, grill. Sure. Sounds great."

We talk for a few minutes more before hanging up. I really need to get it together before I scare this man away. I need Patrick time. No matter what happens in my life I will always need Patrick time. I need to feel close to him and know that he would approve of the steps I am taking. With that in mind, I make a cup of tea and head out to my nook. Oh, Justin. After the first retreat, Justin decided that nobody could use my nook so he posted a little sign that says, "This spot is reserved for the Queen of the Manor." Of course, I take it down each time because that's silly.

With my thoughts, a cup of tea, and Tilly at my feet, I think of Patrick. We had so many plans and in the end I think I am on the same path, only alone. I remember one night when we were first married and sharing a pizza and a cheap bottle of wine, I was worried that we would never get past that cheap bottle of wine. I never saw the light at the end of the tunnel. Patrick, on the other hand, always did. That night specifically, I was being honest and open . . . and probably a little tipsy . . . when I told him I was scared we'd never not be struggling. He looked at me, took my hands, and laughed. Not chuckles or a small laugh. Like full-on belly laugh. Jerk. Then he broke it down for me.

"Oh sweetie, don't be upset." I hadn't realized I was crying until he took my face in his hands and used his thumb to catch a tear. Looking in his beautiful emerald eyes, I sighed, knowing I was safe.

"This is our time, Vic. When we look back thirty years from now we'll see this moment as *the* moment that we cherish. One day, we'll be successful. We'll have the big house, a family, and always rushing from here to there. That is when we'll sit by the fire in our big house and remember the moment you were scared, the moment *we* were scared of what the future held. And that is the moment when I will hold your hand and remind you that even when we only had enough money for a pizza and a bottle of Boone's Farm, our love was forever. No matter what the future holds, this is the time that proves our love is forever. I don't know what the future will throw at us, if we'll be healthy and happy every day and always. What I *do* know is that in life and death, good and bad and health and sickness . . . this love we have? It is always. You are my world, Victoria, and I love you."

It's okay to cry. I do. I am. He was fantastic. I was lucky. I *am* lucky.

Chapter Thirteen

"JUSTIN, FOR GOODNESS sake, use a napkin." And people wonder why I call him my man-child. I'm convinced my future daughter-in-law is going to hate me. She's going to think, "This woman didn't even teach him to use a napkin!"

"Mom, relax. It's fine. I have to do laundry anyway," he says and smiles. When I've spent the afternoon on the Patrick memory train he busts out the smile. Brat.

"I assume it is in the laundry room?" I ask as I enjoy the chocolate mint shake that I will actually have to get on the treadmill to rid myself of.

"Duh. So, mother dear, tell me about your drunken shenanigans. Any drunk dialing?"

Oh, this kid. I'm telling you. "No, brat. Now quit teasing me or I'm going to think you are embarrassed by me and we know that cannot be the case," I say completely mockingly, and loving it.

We spend the next few hours catching up and doing his laundry. I'm determined to make sure I have taught this boy something. I cannot have the mother of my future grandchildren thinking I completely dropped the ball. "Justin, you really have to get it together. One day you're going to meet a girl and want to get married and have a family. That poor girl is going to hate me if she thinks I taught you nothing."

"Not going to happen. She already knows how much I love you and how much you've taught me," he mumbles as he walks into the kitchen.

Whoa, what? "*She?!*" Yes, I'm shouting. "What do you mean, she knows? There's a she? Why am I just hearing this? What is she like? Where did you meet her? When do I get to meet her? Oh, is she pretty? I bet she's beautiful. And smart. Is she funny? Do you love her? How long have you been together?" All of that in about three seconds.

"And that is why I didn't say anything. Mom, you have to relax." Justin takes a deep breath and smiles. "Look. I know how much you love me. I also know how crazy you can get. I know that you want the best for me, but I kind of want to play this out before I introduce you. I will say that we are very much in-like and enjoying each other."

How can I question that? I respect how hard it is to date. I haven't introduced him to a single guy I've dated for that reason. Well, that's not true, he's met Dillon. And, if I'm honest, he technically met Michael.

I started talking with Michael after Ted the sweater and the debacle at *The Sizzler*. When I came across his profile and it read, "Hard working, sensitive man seeking a woman I can talk to and laugh with," I was intrigued. Unfortunately for me he left off "and doesn't mind excessive crying and breaking the law." Michael was everything on paper - age appropriate (big deal at 40ish), handsome, funny, single, employed, and family oriented. After Michael, I realized the need to ask big questions that initially seemed ridiculous: Are you in this country legally? Do you have moments that you must uncontrollably sob? Do you fall in love instantly? I am not kidding.

Michael and I did the usual messaging, texting, and talking on the phone. I really liked him during that time. We had a few hurdles with schedules and actually didn't meet in person until we had been talking for almost three weeks. That is the point where the feelings can start. He made me feel something and I was excited to see him in person. This is where *technically* Justin met Michael. For whatever reason, Justin was borrowing my car that night and going to drop me at the restaurant for my date. When we arrived at the same time as Michael, I felt I had to introduce them. It was a pivotal moment because Michael could have run for the hills when he realized I had a man for a child. He didn't. If anything, he seemed to roll with it.

Dinner was great, conversation flowed, and we laughed a lot. Since I thought everything *was* great I didn't see anything wrong taking our date to a nearby jazz club. This is where I needed to make like Cinderella and have a fairy godmother. I needed her to say, "Hey, Victoria, cut your losses early." I should have gone out on a high note. Of course, I did not. After grabbing drinks and settling into a booth, Michael began telling me that he and his longtime girlfriend had split up about eight months earlier and he was just getting himself back out in the dating world. I talked a little about being married and a mom. I think that is when the tide turned. Michael told me how he grew up in Canada and came to the U.S. on business. And never left. Okay, cool deal. I asked about Canada and what he liked about the U.S. We talked about online dating and exchanged stories about first dates from Hell. Michael told me that he had even been catfished (don't worry, I had to consult Google too). Sounds awesome, right? Yep. Until he told me that he loved the fact that he could find a wife to keep him in the U.S. by online dating. I was confused, appalled, and a little intrigued.

As it turns out, during that business trip, Michael fell in love with the US and didn't want to leave. One thing led to another and three years later he was still here. Illegally. I didn't even know that was possible for a Canadian. I guess it is. And now he must find a wife. I gently told him that he was barking up the wrong tree. I also frantically texted Justin to get his ass to the club to pick me up.

Michael began his pitch to sell me on the marriage. He was kind of enough to offer me $879 to marry him. Nope, I didn't leave off a few zeros. He offered me $879 to break the law. I said no. And then it started. The tears. At first they were enough to tug at my heart. That was, until I put my arm on his shoulder and he started sobbing, telling me how he thought we had a connection and he was falling in love with me. How could I abandon him and force him into the world alone? Uh, what? Yep. I tried really. I did. I am a good person. I tried to talk him off the ledge. It didn't work. He insisted that I was breaking his heart and that I didn't understand how deep his feelings ran. You're right, buddy, I don't. I excused myself and passed right by the restroom that I said I needed and right out the back door. Now I've added to my profile, "I will not marry you for a Visa - credit or citizenship."

I am looking at my son realizing that he is protecting this girl from me. He knows I will grill her and make sure she is the one for him. I want him to experience all life has to offer, but I really want him to experience love. The love his father and I shared is forever and I want that for him. I want him to know that there is room in a heart for a lot of different kinds of love. Sadly, I am not good at hiding all of that and he's probably scared I'm going to embarrass him - really, who can blame the kid?

"Okay, I get it. Will you just promise me that when you decide this is more than just dating and getting to know each other I can at least have you both over for dinner?"

"I can do that. I love you, Mom," he says while he hugs me. I am really blessed. He's a good egg.

Chapter Fourteen

A FEW OF MY favorite things about living in Abbott Falls are, well, the falls. When Patrick and I first set out to find the town we'd move our new family to, I told him I wanted mountains, water, and green. He kept saying "greenery" and I always said, "Nope. Green. The color. I want it *everywhere*." Then, we ran out of gas and had to walk until we found cell reception.

Along that walk we found it . . . mountains, water, and *green*. I cannot do the amazing background of Abbott Falls justice with words but . . . it's perfection. Like if the creators of the world gathered every person's innermost peace and then painted it in crisp colors of green, aqua, and chocolate brown. That is almost as beautiful as Abbott Falls. I think today is a perfect day for Tilly and I to take a little hike and center ourselves. I mean, today is just a day, right? Oh yeah, it's also date night with Dillon at my house. That's not stressful *at all*.

"Look, sweetie, green. Everything is like six different shades of green!" I'm in awe of this raw beauty.

"Yes, sweetie, I see it, but I do believe they call it moss," Patrick smugly and simply stated. Oh that's just like him, to be logical. Obviously it's moss, it's like a rain forest here, but it's the most beautiful moss ever.

"Patrick, don't be a dark cloud. I love it here. I mean, I don't want to live in the moss, but can you imagine walking along this amazing scenery whenever you want? It's a lot better than that alleged walking trail they put in our complex in the city. I want to live here." I'm now a good ten feet ahead of Patrick on this trek to cell reception, but I am serious so I stop and turn to him, hands on my hips. "What is it you always tell me? If you want it, make it happen? Well, let's make it happen!"

Just like that we found cell reception, a realtor, and by dinner - a house. As Tilly and I make our way along what is now a hiking trail with plenty of cell reception, I realize I have a permanent smile. I also have anticipation brewing. I am aware of all the memories each place in Abbott Falls holds, but I am also finally seeing the possibilities. Not only in my dating life but in my career choice. So what if I can't knit a damn pair of mittens or whip up a soufflé? I mean really, who can actually whip up an anything? It's not like we were all born to be on Top Chef. But, what I am doing is giving at least one other person a few hours of peace and escape. If I'm honest, I'm making things happen one little step at a time.

After a long and necessary hike, it's go time. And by go I mean a minor Victoria moment of freak-out. If I have learned anything from being Anna Crawford's best friend it is that music and chocolate can soothe the soul. So a tiny piece of chocolate and some Kool & the Gang blasting and I can face the little butterflies that have apparently hatched in my stomach.

I suppose this is *technically* my third date with Dillon. But since I'm not counting the whole coffee as friends/scouting a new location adventure as a date, tonight is only the second date. Second dates are no pressure. Well, at least that's what I'm told because in all honesty,

I haven't had a second date since shoulder pads and perms were in fashion. That being said, I am a girl who likes to be prepared.

With that in mind, a long shower, hours of primping, and I think I'm presentable. I didn't even need to call for reinforcements. Okay, so maybe there were a few text messages, but just a few. If *What Not to Wear* was still on TV, the need for reassurance on my wardrobe wouldn't be as necessary.

The house is perfect, I have the table on the deck set, wine chilling, and switched from Kool & the Gang to a little Al Green; you know, sexy time music. A few deep breaths and I know I can do this. Then I feel it, a slight breeze, and I release a small breath, sigh of contentment I suppose. Gone are the butterflies of nerves and now taking up residence in my stomach are butterflies of excitement. I realize this as I hear the doorbell. Showtime.

"You can do this, Victoria. It's just Dillon. Pretend you're talking on the phone three thousand miles apart. That seems to work for your neurotic state." I've never said my pep talks worked. With that I make my way to the front door and as I take a deep breath . . . I trip over the damn runner. And just like that I'm cracking up as I open the door.

"Hey. Don't mind me, I'm just falling over the same rug that's been in this foyer for seven years," I say as I catch my breath . . . and lose it again. Is he kidding me? Dillon is standing there, dark washed jeans, white button-up shirt with the sleeves rolled up to his forearms, collar open, a dusting of chest hair peeking out with his piercing aqua eyes twinkling with mischief.

"It's okay, I almost ate shit on the curb."

"Well, come in and let me help you," I say as I gesture him in and hold the door open. "I can't have the chef falling. If you can't cook we may starve," I tease, but realize I'm not joking as I take his hand. It's strong, ever so slightly calloused and smooth at the same time. Kind of like Dillon. Layers upon layers of man. Slow it down, girl, it's a hand.

I lead him into the kitchen, and just before I release his hand he gives it a little squeeze. I won't lie, I squealed a little, hopefully this time only in my head, and squeezed back. How can a single man and his hand make me feel like a schoolgirl? Is it because he's like a damn Calvin Klein model standing in my kitchen or is it because . . . he's like a Calvin Klein model standing in my kitchen? Yeah that.

"Wine?" I ask as I pull two glasses off the rack. "I know you said steaks, but honestly, after the last girl's night I am not feeling the red, is that okay?"

He shakes his head a little with a chuckle, "It's fine. Actually, I prefer white. It's crisp and clean. Thank you." There's a moment that we just stand there in comfortable silence and then, in true Victoria Bennett fashion, Marvin Gaye breaks into "Let's Get it On." *Awkward*. Only it's not. Dillon just smiles, winks, and turns to the steaks. Holyshitballs. Was that flirting? Did Dillon Laughlin just flirt with me, openly? In my kitchen? I think he did and I think I like it.

"What can I do to help? You are a guest and here I am just sitting watching you chop and whatever else it is you're doing."

With that relaxed and sexy smile he simply says, "Talk to me."

So I do, and my talking turns into us talking and laughing. I manage to keep him entertained with stories of nothing and, again, everything. Why do I feel that way with him? It's so simple and easy. I am not in any way self-conscious or embarrassed like I normally would be. I also am not freaked out and ready to implement an escape plan. I suppose that would be difficult in itself since this is my house. Regardless, it's unnecessary.

"Your turn," I motion to him as we sit down at the table for what I can only imagine is going to be the most delicious dinner these dishes have served. "I feel like all I do is talk about me and if I'm going to enjoy this meal then you need to talk. So, go!"

"Okay. What do you want to know?" If that isn't a loaded question. I want to know *everything*. "Shall I start at the beginning?" I nod while I moan in ecstasy. Seriously, who knew vegetables could taste this amazing? I should be embarrassed reacting to a meal like this, but I'm really not. I look up and Dillon is just smiling at me and shakes his head. Okay, maybe I'm a little embarrassed now.

"Well, let's see, I was born in Ireland. I'm the second oldest of four boys. My parents came to America shortly after I was born so my older brother Liam and I have teased our younger brothers, Finn and Sean, that they aren't true Irishmen since they were born in America. I expect it isn't as funny as Liam and I believe it is."

We both laugh at that and then I proceed to make a fool of myself. "Ireland like Pierce Brosnan Ireland? I can't even imagine."

With a sexy, err I mean sly, smile, he chuckles and then, straight-faced, looks me in the eye and says, "Yes, the Brosnans live just up the road from where we grew up."

"Shut the front door! Are you serious?!" I shout and scream and maybe smack him in the arm.

"No, I'm not serious. Not all Irishman know one another, but yes the same Ireland as your 007," he says between laughing and coughing through his laughs. Jerk.

"Whatever, that was cruel. Getting a lady's hopes up like that." We continue to chat while Dillon tells me about each brother and their accomplishments. As a mother I can only imagine the pride his parents feel for each of their sons.

"Seriously, Dillon, what you can do with seasoning is amazing. This steak is to die for." I mean it too. Amazing.

"Well, don't go dying on me. I've become rather fond of you," he says and in that moment I think my little crush just snowballed into a big crush.

"Tell me about your parents. Where are they now?"

"Oh, well, they are still blissfully married after forty-seven years and living in upstate New York. Mum is quite fond of baking and is honestly beggin' for grandchildren to spoil. My dad is a strong and caring man who works non-stop. Don't get me wrong, he's really pulling for grandchildren too. We've been really lucky. How about your parents? You never speak of them."

With a deep breath and hearty drink of wine, I smile. "My parents," I say, almost contemplating how much to share with this man. I don't have the best relationship with my mother and therefore I have been rather distant from my father. When I say I don't have the best relationship, I mean that I can handle my mother in small doses and a few times a year only.

"My parents are still married and actually, they live in Seattle. My father is a great man, always laughing and one of the smartest people I have ever known. My mother, well we have always been hot and cold. I love them, I do. They are good people and I never wanted for anything growing up." I hear myself almost trying to convince myself and I get the impression Dillon hears the same thing. I mean it too, my parents are good people. I don't doubt that they care and even love me but my mother and I just seem to always clash. "Charlotte sees them regularly as does Justin," I say, taking another sip of wine and sending a little prayer he can sense my struggle with this subject.

"What do you say we start a fire and talk some more?" Dillon asks and I am grateful he doesn't push. At that same moment I realize I've gone from crushing on the local coffee guy to having feelings.

"Sounds perfect. You owe me at least twenty years' worth of stories anyway." As we clean up, I put my newfound feelings on the shelf and we just chit chat and laugh while I grab some more wine and he starts a fire.

When I get back out to the patio I'm a little taken aback to find two of the chaises pushed together and a blanket thrown across them. Dillon has his back to me and I realize that I may have the best view as he's playing with the fire. I'm sure he's not "playing" with the fire but, you know, making it a fire. Whatever, those jeans are doing a lot of things for him and now I feel like I'm the one playing with flames.

He hears me walk up and just peers over his shoulder with that smile. Fine I'll say it . . . that panty-dropping smile. I'm not dropping anything, but there is a glimmer that maybe one day . . . things may drop. Enough of that.

"This looks really comfy. Maybe I should look into a few double lounges for couples." Shit, did I just insinuate that we're a couple? Nice one, Victoria.

"Well, let's test out the theory while I put you to sleep with the boring story that is my life."

Chapter Fifteen

HOW DILLON COULD possibly think his story would bore me is rather confusing. I am in awe of the childhood he describes. I've lived in the same area my entire life; never one to really add the "adventure" label to the list of characteristics to describe me. His life, however, has been the polar opposite.

I take a moment to glance at how we are in this moment. Dillon lounges all relaxed and sexy and I fiddle and can't get comfortable to save my life. He must sense my nervousness and calls Tilly up to lay between us. Again, feelings. Sitting here I suddenly realize that Dillon doesn't smell like melted chocolate as I had imagined. I can't quite put my finger on it, but there is a hint of citrus and vanilla, which I kind of expect, but then there is a crispy woodsy smell that just drives home just how masculine he is. Needless to say, I can't help but take in a sniff or two - quietly of course – as he continues to talk about his life.

"So let's see, there was the usual stuff growing up. We didn't have much in the way of money, but my parents were hard workers and very supportive of all of us. The one thing my parents have always pushed is education. Thankfully we each had to work very little while in college and I knew early on that I would be successful as long as I focused on what ultimately made me happy. I vowed never to do anything that didn't make me smile. Anyway, I traveled in my twenties and early thirties and stumbled upon Abbott Falls on my way into Seattle one day. Something about this town stuck with me and I couldn't get it out of my mind. When I was ready to settle and put down roots, I chose Abbott Falls."

I realize at this moment that we are both curled up on our sides, both of us with our hands tucked under our cheek just talking and listening. Tilly is snuggled at my feet and the fire is dying; I know we've been out here for hours but it's almost like I can't imagine the evening ending. Then I yawn. "Excuse me. I guess I'm more tired than I thought."

Dillon smiles and says, "Maybe I should get going," and at the same time I smile and ask, "Coffee?" We laugh and agree, coffee and the couch it is.

I head in and start a pot of coffee while Dillon puts out the fire. I meet him in the den and, making a move so unlike me, pat the spot next to me as I lean against the armrest. Dillon looks like he has something to say and then shakes his head and smiles.

"What? Is something wrong?" I ask him. This is the moment he tells me he likes me . . . as a friend. This is the moment my forty-something, single mom, dog loving, frumpy status takes front and center.

"No, it's just . . . .. I'm really enjoying this date and I'm a little nervous."

"Nervous? Why on Earth would *you* be nervous?" I am so confused by this concept it's likely I'll actually have to invest in some Botox for the face I'm making.

"I feel like a damn teenager," Dillon says with complete frustration and humor in his voice. I can assure him he is not a teenager.

"Okay, look. I like you, Victoria. Not in the 'oh let's be friends and share a cup of coffee here and there' kind of way. No, more of 'I enjoy being around you, I look forward to your daily trips into the shop, and I *really* enjoy our dates and conversation' way. I just don't know where you stand."

Yeah, so that just happened. I've been sitting here all night worried this unbelievably sexy man thinks I'm a boring middle-aged mom and he's concerned I'm interested in a friendship? It may be time to channel my inner Anna and lay the cards on the table. Here goes nothing.

"Wow. Okay, that was a lot. I'll start at the top?" He nods. "Before I say all of this, how about that coffee? I'll be right back." I need a minute to get my shit together. I also need to think. A normal person may think this conversation is too soon. I, on the other hand, am not normal in so many ways, plus I've learned over the last few years not to waste time. There is no guarantee of a tomorrow and we must embrace today. That is what I need to do.

Once I have a tray of coffee and dessert put together, I glance at my phone, contemplating a quick pep talk from Anna or Charlotte. Then I look back toward the den and realize I don't need to. I know where I stand and what I'm feeling. Well, I don't *exactly* know what I'm feeling, but I can tell you it is not "let's just be friends." I'm also not feeling nervous.

Well, that's not true, I feel nervous as hell as to what I'm going to say, but not about the man. Not about the moment. This all seems so natural. Why am I not completely freaked out? That is just weird. I know why, it is because Dillon calms me. With my head high, shoulders back, smile on my face, and confidence through the roof I head back in to have *the* talk.

"Here we go. I threw on the dessert too." I remind myself to breathe and smile as I settle back into my spot, but don't take my cup; neither does Dillon. I turn toward him, gather my legs in a cross-legged position, and reach for his hands. He really does have nice hands. Goodness, he smells good. A few deep cleansing breaths, which are making me light-headed since they are coming out more like Lamaze breathing. Just another reminder I should really stay for the entire yoga class.

"First, thank you for cooking and coming to my home. I know it's not a traditional date but I really enjoyed not worrying about a restaurant or having constant interruptions." I offer him a smile that I hope is sincere, but shit on a stick I'm nervous as all get-out.

"So, I was married. Obviously, sorry." I sound like such an idiot but manage to look him in the eye as he chuckles and squeezes my hand in a gesture for me to continue. "Patrick and I were together over twenty years. We had a great life and have an amazing son. When I lost Patrick just over three years ago, I never imagined I would start dating again. That being said, I have been *trying* to date for just over a year. You are my first second date in over twenty years."

I begin to giggle when I realize how I just admitted to this amazingly handsome man who could date a *Sports Illustrated* model that he is my first second date in two damn decades.

I notice the moment he realizes what I've just said. "What do you mean, first second date? None of your dates called you for a second date? That's absurd. I don't believe it!" He's a little confused, I can tell.

"Oh, they called. I just said no. No spark, no real reason to pursue it," I reply almost casually with a shrug.

"I am a horrible dater." It's true, I really am. "Well, I mean, I suppose I'm fine *on* the date but perhaps my dating picker is broken. Or the online dating site is broken. Either way, no second dates." Dillon still seems a little confused but he nods for me to continue. "You said you wanted to know where I stand. Well, nothing in this world would make me happier than having you as my friend."

Dillon goes to move his hand away and I squeeze it again, "Let me finish. Nothing would make me happier than having you as my friend *other* than having you as *more* than my friend. Dillon, you are the first man I have wanted to spend time with. The first man that makes me smile and laugh and you never make me feel like I'm only Justin's mom or the poor widow. When I talk, you listen. I don't want to overstep or move too fast because, that's the whole 'I'm a horrible dater' thing." I pause long enough to recognize how much I am saying. These are more than just words for me, they are the first steps to the new version of my life.

I release my hands and try to casually wipe my palms. Why is it suddenly so hot in here and why in the fresh Hell did I pour us coffee and not some damn ice tea? Another deep breath and I continue, "I would love to spend more time with you and I want to see where it goes. I just need you to be patient. I'm scared shitless."

Almost done, Vic, you can do this. "You have to know that by saying all of this, I am freaking out inside. I know one thing for certain. You are a good man, Dillon Laughlin, and I trust you." There. I have officially vomited my feelings and fears and hope that he doesn't make a run for it.

"Oh thank God. I thought it was just me. You really want to see where this goes? What about the online dating thing?" he asks as he hands me my coffee, and it's as if he has flipped a switch and a thousand pounds of stress has been lifted from his shoulders.

"Oh," I say while sipping my coffee; damn that's good. "Yeah I gave that up before you and I even went out the first time for our non-date. Which, by the way, is still a non-date so that makes this only our second date. Just so there's no confusion." I wink and smile. Are the winks contagious and when did I become a winker?

"So this patience part. Are you prepared to be patient with me too? We haven't really talked about my past relationships, but if you have questions, I'm willing to answer them."

"Well, I do have a few, but we can always get to that. Answer me this - are you dating anyone else?" Please Lord in Heaven don't say yes. I can only imagine the super models lined up to date him.

"Are you saying you don't want to be part of my harem?" he mockingly asks me as I huff a response and roll my eyes. "I'm kidding. I am a one-woman man, Victoria. If we are dating, it is you. Only ever you." Whew, thank goodness for small favors. "Victoria, I mean it. I want to see where we go. I should be scared, being a man and all, but I'm not. I feel the most relaxed and myself than I have in years. I feel inspired because I don't feel like I'm searching anymore. My creativity is back and I have you to thank for that." Holy shitballs. What happens when you have more than butterflies and dragon wings in your belly? Do you pass out? I almost feel like I want to because maybe there'd be some mouth-to-mouth action. Yes, Victoria, *that's* taking it slow.

"Well then, that's all I need to know for now. So P&Q. . ." We continue to sit and talk for another few hours, holding hands and drinking coffee. I tell him that after this weekend, P&Q is booked for the next few months. I have a few small weekday book clubs that want to start holding their gatherings here and I've been corresponding with the publisher for the big author event in September. Once I notice the clock says we're closer to sunrise than sunset., we decide to call it a night. The butterflies and whatever else are back as I walk Dillon to the door.

"I'm glad we did this, Victoria. I'm not trying to put labels on anything or pressure you but I want you to know that I think this means we are officially dating and I can freely say that I like you."

"Well, thank goodness you like me. I'd hate to date a man that could only tolerate me," I say with a giggle and a tug of his hand. *Please kiss me. Please don't kiss me.* I'm so confused.

"I won't," he says.

"What? You won't what? Shit, I did it again, didn't I?"

"What? You didn't mean to tell me to kiss you then tell me not to kiss you? No wonder you're confused." Damnit. "Don't worry, Victoria. I know you're a cautious woman and I want to ensure you are one-hundred percent certain and comfortable with me when I do kiss you. For now how about this?" He leans in and gives me the softest kiss on the cheek. This man and his cheek kisses. It's like feathers stroking satin. His breath is sweet and somehow still minty. It's so simple, but it says so much. A kiss to my cheek tells me that this is the path I am meant to travel. This man will change my life and if I'm lucky when those lips touch mine, I won't actually self-combust.

"I'll call you tomorrow. G'night." As I stand there watching my unlabeled 'I like you and we're officially dating' guy walk to his truck, a sense of peace washes over me. Once he's driven away, I step in the house and close the door. Unable to stop myself, I once again entertain Tilly with my own personal dance party in the foyer. Again, Tilly is not impressed.

As I close up the house, I take a peek at my cell phone and see I have one text message.

I just wanted to tell you goodnight again and . . . you are not frumpy or middle aged. You are beautiful. Talk to you tomorrow.

Oh boy, I'm in trouble.

Thank you for making me feel beautiful. Goodnight.

Chapter Sixteen

*L*IVING IN THIS part of the country, we are more often than not blessed with gloomy, rainy days. For some, this can cause darkness and a slight funk to their mood. I am the opposite. A nice cool and foggy morning can actually put me in a spectacular mood. I'm sure it is only the weather that is responsible for this mood and it has nothing to do with having chosen to officially date a man. A man who, until last night, I hadn't admitted to having feelings for. Nope, not at all.

After a quick hike with Tilly and my daily drop in to Irish Coffee, I am ready to get the day started. When I started P&Q I wasn't sure how this would pan out. I knew that I could book a few little retreats each month, but when I open my email and see the dozens of inquiries from businesses for corporate retreats, book clubs for weekly meetings, and mom groups looking for some "me time," I am beyond giddy. The upside to a lot of these new inquiries is that they are short time periods and want to set up a package deal. I decide to put together a few package options, handle the inquiries, confirm some reservations, and call it a day. This whole being your own boss is kind of fantastic. Considering I now have the entire rest of my day to do whatever I want, I call Anna and Charlotte and see if they are up for lunch and shopping.

It's as though all of the gods and goddesses are looking down on me. The weather stayed cool and my drive into the city is a breeze. I'm feeling pretty good about life. That is, until I walk up to the restaurant and see Anna in a velour sweat suit. Don't get me wrong, I have two or three (five) myself. Anna? She doesn't even wear her yoga pants *to* the gym. She changes there and then changes after. "Just because I have to wear these things to actually exercise doesn't mean they make any sort of fashion statement." So a velour sweat suit (in yellow) is beyond weird.

I look at Charlotte, who is walking up at the same time with wide "What the Hell?!" eyes and a quick nod to our velour-wearing friend. I didn't even know Anna owned anything this casual. She must have either raided her mother's closet or hit up a thrift store. That's the only thing that makes any sense.

"You're here early!" I say to Anna as I quickly ignore Charlotte's eye communication.

"I told you I was up for spending the afternoon with you," Anna replies as if nothing is amiss. That means something is seriously amiss. "Charlotte, seriously, close your mouth. Velour is quite comfortable," she says dismissively and falls in step behind the hostess. Charlotte and I numbly or dumbly walk closely behind and take our seats.

Once we sit down and listen to the hostess explain the special, an awkward silence takes over our table. Not only is it awkward, but it is completely out of character for all three of us, especially together. As I take a sip of water, I peer at Anna over my glass with a raised brow. She releases an almost resigned sigh of frustration and looks at both of us before she says anything.

"I don't suppose there is a chance you both will just let this go?" Before either of us can muster a response, she continues," No, I don't suppose you will. Fine. I quit my job. Well, actually the partners and I have decided that it was no longer 'a good fit' and so I've decided to embrace comfort," she says while nonchalantly looking at the menu.

"Oh well, then if that's all," Charlotte snarkily replies while reaching for the drink menu. "Let's have a drink with lunch!"

And we do. Well, we decide champagne to celebrate Anna embracing "comfort" is more in order. We laugh and have the best time at lunch. I've been stewing on something since I left the house and figure I'll just gradually bring it up. Kind of like that movie *For Keeps?* where Molly Ringwald just says, "I'm pregnant! Can you pass the potatoes?" like she didn't just drop the biggest bombshell.

"So, ladies, I need to do some major shopping. This whole suburban mom look I have going on is kind of boring and so I thought maybe we could hit some cool boutiques and a lingerie shop. How much do I owe for lunch?" See, just like Molly Ringwald. Except in the movie she isn't sprayed in the face with water by her sister's mouth. "Geez, Char, really? I already had a shower!"

"Well well well, do you have something to tell us, Ms. Bennett? I do believe I see a hint of blush forming on your cheeks," Anna coolly replies. She's so damn observant.

"What? I just think that maybe I need more than some panties you get in a six pack and a bra that doesn't scream 'I live alone in a drawer,'" I simply say with a raised brow.

Nothing. No comment from the peanut gallery aka Charlotte and no snide remark or cackle from Anna. Shit. They just sit there, looking at me. For a minute I wonder if they think I'm rushing things and are upset. Then I realize they want an explanation that is perhaps a little more truthful.

"Okay fine," I say with what could be described as a huff and a puff. "Dillon and I are officially dating. Like officially *dating*." I am smiling like a damn fool at this point but just saying it aloud makes it even more real and fan-freaking-tastic! "Oh girls, I really like him! He's so damn sexy it's almost ridiculous. Plus, he's kind and funny and he likes me. Me, Victoria Bennett! Can you believe it? And? He's willing to wait for me to move things from hand holding to more but last night when he left my house . . . he kissed my cheek and I swear I felt my toes curl." Smiles and nods. Seriously? These two show more excitement when I show up with donuts. I tell them I am officially dating a God-like man and they freaking nod?

"Well hot damn. I'm proud of you, Victoria. You have a boy-friend," Anna supportively says.

"Yeah, sis, it's really cool. You deserve it. But you're right, Dillon is pretty hot and some six-pack cotton briefs aren't going to cut it. To the panty store we go!" Charlotte, or more appropriately Champagne Charlotte, proclaims. For a slight moment it's like we're off to see the Wizard of Oz with our arms linked. I guess panty shopping does that for a trio of ladies.

Four hours, a new "intimates" wardrobe, and a few updates to my boring regular wardrobe and we're at Anna's for takeout. Shopping is exhausting. Don't judge. When my phone alerts me to a text message, the "oohs and aahs" are almost funny. Almost.

Hey there. Sorry I missed you this morning. I was stuck on a conference call with Liam and another investor.

That's okay. I was in and out pretty quickly. I'm at Anna's now.

Another slumber party? Please tell me you don't love Anna's pillows too.

I can't help it, I'm swooning.

I'm sure her pillows are lovely. Fortunately, I do not feel anything for them :)

Killing me. I guess dinner tonight is out?

Yeah, I'm going to spend the night here. Rain check?

Most definitely. Night.

Night.

The girls don't even harass me about my texts from Dillon and we have an amazing night of laughing, maybe a little dancing, and a lot of movie time. Charlotte heads home close to midnight and Anna and I snuggle in her bed. I know I need to talk to her about everything that is going on. It's what we do. We support each other unconditionally.

When I was first dating Patrick and completely absorbed by the newness, I was not the best friend a girl could have. Anna and I went to different schools but were still close enough to see each other all the time, and we did. Until I gave Patrick a chance and fell head over heels in 2.1 seconds. In all honesty, I kind of dropped off the face of Earth and became consumed by my new life and figured Anna was enjoying the college life. She wasn't. As strong and independent as Anna is, college was not a cakewalk for her. I didn't realize how hard it was for her until Patrick and I ran into her one night at the movies. She looked plain. Anna does not do plain. Seeing her in what is now a Target uniform was bizarre and hit me like a ton of bricks. After an uncomfortable five minutes of small talk, Patrick could sense my uneasiness.

"Victoria, are you okay? You have seemed kind of bummed since we ran into your friend." Patrick was so observant even from the beginning. I think that is why I knew by day ten of dating that I loved him.

"I am a bad person, Patrick," I said with a flood of tears.

"That is simply not true. You are a wonderful person. Tell me what is wrong," he said as he let me destroy his shirt with my ugly crying.

"Anna, I'm sorry. I think I'm about something twenty years too late, but I'm sorry," I say as I snuggle into her Cadillac of mattresses. Seriously, I need to look into getting one of these. The look on her face tells me I need to explain myself. "I let you down after I met Patrick. I was a bad friend. I'm sorry. I just wanted to say that. Now, let's talk Dick. Shit, I mean Richard - Dick. Not like *penises*." I whisper the last word. I'm not a prude but it happens sometimes.

"Did you just whisper? Good Lord, Victoria, lighten up. Anyway, you were not a bad friend. You were in love. I wasn't and I was a little jealous. I got over that once I got to know Patrick and saw you two together. I really don't want to talk about Richard - Dick or anything about myself. It happened. I fell in love. I chose a man not worthy of my heart and handed it over on a silver platter. I knew the game and I changed the rules. I just thought he was serious about me. I guess I was wrong. I couldn't work in that firm anymore. It was too intertwined with Richard and Mrs. Richard. I need some time to figure things out."

This is the moment I realize I'm crying. Anna is amazing and I am blessed to have her as my best friend. "What can I do, Anna? I want to help you like you helped me. I've been in the dark and I'm scared this will put you there. It's not death but it's a major loss and life change. Let me help," I say as I reenact the ugly cry scene with Patrick.

"Just be you, Vic. I am going to take a trip though. I will stay until your big author event in September but then I'm going to take off for a while. I need space and alone time to figure out the next phase of my life."

And with that declaration, we fall asleep like we did so many nights growing up.

Chapter Seventeen

HERE'S THE THING about the new "intimates" wardrobe I purchased: these are not cotton comfort briefs. I get it. Panty lines are a no-no, but come on already! Isn't the point of undergarments to *cover* all your parts? Thongs may not be my thing. Nobody is less surprised by this revelation than I am. I'm all about comfort, no nonsense, and did I mention comfort? I'm giving it a go because . . . well, I do plan on being "intimate" and would like to put the effort forward.

I know, I know. Some may think I'm jumping the gun on the whole sex thing. I don't really see it as jumping the gun. I consider it as *planning*. I know I *plan* on kissing Dillon at some point. Of course I hope that kiss happens sooner rather than later and for that reason I must have a plan. What happens if, when Dillon and I do kiss, my body, which has been hibernating like a bear in winter, realizes that it's been *years* since a man has touched it? Then when that happens I am suddenly overcome by some phantom seductive woman and throw myself at him? I can't have on my comfortable, clean the house, everyday, no big deal cotton briefs. Nope. I must have on the proper panties. Yes, even if those panties are more like dental floss. See. *Planning.*

I'd like to say that I'm going to channel that inner phantom tonight and maybe finally initiate a kiss with Dillon. I'd like to say that, but I can't. I haven't seen Dillon in a few days, yet another trip to the East Coast for him and a ton of work for me. If we hadn't already fallen into a routine I would probably worry he has some secret life in New York. But, we have fallen into a routine. While it may seem fast, it doesn't feel fast at all. Texts, phone calls, emails, and of course flirtexting throughout each day and night has made our relationship a little like old-fashioned courting. And a lot like perfect.

Stepping out of my comfort zone, I've taken the initiative and asked him out on our next date. Which means, of course, that I must now plan the damn thing. I'm not the most creative and spontaneous gal, but can and will go into the archives to see what kind of contacts I have to make this a great time for both of us.

Ellison's Luxury Car Rentals is the first step to plan this date. I know, John Sweat, Mr. *The Sizzler* himself isn't the first person you think of when planning a date for the guy that was responsible for sending you out for new panties. John and I were never meant to have a romantic relationship, but like many of the men I've met through online dating, I've maintained a friendship with him. John is a really a good guy - funny and easy going. Sweaty, but easy going nonetheless. Dillon is a guy and guys like cars, right? What guy doesn't want to drive a fancy car, like a Bentley or a Lamborghini?

"Hi, John, it's Victoria Bennett. How are you?" I ask and I realize that I really am curious.

"Hey, Victoria. I'm well." He sounds a little scared. Scared? That's weird.

"How's life been treating you?" I ask, trying to make small talk but avoid the weird stuff like weather and the stock market.

"Oh you know, I've been dating. I gave up that online gig and wouldn't you know it, one day I was at The Sizzler and struck up a conversation with the girl at the counter. Her name is Lettie and we've been dating about a month. Just shows that you never know when you'll meet the right girl. No offense." Huh, imagine that. Good for John.

"Oh stop, you know we're better off as friends. I'm glad you met someone. That is why I was calling. I am planning a date for the man I'm seeing and I was hoping you could help me." After I explained that I needed to rent a luxury car and since John is *the* premiere luxury vehicle salesman, I figured he could help me out. John instantly went into work mode and I must admit I was a little impressed. After about thirty minutes of him telling me all there was to know about every "Lambo" and Ferrari available, it hit me as to which car I needed. We made arrangements for delivery and just like that I had the first part of my next date with Dillon planned.

I am, admittedly, a little impressed with myself. Yet, I am still a realist and know that it is likely I will trip and split my lip or pee my pants on our date. It's how the universe works, right?

At least Dillon and I have talked about food over the last few weeks. While he loves to cook and experiment in the kitchen, I like to eat and watch a lot of cooking shows. During one of our foodie conversations we debated over seafood. I'm partial to shellfish while Dillon thinks that anything from the ocean by way of a hook is the "best damn thing there is." His words, not mine. I wanted to plan a day on the coast, by the ocean, where the seafood lives. I've realized in this moment that even when I'm just planning and thinking of time with Dillon I tend to sound like a complete ditz. I fully acknowledge this little tidbit about myself except that I am going to call it being smitten. I am smitten.

I spent half the afternoon after I spoke with John looking at upcoming events and festivals along the coast. I was thrilled to find that there was a sandcastle-building competition the same weekend I planned our date. Everything is falling into place and I'm feeling pretty confident. Again I'm a realist so I'm not getting excited, just *feeling* excited. See, feelings are okay, not overly confident and still keeping it real.

The next few days fly by, and with less than two months until the D.L. Cardwell event on Labor Day weekend, I am beyond busy with P&Q. Of course, when I had this idea I didn't realize how crazy busy I would be. Thankfully Ms. Cardwell has opted to not stay at my house for the event and instead is staying . . . well, I don't know where but it's not here. I would probably have a minor panic attack if she was so at least I can be grateful for that. I can see myself now, walking the halls like some horror movie throwback in my pajamas with crazy hair and just mumbling to myself about scones, coffee, and books. It's a vision I'm sure everyone would want to see.

While I am thrilled to know that Justin has a girlfriend, I must admit that I miss my kiddo. I know, girlfriend trumps mom and I'm lucky to still get my one dinner a week, but our conversations are much more rushed and less substantial than they were. I suppose in some ways we are both growing in our friendships and relationships but I'm not loving the whole change thing.

Speaking of change, Anna has possibly gone off the deep end at this point. She sent me three texts this week - *from the gym*. At first I was thinking she was at the juice bar, but nope. Each time was her just leaving after a "kick ass workout." Traitor. How can I continue to not be motivated if Anna is suddenly . . . *exercising*. Just so you know, I whispered that in my head. I'm that girl who loves how I feel after I work out but the actual going and doing part, nah. Now here I am, the lone warrior on this fight of not being much of a workout gal.

The only option I have with this sudden status of lone warrior is to visit my favorite coffee shop and have a pastry - obviously. I've thrown myself into such a world of change these past few months that I find myself needing familiarity and comfort. The only place I feel that sense of familiarity and comfort other than being around my friends and family is at Irish Coffee. Perhaps it is my new relationship with Dillon that solidifies the feeling, but I don't think so. I think it's how reliable it is, nothing changes. I can depend on this place to be my constant. That is, until I walk in the door and I notice more change. Sara, with her beautiful and long crimson hair, isn't standing at the counter. There's a new girl there and I don't recognize her. Why oh why are so many things changing?

"Good morning, welcome to Irish Coffee!" new girl says excitedly. Let's scale it down a bit, new girl, I'm not sure we've reached exclamation point status.

"Hi there, ummm where's Sara?" I ask, perhaps a little gruff. I'm trying to be kind and all that, but I need my normalcy right now and this girl is not my normal.

"She's gone out of town for the weekend. I'm Tasha; you wouldn't happen to be Victoria, would you?" she asks me with a lifted brow and kind smile.

"Yes? Sorry, I don't mean to sound confused as to who I am, but I'm curious how *you* know who I am. Tasha, is it?" How in the world does this girl know me? Is there a weird poster of me somewhere that says, "this lady is high maintenance right now, beware" or something?

"Yes, Tasha. Short for Natasha. Don't get me started on my parents and their love of everything Bullwinkle. It's just weird. Umm, well, when I agreed to cover this shift for Sara she told me about you. She said, and I quote, 'Victoria will be by for her morning coffee and treat. She's the coolest lady and has the best hair like ever. You'll know her when you see her and like every day she'll ask what's good today. The answer is the special and Dillon's banana nut bread.' And, here you are. Cool and with awesome hair," Tasha tells me and I just stand there with my mouth open. Huh.

"Oh, and Dillon called a few minutes ago and asked if the beautiful Victoria had been in yet." She winks and begins pulling the banana nut bread from the case.

"Umm, well, uh okay. So this is weird. Can we start over? Hello, I'm Victoria. You must be new!" I say with a sincere smile and extend my hand for a shake. Tasha laughs, shakes my hand, and hands me my tray of goodies. I head to my table just as my phone alerts me to a text message.

Hey mom, just wanted to let u no I went camping this weekend b back Sun nite Luv u

Good gravy, really? Have I mentioned how much I hate the way Justin text messages?

Sounds fun. Be safe. I love you Justin.

Is this the time in my life that I realize that my child, my only son, has grown up? Yes, Mom, I believe that's the case. Goodness, this bread is good, I should probably tell Dillon.

Mmmmm. . .this banana nut bread is amazing. You've outdone yourself. :)

Good morning sunshine. I just called in and Tasha said she hadn't met you yet. I gather that has changed?

Yes. I may have scared her a bit. I'm not doing great with all the change.

Change can be good, right?

Yes, change can be good. I'm just having a ho-hum day. How's your day?

It's going well. I fly in late tonight and expect I'm going to sleep until lunchtime tomorrow. I'm so tired.

You need to take care of yourself. Are you at least eating and drinking water?

Oh great, now I sound like his mother.

Yes. You sound like my mother. Wait. . .not like my mother-that's weird. You sound like my girlfriend.

Holy shit. Girlfriend. Wait. That doesn't seem weird at all. Interesting.

Victoria? Shit.

Crap. Apparently day dreaming of being Dillon's girlfriend and it not being weird distracts a girl because my phone just flew across the floor like a hot potato. And it's ringing. I manage to grab it just before the voicemail picks up. I may be hyperventilating, but I've got it.

"Ello? Victoria? Are you there?" It's Dillon. Of course it is.

"Sorry. I'm here. Hold on, I need a second," I reply while taking deep breaths and realizing I'm sitting on the floor of Irish Coffee and Tasha is laughing like she just got the joke. Don't worry, Tasha, this is nothing. And maybe I need to go to the gym too. "Okay, I'm here. Sorry. My phone just flew across the room and I had to chase it. I'm here. Whew." That laugh. Oh boy, I'm in such trouble with this guy.

"I blew it, didn't I. I shouldn't have said girlfriend. I was kind of kidding but if I'm honest, not really. Shit. I'm doing it again," Dillon spews out in what could have been one huge sentence. I'm too busy smiling to really pay attention. Flustered Dillon is fun and sweet.

"You didn't blow anything, Mr. Laughlin," I say with what I hope sounds like a seductive whisper. "Are you asking me to be your girlfriend? Go steady? Wear your letterman's jacket?" I tease.

"Why, Ms. Bennett, I do believe I am. However, all I can offer is that banana nut bread you're enjoying and all the coffee your heart desires. Sadly, I didn't letter in any sports." The smile I have on my face can probably be seen from space. It's huge. And a change I can embrace.

"I graciously accept the offer and title of girlfriend. You know, this is only for the promise of bread and coffee. Although if I get chilly I'm going to have to ask that you find me a sweatshirt or something," I say, hoping my huge smile can be felt three thousand miles away.

"Oh of course, I expect nothing less," he coolly replies. And like that I am Dillon's girlfriend. I am Victoria Bennett, age forty, and I have a *boyfriend*. Shit. I have a boyfriend I haven't even kissed yet. I need to handle that situation or in the very least address it with my *boyfriend*.

"We're still on for Saturday right?" I ask hopefully.

"Absolutely. I'm looking forward to seeing what you have planned. Are you going to give me a hint so I know what to expect? I would ask what I should wear but I do feel like that may be like turning in my man card, so to speak." Oh please, he can't be serious. Dillon could show up in a dress and he'd be a man. Goodness, is it hot in here?

"Hardy har har. Just get home tonight, rest up, and be at my house at ten AM Saturday morning."

"I'm coming. Sorry, Vic, I have to go into a meeting. I promise to be rested and I will be there Saturday. I can't wait. Umm . . . I've missed you." Swoon. This man.

"I've missed you too. Be safe. Oh, and Dillon? I'm at one-hundred percent," I say and end the call. I'm not going to chance him even questioning if I'm ready.

100% is perfect. See you Saturday!

Suddenly all those changes that were scaring me? Causing that anxiety? Suddenly they aren't so bad, and the change where I became Dillon's girlfriend? That change may be my favorite. Crap, now I have to find the perfect first kiss outfit.

Shopping emergency!! Meet you both at Charlotte's at noon tomorrow!

I'm in. ~A

Yay!!!! Char

Yep, this change is okay.

Chapter Eighteen

ERE'S THE THING about build-up . . . well, it is like inflict-ing pain on yourself. At least, that's how I am feeling. It's Sat-urday and it's go time. I've planned this date and day down to almost the minute and that was probably the worst thing I could have done. I mean, at this point, I'm stressing that when Dillon gets here I'm likely to squeal like a thirteen-year-old girl meeting some boy band. That reaction is not on my agenda and I don't have time for the fallout.

I take a sip of my water and am rubbing Tillly's ears when the doorbell rings. Deep breaths, a quick check in the mirror. I want to wow Dillon and make sure he doesn't regret the girlfriend title he has bestowed upon me, and according to Anna I have succeeded. A quick fluff of the hair and here we go.

"Hey, you . . . umm, oh hello, can I help you?" It is not Dillon. It's a Girl Scout.

"Hello, ma'am, my name is Lucy," this sweet girl of about six says as she reads from what I expect to be a script. I look up and see who I assume is her mother watching and encouraging her from the sidewalk. "I am selling Girl Scout cookies. We have great choices and I just bet your family would love a few boxes. Would you, uh, oh uh . . . like to order some?"

Cookies. "Oh sweetheart, I'd love to but. . ." There he is. Thump. That was my heart. Is it possible for the perfect man to exist? Even the little scar above his lip is perfect. It almost adds to the perfection of his.

"Ma'am? How many?" Good gravy, Victoria, get it together.

"Oh sorry," I quickly reply with a small smile and catch Dillon's eyes full of . . . something, but I'm not sure what. I only know that I like it. "I'll take six, yep six boxes. You pick which flavors, okay? Where do I sign?" I've got to get this kid out of here so I can touch him or throw up, 'cause suddenly those damn butterflies are back. Stupid insects in my stomach. Once I have confirmed my cookie purchase, little Lucy skips away waving goodbye, and Dillon is on the steps in what appears to only be a few short strides.

"Hi. So that was a Girl Scout. I just bought some cookies," I say as I look at him and momentarily lose my train of thought. Oh, that smile of his again. It's as if with each millimeter his smile broadens his eyes light up a little more. This smile though, it seems different. Why does he look like something is brewing in that . . . Why is he holding my face, his fingers just brushing the hair behind my ears?

"One-hundred percent?" he asks and I nod. Holy mother of all that is sacred. Those lips. On my lips. His hand in my hair. The feeling . . . like those butterflies have left and a volcano is erupting.

The warmth starts in my toes, and as he slowly parts my lips, that same warmth makes its way to my chest. It's as if I am woken from a deep sleep, complete with a little moan. Was that me? Without even thinking I am so consumed by the overwhelming desire I have for this man.

As he slows his appreciation for my mouth, his forehead resting on mine, a quiet, "Hi" is all I hear. No birds, no breathing. Just "Hi." One simple word and I can't help but smile. The smile seen from space.

"I've thought of nothing but that since we hung up the other day. I've missed you," he tells me and I can still only smile while he continues. "I thought I could wait until the end of the date like a gentleman, but I got here and you are just so beautiful and were so kind with that girl I was overwhelmed. I'm sorry if I frightened you."

Without even thinking I grab him and show him just how far from frightened I am. Until a damn horn honks and I hear, "Yeah, baby!" Really? So much for my detailed plan.

"Umm, Victoria, who is that?" Dillon asks me with a nod toward the street.

"That, is part one of our date. Not the man, that's John, but the car."

Dillon turns and really looks. "You bought me an Aston Martin?!"

I giggle and grab his hand, tugging him toward the street. "While I do hold the title of girlfriend in high regard, I am not the Queen of England, so no I didn't *buy* you an Aston Martin. I rented you an Aston Martin," I reply. In that moment, when I look over at him and see the look in his eyes that is equivalent to a child on Christmas morning, I high-five myself. Well done, Vic, well done.

After a few minutes of Dillon running his hand interchangeably between his hair and the car itself, I manage to introduce him to John, sign the papers, obtain the keys, and steal a few more little kisses. When he wraps me in his arms and looks me in the eyes with his personal pieces of the ocean, I know that this is a turning point for us.

"Victoria Bennett, you are the best girlfriend ever. You do know who drives an Aston Martin, right? James freaking Bond! When I was a boy and saw James Bond driving an Alpha Romero I thought that was the best thing ever. Then, 007 got an Aston Martin and I knew that James Bond was officially *the man!*"

I can't help but laugh. He is seriously adorable right now, in this moment, in the middle of my street. "Well, I'm glad you like it. I thought we'd take a drive down the coast and hit up the sandcastle festival. What do you think?" He nods and continues to pet the car. I get it, because I do that with a new handbag. He isn't talking to the car yet so at least he isn't as odd as I am.

I tell him I'll give him a few minutes with his new friend and head inside to grab my things. When I come back he's leaning against the car, arms folded, and I snap a quick shot of him on my phone. That man, sexy and loving, is staring at me like I am the best thing he's seen. I want this moment forever. I want this moment for the rest of my life. Holy shit. Where did that come from?

I've finally found the crack in the armor of my Prince Charming: his choice of travel snacks. I packed us a nice little bag of simple snacks for the road. You know, nuts, grapes, *water*. Dillon, on the other hand, insisted we stop by the gas station for corn chips, some sort of cheese things, and Mountain Dew. I'm obviously on a lovely scenic drive in a beautiful car with a . . . a preteen boy. When I pointed this out there was a lot of laughing and maybe a snort or two. I've always enjoyed a nice long drive with good music and even better conversation and today is no exception. Dillon is having a blast driving this car and after a few hours we're hand in hand walking along the sandy beaches of the Pacific Ocean.

"You should give up P&Q and start a business professionally planning dates," he tells me with that wickedly handsome smile of his. It may be obvious at this point, but I'm pretty smitten and giddy. And that may be why I didn't see the sand cannon . . . Okay, it wasn't actually a cannon, but it was sand. In the air. And then on my chest and face. I suppose when you attend a sandcastle-building contest it is possible there will be flying sand. Or even sand cannon balls. I guess I just never expected them to smack me in the face.

"Lady, lady! I'm so sorry! Sorry! Oh boy, oh boy! You sure are a mess!" All of that is what I hear as I sit on the sand in my beautiful new dress and cardigan, my good hair and makeup day down the drain. And I've never laughed so hard in my life. I'm pretty sure the guy who flung the sand thinks I'm nuts but I can't stop laughing. Soon Dillon joins me as does the entire crowd. I stand and take a quick curtsy before grabbing Dillon and heading for the water. Turns out, just because it is warm and doesn't mean the water is as warm – or warm at all. I realize Dillon is no longer holding my hand as I turn around and see him standing there, with just his toes in the water.

"Oh my gosh it's cold! Dillon! It's freezing!" I shout at him as he stands there smiling and shaking his head at me like he cannot believe I'm in the water shin deep. Damn, it's cold! My toes are little ice cubes now.

"Well, yes, I s'pose it is, Victoria. Come out of there, you nut!" I laugh and stomp up to him brushing off sand to no avail.

"I think I need to buy a new outfit," I say and hope I don't look as awful as I feel at this point. As we walk toward Main Street, Dillon is shaking his head. Oh no, does he think I'm a complete idiot? I mean, it's not like I planned getting smacked with the sand cannon. I should apologize. "I'm sorry," I say shyly.

"Sorry? For what? Giving me the best day I've had in . . . well, too long. Victoria, that was hilarious, perfect, and absolutely worth the pain in my side from laughing." Whew.

"Oh good, because I'm not really sorry. I'm freaking freezing my ass off. Let's find me a store!" After a quick jaunt down Main Street, I manage to find a little boutique where Dillon and I debate over who will purchase the T-shirt and pair of shorts I need. I compromise and let him pick and buy the T-shirt while I buy the shorts. While I'm getting myself together, Dillon runs my sandy dress back to the car.

Dillon is waiting for me outside of the store and when I reach him, he grabs my hand, gently pulling me to him. His hands are once again on either side of my face, his beautiful eyes staring at me without blinking, and with that oh-so-sinister smirk on his face he gently kisses me and I melt. Dillon's kisses are almost like I imagined they would be. I say almost because there is no way a single person could imagine the gentleness in each kiss that is, at the same time, just strong enough that he claims me.

Don't get me wrong, I've kissed guys. I was a teenager and played my share of Truth or Dare and of course I dated in high school. Obviously, Patrick and I kissed. It was one of our things. But this? These kisses from Dillon - it's like each time his lips touch mine, something new is ignited in my soul.

My soul? I pull away and smile, but am suddenly hit with sadness. Is this wrong? Should I love these kisses so much? How can I compare these kisses to Patrick's? I can't, yet I do. I loved Patrick, he was my heart and soul. I still love Patrick. I always will. But there was never this . . . passion. This deep need for him like I suddenly *feel*. This is way too much for me. "Lunch?" is all I have in response. Dillon nods, interlocks our fingers, and we head for a nearby restaurant.

"Mmmm . . . smells delicious. I didn't realize how hungry I am," he tells me.

"Well, I can't imagine why. Everyone knows that Mountain Dew and corn chips are the equivalent of a Thanksgiving dinner," I tease him.

We settle in and enjoy a wonderful meal that I insist tastes even better because we are eating on a patio just feet from the ocean. The rest of the afternoon is relaxing and fun. That moment I had on the street when he kissed me seems to have passed, but he hasn't tried again. Once again, showing me that he understands what I need even when, perhaps, I don't.

The drive home is relaxed and beautiful as the sun is beginning to set. Dillon seems to *really* enjoy the car. I'm not just guessing here, he's basically said, "This car is freaking awesome" every fifteen minutes or so since we started our drive back.

"Victoria, are you alright?" he asks as he grabs my hand and links our fingers.

"Hmmm? Yeah I'm fine. I'm just a bit tired, the sea air and all that," I say with a simple smile and a hope and prayer he'll let it go.

He gently squeezes my hand. "I'm not going to push, but you know you can talk to me about how you're feeling. About Patrick." And there they are, the tears I've held at bay all afternoon. I glance out the window and take a deep breath before turning to him.

"I know. And truly, I am grateful. I don't really know what I'm feeling so I don't think I could talk about anything. You've been so patient with me. This is all just overwhelming. Please don't second guess my feelings." I hope he hears the sincerity in my voice. I think I realized today that I could take these feelings of like and giddiness and easily find myself with Dillon forever. That scares me. I almost feel like I'm betraying Patrick. Then I remember one of our talks during his last days.

It was late at night and during the final few weeks of the fight. I often found myself sitting next to his bed just watching him breathe. Every so often, he'd wake up during these times and we'd have talks about our past, our families, Justin, and the future. Patrick always wanted to talk about the future. It was frustrating for me to go there - how could I talk about my future when he wasn't going to be part of it?

"Victoria, I know how much you hate talking about these things but we do need to talk about it. I will not allow you to ignore facts. You are young and beautiful. You need to promise me you will get out there and find someone for the rest of your life."

"I'm not discussing this, Patrick. We've gone over this. I can barely think of next week let alone this forever you keep talking about.

I promise I won't become some recluse cat lady if you'll promise to stop talking about it." I smile the most I can at 3:00 in the morning on virtually no sleep.

"No. I am a dying man. You are expected to listen to whatever I want to say," he teases me. "Fine, we won't talk about it anymore." I smile. "Instead I'll talk and you will listen." Great. I decide this requires contact. When he's like this I need to feel him and I need to let him talk. I climb into the bed next to him and snuggle in.

"Fine, Patrick, I'll listen. I won't agree or like it but I'll listen." And I did. For the next two hours I listened to him tell me how much he loved me but how much love I had left to give. That he would never expect me to be alone for the next fifty years. He expected me to meet someone, fall in love, share a life, and maybe, just maybe, have another baby. He was obviously on some good drugs at this point. I was not having another baby.

"Victoria?" I am pulled from my memory and look over at Dillon. It's like seeing him through Patrick's eyes for a minute. Almost like a blessing to let myself feel.

"I'm okay, Dillon. Truly," I say as I grab our linked hands and press a simple kiss to his hand. I realize then that I really am. I'm scared as hell, but I think this is all going to be okay.

Dillon and I return to my house after stopping off for a quick dinner. I am exhausted and, turns out, so is he. We decide to just call it a night. After a kiss . . . okay a few kisses. Hell, we went at it like teenagers on my porch. Thankfully nobody was peeking through my curtains like when I was an actual teenager, before we say goodnight. I put the Aston Martin in the driveway for pickup in the morning and head straight in to bed.

Chapter Nineteen

I N THE THREE years since Patrick died I have been able to fib and deflect my way through a lot of situations. I was a master fibber - aka liar - during Justin's senior year of high school. Perhaps that is when I mastered my super power. I'm not sure, but I know for that entire year I pretended that everything was fine.

I was very good at convincing everyone, including myself, that I wasn't hurting every time a senior year moment happened for Justin. I didn't let on for a minute how much pain I was in knowing that his father was missing out on seeing our son grow into this magnificent man. I didn't let on how often I cried when I would hug Justin goodbye as he headed out for his last Varsity lacrosse meet, final homecoming dance, his final history exam, or his prom. I didn't let on that I felt like a shell of a person during his graduation. I refused to be that widow anymore. I didn't want to put that memory on those moments for Justin or even myself.

Learning how to master the picture of stability and "okay" took work, but I handled it. Then I truly became okay. And now, three days after my wonderful Aston Martin date with Dillon, I'm lying in bed. In the same pajamas I put on after he dropped me off. I've managed to avoid talking to him directly because he had yet another emergency meeting in New York and had to leave town. I really need to talk to him about these "emergencies." It is almost as if he's some version of Clark Kent leading a double life I'm not part of. I feel like I'm right back to the fibbing and deflecting year of my life.

When I don't think, when I let myself feel, I am so unbelievably smitten with Dillon. He is handsome, smart, kind, amazing in the kitchen and unbelievably humble. But it's when I stop and feel, I realize it is so much more than all of that. It is the kindness in the words he speaks, it is the manner in which he looks me in the eye like everything I say is important. It is how I *feel* when he looks at me. I felt loved by Patrick, but with Dillon, I feel powerful. It's almost as if he believes I can do more than I really can. I feel this awakening within me and it scares the shit out of me. There's no other way to explain it other than I feel like I am standing at the edge of a cliff ready to jump but I can't see the bottom. It's an abyss and I don't know if I can take the leap. Okay, that even sounds ridiculous to me, but it is the only way to explain how scared I feel.

I was honest with Dillon when we talked in the car after the date. I was okay. I *am* okay. But then I'm not. I hate being so emotional sometimes. My father always told me growing up that I wear my heart on my sleeve, that I have the worst poker face ever and that if someone really looks at me they can read me like a book. If that is the case, I pity anyone trying to figure out what is going on in my head right now. It's almost like my mind, my heart, and my soul are all on a different path. I am ready to move on. I'm just scared to let myself feel the feelings I have.

I will say this because I want to be honest - I feel like I'm betraying my years with Patrick. I feel like I am shoving a new relationship in his face and telling him he wasn't enough. He so very much was. I just think that I'm a different person and I don't want to be a different person. Would Patrick love this person? This new version of me? Do I love this version of me?

I've spent three days hiding from my life. I haven't talked to Anna or Charlotte, but I did respond to their hourly texts. I didn't tell them I was a hot mess, I just said I wasn't feeling well. Sometimes you have to blur the truth to save your sanity. I haven't been to Irish Coffee and I told Dillon I couldn't talk because of P&Q business. He knows I'm busy and that seemed to pacify him. I know I need to get up. I know I need to suck it up, but I just don't know that I can. Tilly is grateful I have enough energy to take care of her and I am grateful I have enough energy to eat the cookie dough I had stashed in the freezer.

I'm laying here, two tissue boxes in, and feeling like I spent the weekend at some hippy compound that didn't have running water when I hear Michael Jackson blasting through the house. What the actual fuck? I mean, I love a good dance party, but not when I'm wallowing. Then I hear all kinds of noise and know Anna is downstairs. I pull the covers over my head and lay there like she can't see me. Maybe if I stay really quiet she'll leave.

"Get your ass up!" Anna shouts as she yanks the covers off me.

"UGH! What the hell, Anna? Can you not see I'm *wallowing*?! Can't you just let me be?!" I wail as I roll over into the fetal position and start sniffling. I can't actually cry because I'm pretty sure I've used up every tear available for the next five years. I'm pretty confident I have broken my tear ducts. They are now officially out of commission.

"Oh give it up. Quit being such a little baby. What's the problem? Figure out you're falling in love with Dillon and decide to throw a pity party? A party you obviously didn't feel you needed to dress up for or even shower for that matter. GET. UP!" Did I mention Anna can be a real bitch? Well, she can.

"No. I don't want to. I want to wallow. I want to be sad and miss my husband. I want to feel lonely and I want to fucking cry!" I scream and realize I sound like a complete asshole.

"Feel better?" she asks, and I nod. "Good. Now first things first, I'm opening these curtains. You should probably close your eyes. I would hate for you to go blind from the sunshine." I don't close my eyes but I do roll them - like a boss. "Now, shower time and then we need to have a talk. It's time."

I grudgingly let her push me toward the shower. Oh sweet lord, this feels good. I take the longest shower imaginable. In part because I'm hoping she'll be gone when I get out, even though I know that's unlikely, and also because it feels like heaven. An hour after being thrown into the shower I meet Anna downstairs in the den.

"That's much better. Sit," she orders.

"Bossy much? I don't suppose you made me food in this quest to get me up and moving?" I ask hopefully. Suddenly, I'm starving and could eat anything put in front of me - sans cookie dough. I think it's going to be a while before we are reacquainted.

"Nah, but I brought you a bacon cheeseburger, onion rings, and a side of ranch. Comfort food, sister. I've got you covered." I sigh with relief. That, ladies and gents, is a best friend.

"I love you. And I don't mean because you brought me heaven in a greasy paper bag. Thank you for coming by," I say as I stuff this amazing feast in my mouth.

Before I can say anything more, Anna takes a deep breath, turns to me, and smiles. "I'm going to speak and you are going to listen. Then, I'm going to give you something and we are going to work through it and you are going to be okay. Capisce?"

Capisce? "Um, okay. I have to say . . . I get a little nervous when you get all lawyer-y with me. Can I finish my food first? I think I may need it," I ask and she nods. I finish my food while she chatters on about her quest for the perfect vacation spot to "decompress" and figure out the next step in her life. When I finish my food I have a slight feeling of dread. I'm not sure I'm going to like what Anna has to say but I equally know I need to hear it.

"I'm ready," I say, almost believing it.

"First, I love you. You are more than my best friend, you are my sister. I know that I cannot possibly understand how much you have suffered in losing Patrick. That being said, I want you to know that I know you are a strong and fucking amazing woman who deserves happiness. We all know this. Including you."

She pauses so I can give her a nod of understanding. "You are such a giving person and always have been. But seriously, Victoria, I think it is high time you be selfish and take something for yourself." I absorb what she's saying and try my hardest to not disagree with her. It's very hard for me to consider putting myself first or asking anyone to put themselves second to me.

"Now, I'm going to give you something. I've held on to this under strict instructions. It was to my discretion when I would give it to you and I think today is the day. In fact, I know that it is the day. Victoria, this is the first day of the next part of your life. Today is the day you put your happiness first. It is the day that you make it all happen."

With that she hands me an envelope. I know instantly that it's a letter from Patrick. I gasp and the tears are back. I look at her and she just smiles, pats my hand, and walks to the kitchen. I need to be outside. I need to be in my spot. I grab a throw from the couch and head outside. With a deep breath, I open the letter.

My sweet Victoria,

This is the final letter. You're probably wondering why I gave this to Anna and didn't stash it with the rest of the others. The reason is simple, you need this letter today. I sat with Anna and told her what I wanted for this letter. If you have it that means you have met someone.

Someone special and someone you are scared to give your heart to. Oh Vic, you are such an amazing person and have so much to give to the world. I wish you could see yourself like we all do. When you laugh it lights up a room. Your smile is so magnetic you could draw even the shyest person into your heart. It is for those reasons I need you to be okay with this feeling you have.

What we have together is so special and amazing Vic but I'm not here anymore. I've fought a good fight but I lost baby, I lost. You are still living. I need you to live. I need you to live for both of us. I want for you to live.

When we met you were so full of sass and so damn confident. I knew the first time you turned me down for a date I would marry you. Have I ever told you that? I knew I would love you until my last breath and I do baby I really do. As I write this, you are curled up in a chair next to me. You look so beautiful and all I want to do is hold you and tell you all of this. I am choosing instead to write this letter because I want you to know that I'm okay with you meeting someone. I know that if I wasn't sick, if I was with you right now, there would be no other man. I know we would be together and so unconditionally in love. But I'm not there. Is he there? Have you let him in? Oh baby let him in. Let him love you. You deserve the moon and the stars. You are an amazing woman and any man who is privileged enough to get close to you is damn lucky.

This man, I know he is good. He is kind and giving and makes you laugh. I know that if you are close enough with someone that Anna gave you this then you need to take the leap. You need to open your heart and your soul to him. Let him in and let him take care of you.

I love you more than words Victoria Leigh Bennett. You are my shining star and I will love you for eternity.

All my love,
Patrick

I don't know how long I laid in my chaise and cried, clutching that letter to my chest. I know that eventually Anna came out and held me and cried with me. I know that when I finished I felt like I had been hit by a truck. I also know that I felt at peace.

"Are you okay?" Anna whispers as she lets me destroy her perfect silk blouse with my ugly cries.

"I think so. How long have you had this?" I ask her in a voice I don't recognize.

"He gave it to me that day you and Charlotte visited your parents, about a month before he passed. I hated keeping it from you, but I promised him. I refused to go back on that promise."

We sit there for a few more minutes and eventually get up and head into the house. I spend a little time alone and meet her in the kitchen where she has some food out, a tender smile, and a cup of tea. "Here, you need to eat something and we need to talk this out."

"Did you read the letter at all?" I ask and she shakes her head no. "It is his final letter but I suppose you knew that. It's his goodbye and his permission for me to move forward with Dillon. Well, obviously not specifically with Dillon, but someone." I'm quiet for what feels like forever.

"Anna, how do I move forward with these feelings for Dillon? I loved Patrick. I love Patrick. He was my husband and he is the father of my son. How can I betray him with this relationship with Dillon?"

"Oh sweetie, I don't know what that letter says but I know that Patrick wanted you to be happy. He wrote me a letter too. Did you know that?" I can't believe it. That's not true; I can believe it. I shake my head no and she continues, "He did. Of course mine wasn't all that sappy. It was kind of more like 'Hey Anna! Don't be such a bitch and you better take care of my family or I will haunt you from the grave,' but much more sincere and with less attitude," she says and I manage a real smile. "In reality, he just wanted me to know that he loved me too and that he wanted to make sure I stopped pushing people away and let someone in other than you. He really was smart, wasn't he? A real Dr. Phil, ya know if I liked Dr. Phil, but much more handsome." We laugh at that and suddenly I feel a weight lifted.

"Answer me though, how can I move forward? I have so many different emotions. It's almost like I'm battling myself but the thought of not being with Dillon almost makes me sick. Then I realize we've only been dating a few weeks and I truly cannot imagine him not being part of my life. What does that say about me? Am I horrible person?" She grabs my hand . . . ouch! No she doesn't, she smacks it. "What the hell, Anna? That fucking hurt!"

"Sorry, but really enough. I'm not asking to read that letter because it is between you and Patrick. I am going to say this though — that man loved you, Victoria. He adored you in a way that I don't think many people can say they experience. That being said, Dillon? That man looks at you the same. I've seen him watching you and the look in his eyes, well, it's not only primal like he wants to toss you over his shoulder caveman style and do many naughty things to you, but like he wants to hold you and love you and care for you in a way that makes even my blackened heart turn to goo. Victoria, you are being given a gift of a second chance at true love. Do not pass this up for some unnecessary sense of duty. Patrick didn't want that for you and you shouldn't want that for yourself."

Hearing someone who I know loves me unconditionally say those words, express those emotions, and lay it out on the line like that makes me start to believe I deserve this. "Caveman style? Really? Have you been reading my romance novels?" I tease and that is the moment that I know she's right. I feel that when Dillon looks at me and I want it and oh so much more. I just have to be willing to let go of my guilt and let it happen.

Chapter Twenty

AFTER THE EMOTIONAL rollercoaster I put myself through last week, I'm so excited to throw myself into work and push forward to give my relationship with Dillon the ability to grow. The day I decided to really give P&Q a shot, I never imagined how quickly it would take off and I suppose the same could be said for my relationship with Dillon. The man I insisted was aloof is, in fact, hilarious and supportive. I've said it before and likely sound like a broken record, but the man is close to perfect.

On the business front, I'm shocked at how my town has really embraced the idea. What started out as me wanting to just do something simple and fun for fellow book lovers has turned into so much more. I've been tossing around the idea of hiring on a part-time assistant and a quick double check confirms that I am now officially booked for the rest of the summer. I can see how so many business owners can find themselves working 24/7 and with my business in my home it's almost impossible not to. Dillon is the one who suggested an assistant. Of course, he also said that he's afraid I won't have time for him if I continue doing everything myself, so an assistant is the only answer. Perhaps he has a point. I am headed to his place now for a cooking lesson/date and I had to consciously not forward calls to my cell.

I haven't talked to Dillon about my meltdown last week, and even though Anna doesn't think I need to, I want him to know. I am far too old to waste time on games. Holding back something like this feels almost like a lie, or at the very least, a lie by omission, which regardless of what anyone says is just as bad.

As I pull up in front of Irish Coffee, I laugh at the fact that my successful, forty-three-year-old boyfriend lives in an apartment above his shop. Yes, there is a separate entrance and I'm sure it's nice. It's just that I can't help but wonder if this is some sort of red flag. I asked him why the apartment and not something more permanent. He assured me there wasn't a story there other than it's just him, and with his crazy hours at the shop there has been no reason to live anywhere else. This is my first time at his home and I'm quite nervous, which is evident by the fact that my face has melted off in a nervous sweat. Lovely.

As I make my way around to the private entrance to Dillon's place, I take a minute to compose myself and give myself a little pep talk. *"People do this all the time. I don't need to be nervous. This is just like him coming over to my hosue. Plus, he is my boyfriend so this is nothing. Just put a smile on your face and suck it up, sister."* I'm ready, and before I can knock the door flings open and I'm overwhelmed by the delicious aroma that fills the air.

"Hey, you. I saw you walking up," Dillon says as he grabs my hands and pulls me to him. Hot damn this man is sex on a stick. Meow. "Thanks, I'm still not used to being referred to as being on a stick." Damnit, not again.

"I'd be embarrassed, but at this point I think you've figured me

141

out so I won't. You do look mighty sexy standing here in your apron with chocolate on your nose," I say as I reach up and lay a tentative kiss on his lips. This is new for me, being assertive, but that's part of the next phase of my life. Tentative lasts for about 2.3 seconds before he has me wrapped in his arms and is making my toes curl and little moans escape my throat. How does he do that? Seriously, it can't be natural how he makes me melt like that chocolate on his face.

"No more of that. We have a lesson to get to and if I don't stay focused I'm likely to struggle staying a gentleman today. Come on." I can't help but giggle at the thought. Since Anna referred to him throwing me over his shoulder caveman style I can't imagine anything else.

After nearly burning my house down the first time I attempted to cook something with Dillon, I was surprised when he invited me over for a lesson in his home. He *said* that he has a very simple recipe that not even I can mess up. I still don't know if I should be offended, but he does have a point and he promised me there would be no actual use of the stove or oven. As I put on the apron he hands me and wash my hands in the sink, I coyly ask, "So tell me exactly how you plan to teach me how to make something and guarantee I won't burn down your place."

"Ah, yes, well after the 'incident,'" he uses air quotes for that, but let's be honest it really was an incident, "I decided the best route for today was a no-bake peanut butter and chocolate dessert bar," he says with a smile and nod of confirmation.

"Uh-huh, and let me guess, you've done all the prep that requires a stove, which is why you are all chocolatey." He laughs and winks at me. As we settle into making our dessert I figure now is a good time to talk about my meltdown and a few things that are driving me crazy not understanding.

"So, how was your trip? Sorry I was kind of M.I.A.," I say.

"Oh, it was fine, more of the usual, you know," he says with almost a dismissive tone.

"Actually, no. I don't know." I'm not trying to sound jealous or snarky, but this mystery man thing is driving me crazy. "What do you do when you go to New York? Please don't tell me you have a secret family and I'm your secret mistress," I add with what I hope sounds like humor. I don't need this conversation to be overly serious. I just want it to be honest and, damn it, I need to know what is going on in New York! He stops suddenly, turns the burner off, and wipes his hands as he faces me. Oh shit, am I a mistress? No, he wouldn't . . . would he?

"I guess I haven't been very forthcoming have I?" I shake my head and try to keep a smile on my face while I stir whatever is in this bowl I have in my hands. He takes the bowl from my hands and leads me over to the two stools at his counter and sits down, facing me. With a deep sigh he says, "First, there is no secret family or anything remotely close to that. I would think by now you know me well enough to know that I would never be anything but faithful to you. I care for you, Victoria, a little too much, I fear, and I could never cause you pain. That being said, I'm there for work. Not Irish Coffee, but other ventures I've been involved in for years. I wish I could say more, but there's all of this confidentiality bull that I have to follow. But just know, I'm hoping that I won't have to do as much traveling after this summer and once that ends I will tell you everything I can. I can tell by the look on your face you are imagining that I am either a spy, a criminal, or something else equally fascinating. Trust me, I'm none of those things. I'm still just Dillon, a guy who makes muffins and a mean cup of coffee."

Whew, thank baby Jesus for that. I hadn't thought spy, but damn if this man couldn't pull that off. I can just see him off in some foreign country all decked out in a tux and making the ladies swoon. Okay, well, I'd prefer there were no ladies, but the tux part, yeah that'll work.

"Hmmm . . . well, I'm trusting you, Dillon. I care too much about you, but I have to say that I do not like secrets. I'm willing to table this because you've been honest with me about some sort of confidential status. That being said," I add as I take a deep breath, "I wanted to tell you something. I've been thinking about it for the past few days. I've decided, while most people wouldn't tell you, I don't want there to be secrets. I am just too damn old and frankly don't have the patience for games. So, I figure if I'm upfront with every-thing we can continue to keep moving forward. Or, if you think it's too much we can end things before either of us gets too invested." As I speak, I realize I'm already so far invested in this relationship with Dillon I may lose my mind if he breaks up with me.

"Well, I'm already pretty invested. I'm quite certain that there is nothing you could possibly say that would change how I feel about you. Well, that's not true. You could tell me that you really don't like my coffee. That would be a deal breaker."

That is the moment I realized I am falling in love with Dillon Laughlin. His ability to put me at ease when he knows I am about to tell him something that is eating me up and has me stressed out is exactly what I need right at this moment.

"Okay then. Well, last week I wasn't busy with P&Q stuff. I had a meltdown. An emotional breakdown really and spent three days crying and being a recluse."

I hold my breath, waiting for his response. Then, in true Dillon fashion, he throws me for a complete loop when he says, "I know. Are you feeling better?"

Wait, what?

"What do you mean you know? How could you know? Oh my gosh, you called Anna, didn't you? Damn her! I told her to keep her trap shut. This is what she. . ." Suddenly his fingers are on my lips and then his lips are on my lips.

"Hush," he says, still lingering with his lips near mine, heaven help me, "I did not speak with Anna. I know simply because I could tell something happened on our last date. I wasn't sure what that something was but I could feel you struggling. Victoria, I haven't been married and truthfully I have *yet* to love someone as I know you loved Patrick. I cannot imagine the emotional rollercoaster the last few years have been and how taking our friendship to the next level and having a relationship with me is probably the most frightening thing you've faced in a long time. Just know that I am willing to take this as slow as you need, but I'm here because I want to be with you."

Oh sweet mother, this man and all his words. Where does he get them? Does he read my romance novels too? Oh does that mean he plans on doing that whole caveman thing too? Focus, Victoria, focus.

"Wow. That was kind of perfect. Thank you. I am feeling better. In fact, I feel better than I have since be . . . well, in a long time. Dillon, I want to see where this goes, and if I'm being honest, which is what I'm trying to be, I'm scared shitless. But as scared as I am, I know that I have some real feelings happening here. I just didn't want there to be secrets between us. It's important to me that anyone I'm in a relationship with, we have honesty. I won't keep things from you and so I just wanted you to know I freaked out. Anna gave me a letter and I feel at peace with it all."

I lean in and kiss him; he feels a little more tense than usual, but I did just kind of dump on him. "Now, how about we finish these bars so we can maybe revisit my teens and make out on that couch of yours!" I say as I hop up from the stool and head back toward my mixing bowl. "What's wrong, don't you want to play teenager on the couch?" I tease. He's still sitting there.

"What? Oh, I want nothing more than to play whatever with you on that couch and frankly anywhere else. I was just thinking, I apologize. Letter? Why did Anna give you a letter?" he asks as he makes his way back to his station.

I explain the letters to him and how this was kind of a special circumstance. He seemed to understand what I was saying when he asked me, almost frightened, "So Patrick didn't leave a letter for the man he knew you'd be dating, did he? Frankly, if I'm honest, that is kind of intimidating." I can't help but break out in hysterical laughter. "Victoria, it is not funny. Okay, maybe it is a little funny but not *that* funny."

I finally calm down enough to speak, "Oh I'm laughing because I said the same thing to Anna. She assured me that there were no letters for you. I guess he wrote this letter and there is one for Justin that she's supposed to give him at the same time. They see each other regularly so I'm sure he's getting his this week too. I don't know what it says so don't ask, but I imagine it has something to do with telling him to be kind to you." With that we finish our lesson, and while the bars cool in the fridge we snuggle into the couch.

When I was a teenager I had a few boyfriends and we had our share of make-out sessions. Let me tell you, a good make-out session with a man like Dillon is far more memorable than any teenage boy's effort. I'm not one to kiss and tell, but I can say that there will be no more comfort cotton undergarments for me. I'm sticking strictly with the fancy intimates I bought.

It appears that having a breakdown, getting Patrick's letter, and being honest with Dillon has opened a floodgate of emotion and, I suppose, needs, which I have pushed deep into the archives. If the rush his kisses give me are any indication of what I can expect with more from him, I can truly say I cannot wait. I wonder if I can channel my inner vixen and make that happen. From what I've read, men like an assertive woman. Maybe it's time I go for it.

Chapter Twenty-One

OVER THE COURSE of the next several weeks, we fall into a routine. Dillon has had to make a few out-of-town trips, but we've been spending at least a few dinners a week together and have taken a few hikes. I have managed to hire a part-time assistant, Elaine. Elaine was at my first mini-event for P&Q and has come back a few times. We were talking one day and I mentioned I was going to run an ad for an assistant. When I did, she applied and now here we are.

She's working in my dining room while I'm on a conference call in the office. I'm only about a month or so from the big event with D.L. Cardwell and so excited. Elaine is equally excited since she is an even bigger fan than I am. Her love of books is one of the reasons I hired her; well, and that she was willing to take the minimal hours and very minimal pay. This conference call is with Elizabeth Barnes, publicist extraordinaire for D.L. Cardwell. Elizabeth seems nice enough, if not perhaps a little snobbish. I don't even care if she makes me curtsy upon her arrival as long as this event goes off without a hitch.

Once the call ends I turn my cell back on and see a text from Dillon.

Just thinking of you and can't wait for dinner.

I can't wait either. 7:00 still ok?

That should work. I have a conference call at 5:00 but it shouldn't last long. See you then.

Sounds good. See you then.

I have four hours until dinner. Which I am also calling Operation Seduce Dillon. I told you he stirs up *needs*. A girl cannot expect to live by kisses alone. I mean, the kisses are phenomenal, but I *am* in my sexual prime. It is time to turn this part of our relationship up a level. I finish up what I'm doing, send Elaine on her way, and order dinner from Salvatore's to be delivered. There is nothing left to do but get ready and avoid a nervous breakdown.

I'm going all out and giving myself a mini spa day while I prepare for the evening. Once I've applied the mud mask to both my face and hair, I sit down to paint my toe nails. In my preparation for Operation Seduce Dillon, I have spent countless hours on the Internet researching exactly how to seduce a man when you have only slept with one man in twenty years.

Turns out there are a lot of women out there like me. Almost every article or blog I read referred to the over-forty body and ways to camouflage the "flaws." I had planned on just keeping all the lights off, but after reading at least six different recommendations to use a self-tanner to contour, it seemed obvious this was the right idea. So once I'm all conditioned and painted up I'm going to give myself a tan and contour the "flaws," so to speak. Since I'll need time to air dry before I can even get dressed for the evening, I have to do this hours ahead of time, and thankfully I have a huge walk-in shower for this kind of project. I suppose I could ask Anna or Charlotte to come over and help, but can you imagine the shit show that would be?

I'm adding professional tanner and contour extraordinaire to my list of potential future jobs. I rock at this, but once again am reminded I really need to go to yoga more often. Some flaws are harder to reach than others, if you get my drift. After what feels like an eternity of standing around naked in my bathroom, I am finally dry enough to get dressed and ready for the date.

I spritz a little perfume on and head downstairs just as the food is being delivered. Everything for Operation Seduce Dillon is ready - candles are lit, Marvin Gaye is serenading us, and the house smells amazing. I pour myself a glass of wine and can feel the nerves as if they are crawling up my skin. This is going to be great.

At precisely 7:00 and only a few sips into my wine, Dillon arrives. And by arrives I mean he's only missing his white horse. He's once again standing on my doorstep in dark jeans and a white shirt, but this time, I'm not stunned that he's there with groceries like the first time. This time I'm stunned that he's here for me. That tonight, if things go right, he'll be leaving here tomorrow morning in the same clothes. I feel almost naughty thinking it, but damn if I don't want it to happen.

"Hi, come on in. You know you don't have to ring the bell anymore," I say as I lead him into the kitchen. He has, of course, brought dessert. I do know my limits and his strengths, and baking is definitely a strength for him.

"I didn't want to assume, but duly noted for next time. Do I not get a kiss hello? I've missed you," he says as he slides his arms around my waist.

"Did you now? I did see you this morning for coffee, you know," I reply with a smile that I pray looks coy and sexy.

"Yes but that was twelve hours ago. I can't help it if that was too long," he replies as he claims me with one of those kisses that sets me on fire from my toes to my heart. Maybe I should just plan on skipping dinner all together. Maybe then these tingles I have will go away.

Instead I pull away and smile at him. "Hungry? I ordered your favorite from Salvatore's. Would you grab the wine?" This is where I realize I should have read up on seductive gestures and lingering moments. I *want* to ever so gently linger my hand on his bicep like I'm flirting. Of course, now that I've had this thought, the moment has gone so long and my hand is kind of in midair. Instead of looking flirtatious I think I look like I want to high five. Thankfully, he's oblivious to what is happening and it gives me time to recover and notice how strong and amazing his body is. When does the man have time to work out? I'm so glad I took the time to contour.

As usual, the food is delicious and the conversation is natural. "Honey, are you okay? You are really fidgety over there?"

Honey? Oh, I like it. "Umm, we'll revisit the honey thing, but gosh I feel tingly. I thought it was some sort of nervous twitch when you got here but it's getting worse. I'm just going to excuse myself for a minute." I get up, but first I lean over and right before I kiss him I say, "Honey, I like it."

I decide I need good lighting and head for my master bath to see what in the world is going on. As I flip on the light and pull up the hem of my dress, I scream. Not a little "Oh goodness me" screech, no, a full-blown "I am starring in a horror movie and just found my best friend dead" kind of scream. Dillon is in the bathroom in seconds and the look on his face tells me everything I need to know. It's bad.

"Oh my God, Victoria, what happened?" He is concerned now. I, on the other hand, am mortified. I probably should have taken the whole "apply this to a small area to determine an allergic reaction" part of the directions to heart.

I burst into tears. Sobbing and scratching and sobbing some more as he starts to come near me. "Stop! Don't get close or this shit will get all over you and you may be allergic too. I'm such an idiot!"

I can't stop scratching, damn it.

"Oh Victoria, you poor thing. You need to shower and get this off of you. Then we need to get you something for the itch. Do you have anything like that?" I sniffle and nod as I point to the cabinet with something I use for bug bites. Dillon hands me a tissue as he unwraps my dress and I realize suddenly I'm standing in my bathroom with only panties and a bra on with my body covered in mini welts in front of the man I was planning to seduce.

Suddenly I'm overcome with hysterical laughter to accompany the hysterical crying. Dillon just kisses my forehead and walks me to the shower. He turns it on and nudges me inside. Once I'm in he leaves me alone to shower. So much for Operation Seduce Dillon. If I'm lucky he won't run for the hills.

I manage to scrub off the tanner and most of the welts seem to be going away. The few that remain will need some of the medicine I have, but for now I think I'm okay. I put on my fluffy robe and head out of the bathroom and toward my dresser to find Dillon sitting on my bed. I imagined tonight's seduction in so many different ways. They all came flooding at me seeing him there on my bed. There are no words. I'm sure there are, but my brain is mush right now and I feel like such a dumbass.

"I'm so sorry you had to see that. Let me just get dressed and we'll have dessert," I say, but before I can move he has my hands and is tugging me onto his lap.

"You have nothing to apologize for. Why in heaven's name were you using a tanner anyway? You have beautiful skin and I love the little tan you have going on. Why would you mess with that?"

How do I explain the "flaws" to him?

"Well, I was doing some contouring. I'm not eighteen anymore, Dillon. I didn't want you to be disappointed that your girlfriend's body is obviously *old*," I say with a small and sad voice I almost don't recognize.

"Wait, you did this for me? Why would you think I want you to be any other way than how you are? I love that you aren't eighteen," he states and I must look confused. "Not just because I have zero desire to be with a child, but because that makes you a woman. A beautiful and sexy woman I love being with." Again, with all the words. If I wasn't starting to itch again I might just jump him right here. But nope, the itching is starting.

"Dillon, I'm getting itchy again. I need to get medicine on my legs. Once I get dressed will you help me?" He nods and as I get up he pats my butt. I yelp and turn to him.

"How exactly was I going to see this so-called contouring? Were you planning a little more for dessert, honey?" he asks in a slow, sexy voice that brings out his Irish brogue and I about melt into the ground. Two can play this game.

"Perhaps. I guess we'll never know. I'm going to change so why don't you take the medicine and meet me in the den?" I reply as I sashay into my walk-in closet and let out a deep breath and let myself scratch the god-awful itching. This is the moment I realize any career aspirations I may have as a professional seductress are gone.

Chapter Twenty-Two

C ALL ME PARANOID, but after the self-tanner/contouring fiasco, I've decided that perhaps I was rushing the entire Seduce Dillon idea. Or, I have really bad luck. Either way, I'm going to table that for now. While I'd like to think that in my forty years I have learned a thing or two about seducing a man, the reality of it is that when you are together as long as Patrick and I were, you don't really put the work in all that much. That's horrible to say and really even worse to admit, but it is true. I don't want that for this relationship with Dillon. I don't want to get so comfortable I don't put the effort in. That is why I'm calling in the big guns.

Anna.

Anna spends, well spent I suppose, her days in a courtroom making people believe everything she said. Watching her stand before a jury, in her element and full of confidence, is like watching a well-crafted play. Only, with Anna's beauty and poise it is also like watching an exotic creature stand amongst the ordinary. That tends to make her sound like an animal, and while she can be a bit aggressive and like a tigress, she knows when to pull back and not overwhelm a person.

The more I think about it, the entire scene really is more about how she carries herself with such confidence and an aura of . . . well, I suppose, the appropriate word is *seduction*. I don't mean to say that she is overtly sexual yet she is and it's almost as if the jury can't help but want to do what she tells them to do. They can't help themselves when it comes to Anna. She is in complete control and it is amazing to watch.

Unfortunately, as we know, I lack that little bit of tigress/seductress. So of course, since I'm only *tabling* Operation Seduce Dillon and not eliminating it from the plan, I figure I'd have Anna come over and give me some pointers on being in control, seductive, and well . . . less awkward.

"So what is it exactly you need from me?" Anna asks me as I pour us each a glass of wine. I'm noticing while I look over at her that she seems a lot better than she has the last few months. I know leaving her job has been really hard. I also know that even though she isn't talking about the loss of her relationship with Dick, she is still hurting.

"Well, I need lessons on being sexy." That about sums it up, no need to elaborate, right? Wrong.

"What the hell does that mean? 'Being sexy'? You need me to show you how to put on some of that complicated lingerie you bought? I'm confused," she says to me as she guzzles the wine. Oh boy, this is going to be a long night.

"No, ass. I don't need help with the lingerie. I need . . . I don't know, some of your confidence and seduction techniques. I know I've never seen you in the bedroom but I've seen you in the courtroom. If that is any indication then I have to assume you are how I need to be in the bedroom." I kind of regret this for a minute when

I realize that the last man she was with was a complete asshole and broke her heart. Maybe I made a mistake.

"Hmmm, I am pretty good in bed, I'd have to say. Fine, but I'm not making out with you," she says as she guzzles another glass of wine. Good grief, I'm going to have to open another bottle before I finish my first glass.

"Hey," I say while I grab the bottle of wine before she can fill her glass again. "Are you sure? I know the last few months have been tough on you. We can just watch a movie instead." She takes the bottle from me and fills the glass herself.

"Relax. I'm fine, and I want to help you. Shit, if I'm not getting any you might as well be getting it all. Plus, then you can tell me all about it after and I can live vicariously through you. First step, we finish this bottle of wine, put on some music, and dance a bit."

We finish that bottle and start another while we dance and laugh for what feels like hours but wasn't. Anna is not impressed when I pull out my tablet to take notes on seduction. I don't think she believed me when I said I was taking this very seriously. That is, until I pull up my list of questions and "what if" scenarios. She's known me most of my life so you'd think she would have expected the lists.

Once I manage to get through everything and she stops laughing and rolling her eyes, she promises me none of my scenarios would happen. She assures me that I will not vomit all over Dillon - with words or actual vomit. She promises me in no uncertain terms that he will not break out into hysterical laughter when I attempt to entice him with my fancy new lingerie. And, she guarantees he will love whatever I am comfortable with in the bedroom.

"Victoria, look, I'm going to be honest here. I know squat about seduction. I've been sleeping with a married man for years. I've been a dirty secret. Sure, I'm fantastic in bed, but it's not about seduction and setting the mood. It is more about the connection, the feelings, and how you bring those together sexually." She makes it sound so damn simple. If only.

"I hear what you are saying, but have you seen Dillon? I mean, you cannot sit there and tell me you think I don't need to put a little effort to keep him interested. Seriously, Anna, get real." I can't believe she isn't seeing this for what it is right now.

"Enough!" she shouts at me as she jumps up in a huff from the couch we're sitting on. Shouts, literally shouts. "Why are you sabotaging something before it happens? Anyone can be around you and Dillon for ninety seconds and know that you are the real deal. I don't think you need seduction lessons at all. I do, however, think you need some fucking confidence!" Anna turns her back on me and begins to walk out of the room.

"What the hell was that?" I demand as I hop up from the couch. I know we've had quite a bit of wine, but we switched to water a few possible scenarios ago. Anna is either drunk and pissed or just pissed. "Are you mad at me?" I have no idea what I could have said to make her angry and frankly I'm too confused to even be upset she's yelling at me. "Look, I'm sorry, Anna. I'm not you. I don't have the most confidence. You were with me not too long ago when I bought my first matching bra and panty set in years. I don't know what I said to piss you off but I am sorry."

"No, I'm sorry. Look, I know I wear this big facade of being overly confident and self-assured. The reality of it is, I am just a woman, Victoria. You mentioned me in the courtroom. I *am* confident in the courtroom because it's what I do. I kick ass there, but that doesn't carry over to the bedroom. I'm not saying confidence isn't important, it absolutely is," she tells me as she comes back and sits down on the couch.

I sit down with her as she continues, "Look, I'm not some sort of sex guru. If I was I wouldn't have been Dick's mistress just waiting day after day and year after year for him to choose me. I wouldn't have wasted my good years on a man that ultimately threw me away like yesterday's leftovers." Leftovers is kind of a sad way of describing what she's been going through. I can't help but scrunch my nose in distaste but I don't think she notices.

"Vic, I should have been with a man that deserved me. I know that now. But you? You have this second chance at something amazing. I don't want to see you throw it all away because you lack the confidence that we both know you have somewhere in your beautiful soul. Now that being said, I really think you need to just let it happen. When the time is right, you'll know."

When you need a little dose of reality, just ask Anna Crawford.

"You're right. I do tend to put too much effort into a plan and maybe this time I need to let nature take its course. I'm not sure I know how to do that, but I can try. I just don't want to disappoint him. Anna, I'm just so scared. Do you think that's crazy?"

"No, it's normal. Just relax. But since I'm here we might as well talk some technique. You *have* been out of the game for a while. Do you have any porn?" she asks as she gets up and walks to the media cabinet, leaving me there with my mouth open.

Suddenly I hear myself shouting, "We are not watching porn!" just as my phone signals a text from Dillon. Yes, I assigned him his own alert tone.

Just wanted to check-in. How are you?

Hey. I'm good. Just hanging out with Anna. How are you?

Oh that's right. I don't want to bug you.

Can I call you?

Always.

Before I can even second guess myself, I leave Anna alone in her quest for porn and hit the call button on my phone.

"Hey, you," Dillon says and instantly I'm much more relaxed. "Everything okay?"

"Hi. Yeah, everything is fine. I just . . . I . . . I wanted to hear your voice. I kind of miss you is all. Are you with your secret mafia spy family?" I tease him. I know whatever takes him to New York is important and he can't talk about it, so I try to just make light of it until he can.

"Only kind of? I completely miss you, honey." Ah, honey. Who knew such a simple term could set me on fire.

"Okay, fine, I completely miss you too. When are you coming home?" I do miss him. I miss his smile, his laughter, his hugs, and his delicious kisses. Just thinking of those kisses has me catching my breath a little.

"I'm hoping to be home Friday afternoon. I was wondering if you'd be up for a late dinner. I could cook or I can grab us a pizza. I just want to see you."

"Sounds great. Justin cancelled our dinner plans that night to go on some hike over the weekend. How about we keep it simple with pizza?" Initially I was bummed Justin was canceling our weekly dinner again. Since he's been dating this girl, I have hardly seen him. Now, I'll have to thank him.

"Sounds perfect. I'll let you get back to Anna. How is she doing?" He's so kind to ask about Anna. He knows how I worry about her after this Dick situation.

"She seems to be good. I can't ever really tell with her. She's really keeping all of this to herself. She won't even tell me where she plans on going after my author event."

"Well, just be there for her. Liam just walked in and we have to go over a few things before I turn in. I'll talk to you tomorrow?" After saying our goodbyes I hang up and head into the den, where I find Anna scouring my movie selection.

"You weren't kidding. No porn at all," she jokingly says as she makes her way through the romantic comedies section of my movies. Yes, section. "How's Dillon?" she asks over her shoulder.

"He's good. You know, visiting his super-secret mafia spy family," I sarcastically reply.

"He'll tell you when he can. You know that, right?" Anna asks me as she holds up *How to Lose a Guy in 10 Day* and I nod in approval at her movie choice.

"Yes, I know. It doesn't mean I don't hate it. Plus, I miss him. I'm used to seeing him every day and getting at least a kiss. This just sucks and that is why I need the seduction skills of a master. Oh masterful one, please help me!" I say dramatically as she rolls her eyes and tosses a pillow at me.

"Oh shut up. Now, let's get started on technique. How are your blow job skills?" Anna asks as I choke on air. We spend the next few hours watching Matthew and Kate and intermittently talking about things I never expected to come up in simple conversation. I've got a lot to learn over the next few days. I promised Anna I will let things happen naturally and won't force the moment.

Chapter Twenty-Three

THERE ARE MANY perks to being your own boss. The obvious being you don't have to answer to someone else. That is superseded by the realization that you no longer have to wake up to the blaring alarm clock before dawn and you can wear pajama pants until noon should you please. The biggest perk of them all is the ability to sneak away for long lunches with your boyfriend. Specifically, picnic lunches in the park.

Dates in the park may seem cliché and perhaps they are, but for me they are some of my favorite moments with Dillon. First, it is established the man can cook and bake like no other. Then you add in the fact that he looks hot in a pair of shorts and enjoys talking. Yes, *talking*. We talk about everything from our favorite foods to our favorite childhood cartoons and even what came first, the chicken or the egg.

Today I have offered to bring lunch and meet him at our spot in the park. I love saying *our spot*, it makes it a little more special and intimate in a place where we are surrounded by hundreds of people. We sit up on a hill just high enough that we can see children playing on the swings, dogs chasing Frisbees, and various women power walking on the trails.

Like today, we often spend our time making up stories of the people we watch. My stories tend to be slightly dramatic and a little on the soap opera side while Dillon gives great detail and background to each person. If this coffee business doesn't work out, he should really consider a life as an author. He definitely has a way with words. I told him that much after we finished lunch.

"You know, if this little business you've got going doesn't pan out you should become a novelist. You make all of these people sound so fascinating." It is true too, he managed to make a woman dressed as if it was still 1984 and she was on her way to an old-school aerobics class into a struggling actress who is late on her rent and struggling to catch her big break. The way he described her trials and tribulations, I wanted to run down the hill and hug her.

"Thankfully I think the coffee business is working out just fine," he says before changing the subject. "So, Victoria, tell me something nobody else knows about you. Something so secret it would shock even Anna."

"Sorry, no can do. I'm an open book," I firmly respond even though my plans of seduction are all my own and definitely a secret. I know he won't let it go, so I have to think of something and wish for the first time in my life I didn't share everything with Anna. "Oh, wait, there is one thing. You'll laugh at me though," I say as I lay down with my head on his lap and hold his hand. Damn these hands.

"I won't laugh. Scout's honor," he barely says without a laugh.

"Were you even a scout, Dillon?"

He smiles and replies, "Well, no, but for this moment we can pretend."

"Uh, fine. When I was little I had the biggest crush on He-Man.

The cartoon."

Dillon begins laughing hysterically and honestly I don't think it's very funny so I tell him that as I smack his arm and join in his laughter. "Are you serious? He was a cartoon, Vic. A cartoon. You can't have a crush on him."

I can't help but roll my eyes. "Why not? Every boy had a crush on Wonder Woman. Just because that was a TV show with a beautiful woman as well as a cartoon it is okay. I don't think so. He-Man was hot. He was all muscly and alpha male-ish. He was a man before his time that's for sure," I say, sitting up facing him in all seriousness.

"Muscly? Oh, are you mad at me? Don't be mad. You can have your He-Man," he concedes and pulls me back down to his lap.

We sit there for a few minutes in silence before I brave a question that has been stewing in my mind for weeks. "Dillon, tell me about Rebecca." He has mentioned his ex-girlfriend, Rebecca, a few times but never anything specific. I know that they were together almost five years and met in college and that is the extent of it. The silence seems to drag on forever before he answers. I manage to shimmy off his lap allowing him time to gather his thoughts. Just as I settle in with my head resting in his lap and looking up at him, he begins to talk.

"I met Rebecca my junior year of college. I wish there was some fantastic story there but really, there isn't. We met in a study group and I thought she was very pretty with a great smile. One night, after the group finished cramming for a test, I asked her out for coffee. Eventually we started having coffee after each study group and ultimately lunches and dinners followed. After about three weeks of that I realized we were dating. Five years later, we were still together. I wanted to travel and possibly live in Europe for a while. She wanted to settle down, get married, and have kids. We tried the long-distance thing for a while, but when I came home to surprise her on her birthday I discovered she had met someone else."

I pause in my task of tracing perfect circles on his palm and look up at him. He's staring at me with such affection. I offer him a smile to continue.

"Actually, that someone else was my college roommate." He chuckles a little and I sit up to look him in the eye. "It wasn't even an ugly breakup, which should tell you something. I was angrier that I wasted my time coming home to surprise her when I could have been in Rome or London. I received their wedding invitation a year later. Llast I heard they were living the perfect suburban life with a couple of kids and a dog." As I listen to Dillon tell me this story and I am waiting for some sort of emotion. A break in his tone or a hiccup in his voice, but nothing comes.

"Did you love her?" I ask.

"Yes, I did. At least, at some point I did. I know that we weren't ever meant to be forever and eventually the relationship would have ended anyway. There truly are no hurt feelings but I did sort of put up a little wall and not let many women in for many years after that. Do you remember that night you asked me to be patient?" I remember and offer him a nod confirming.

"I told you I would need patience too. I'm sure you thought it was because I suffered some sort of heartbreak. The reality of it is I have spent so many years avoiding relationships, I've had to relearn the entire process with you."

As he links our fingers, I look up into his eyes and offer a smile. "Then I suppose we are learning together as adults. It seems simpler this time, doesn't it?" I ask him. "I don't mean to simplify our relationship, but there isn't that youthful angst and self-doubt. It's almost extremely natural and organic in a sense," I tell him as I lean in and offer a gentle kiss to his lips.

"I like organic," he replies as he grabs me and dramatically pulls me to him as if he has dipped me during a waltz. I can't help but giggle and let him kiss me silly.

Once our little public make-out session ends and we gather our items to head back to our cars, I decide to see what else he'll share. "Dillon, you told me once that you had tried online dating. How amazing was it for you?" I tease him as he puts the basket and blanket in my trunk. As he closes the trunk he offers me a boyish smile.

"Oh, it was so amazing. Especially the girl that spent the entire date telling me about her love of Hello Kitty and intent to cover her body in only Hello Kitty tattoos. That was, of course, after she told me that she could see my future and that our wedding would be beautiful as would our daughter, who would obviously be named Kitty."

I can't help but completely lose myself in hysterics. "Oh no, she didn't. Kitty? Really?"

"Do you think I would even be able to make that up? I am one-hundred percent serious. I am also serious when I say that I told my cousin my online dating days were over and if she even thought of putting my picture up on another site I was going to return the favor. She is a lot of things, but the one thing Alana isn't is crazy. She pulled that profile off the dating site within minutes and Miss Kitty or whatever her name was is only but a memory. Now tell me, do you have plans to cover your beautiful body in kitten tattoos?" he asks me as he pulls me to him.

As I wrap my arms around his neck and nudge his lips closer, I whisper ever so slightly, "I told you I was more of a He-Man girl." He just laughs as he gives me a lingering kiss and swats my behind as he walks away. "Hey! What was that for?"

"You said you liked that He-Man was a little alpha. Just giving you what you wanted. Have a nice rest of your day and I'll see you Friday."

Oh that man! If I'm honest, I kind of liked it.

Chapter Twenty-Four

I AM, ONCE AGAIN, moving Operation Seduce Dillon into play. Since I've thrown the damn self-tanner away and swore off all contouring efforts, this go around is going to require proper lighting. When I promised Anna I would let things happen on their own, I meant it. Then I talked to Dillon on the phone while we both were relaxing in our respective beds. I am pretty certain that the man could just read me the phone book and I would be turned on. Sex on the brain would be an understatement. That being said, I don't think anyone could blame me for a little nudge to nature to move things along. I'm still letting it happen naturally, just when I want it to *and* with a plan.

I spent the better part of Friday morning at Pier 1 stocking up on candles. My bedroom is either going to look like a den of love or a fire hazard. I'm not quite sure which but I'm hoping for den of love. I do have a fire extinguisher nearby just in case. A girl can never be too cautious, after all.

I'm not sure how single women planned nights of seduction before the Internet. Did you know you can just search "Best candles for seduction" and a ton of options appear? It's really convenient. Thank you, Internet. Also important when planning *the night*? Finding a good esthetician for your first Brazilian waxing. Yes, first Brazilian. Both Charlotte and Anna have been bugging me for months to have it done. They swear it is the greatest thing since, well, anything really.

Since I didn't know where to begin I called my regular esthetician, Heidi. Heidi told me it wasn't something she does but could refer me to a colleague. I was grateful because it made me feel more comfortable knowing it was someone she trusted. These *are* my nethers we are talking about, after all. I probably should have asked for some specifics on what to expect and how things would work, but I didn't. I figured I'd go into the room like I do for my facials and we'd chat a bit before she walked me through the process. Not so much.

First, Firenze wasn't at the same location as Heidi. No, she was across town and traffic was a bitch. Plus it was hot as Hades out and since I chose to drive with the top down I needed a gallon of water and a shower by the time I arrived. Firenze is a no-nonsense woman. I was quite flustered after a crappy drive and she didn't seem to have the time or patience for my issues and questions. When I started telling her about the traffic, the heat, and asking about what to expect she simply turned to me with no smile and replied, "Undress."

Okaaay . . . yes, I was ten minutes late for my appointment but that seemed a little rude. However, instead of telling her my reasons I simply did as she instructed. I certainly didn't want the woman handling my lady garden to be angry. That can never be a good thing.

I should also say that Firenze did not leave the room while I undressed, nor did she feel it necessary to turn her back. She just stood there with her arms crossed, tapping her foot impatiently. My initial reaction was to leave because I had a bad feeling about this. Unfortunately, if I wanted to take my relationship with Dillon to the next level on Friday I needed to have this done by Thursday. It was time to suck it up and just pray this went quick and smoothly.

Then Firenze started with the questions. Well, one question really - what type of wax did I want? I kept responding, "Brazilian, Firenze. Brazilian." I guess this wasn't the correct answer because she started saying random words like martini glass, postage stamp, and Mohawk. Since I was desperate for a cocktail at this point I just said, "YES! Martini!"

After the cocktail discussion ended the yoga began. I'm just going to put this out there. If you want to go get a Brazilian you may want to 1. Check your inhibitions at the door; and 2. Do some stretches and yoga moves beforehand. I had no clue I was going to have to pull this leg that way and stand this way. It was really eye opening and Firenze and I have a bond that I have only shared with the labor and delivery nurse before now.

In the end, I *am* smooth and have a martini glass situation happening. I'm not going to say the process was worse than childbirth because, well, nothing really is. But this waxing? Not my thing. Maybe if it was performed by someone who didn't curse in a different language while handling the business. I don't need to speak Hungarian to know she was cursing at me and my lady garden. And, I'm not sure it is common practice to smack said garden after ripping it to shreds with hot wax. At least, I hope not. Regardless, it is done. Firenze seemed to be pleased with the end result. I chose to put the top up and drive with the air-conditioning on when I headed home and left her a fifty percent tip with a wave and promise to myself and my nethers that we'd never go back.

So here I am. Setting up all of the candles for what I hope is *the* night with Dillon. Lord knows I'm ready. Once I am pleased with the setting, I cue up my iPod for the perfect play list and change into something I hope looks casual and flirty.

Since I have some time before Dillon arrives I decide to check the P&Q email. This year has really flown by and I can't believe how much has changed for me in just a few short months. I'm just about a month away from the big author event over the Labor Day holiday weekend. Nobody was more surprised than me when I hit maximum capacity for the entire weekend and had to start telling people no when they continued to inquire. Everything is just falling into place and I am genuinely happy. I only hope that after tonight all of the pieces will be in place for this next phase of my life. While I'm lost in thought I hear whistling and realize Dillon didn't knock or ring the bell and let himself in. For some reason that little gesture makes me happy.

I follow the whistling and find Dillon in the kitchen with Tilly and two pizzas. I just stand there for a minute and take in the scene. Yes, I want to be in his arms and kiss him like crazy, but the view from here isn't too bad. He's dressed casual in cargo shorts and a T-shirt with a pair of flip-flops. How can this look make my knees shake like they are? Then I hear what he is saying to Tilly and my heart swells.

"Tilly, you are a very pretty girl. Yes, you are. I cannot give you pizza, your mommy would kill me if you got sick. She loves you so much, which means I love you too and you need to stay healthy. That's why I brought you this bone. Now take it outside so I can find your sexy mommy." Holy shit. I clear my throat and walk toward him with purpose and a sudden need to skip the pizza.

I'm on him faster than he has time to react and have my fingers threading through his hair and pulling him to me. I cannot believe how quickly his kisses have become as vital to me as air and water. The way his hands grip my waist and he pulls me up to eye level with him. I can't help but start smiling because I know this is going to be a fantastic night.

"Hi there," I say as he slowly puts me down. The loss of his lips is immediate but I need to make sure this is perfect for us.

"Hey, hungry?" he asks me as if we weren't two more kisses from our first time being in the kitchen. Lord in Heaven he looks hot and smells amazing. I really need to slow this down.

"I'm starving! Let's take this to the table. I'll grab us some wine?" I reach for the glasses and he heads into the dining room. Once we're settled in we spend the next little while catching up and the sexual tension is there again. I have this entire plan of seduction, but quite frankly I'm having a little trouble remembering all of my plans.

"Honey? Did you hear what I said?" Shit, no, I wasn't listening I was trying to remember how I'll seduce you in about fifteen minutes.

"Oh, sorry. I kind of drifted off. What did you say?" I really need to calm down.

"I just wondered if you wanted to watch a movie or play some cards," he says as he's clearing the table. Why wait fifteen minutes?

"Oh, I'm not really in the mood for either. I was thinking we could just relax? I'm actually going to run up and change out of this, I'm a little uncomfortable. I'll be just a sex . . . Umm, I mean sec. Just a second," I say and hope he passes right past the sex slip.

I rush up to my room and quickly light the candles and change into a little baby doll I have been hoping will please Dillon. Once I have brushed, okay and flossed, my teeth, spruced up my hair, and pushed the girls up to play, I set the music to play and head to the stairs. Deep breaths, Victoria. Deep. Breaths. I slowly make my way down the stairs and smile when I see Dillon is lying on the couch with some candles lit and low music playing. I guess I'm not alone with the ideas tonight.

Just as I'm about to use my "come hither" voice, I hear my phone shouting Stewie-isms. Justin's ringtone. He's camping and it's late. I want to let it go to voicemail, but my gut says not to. At the same moment I go to grab my phone Dillon stands up and sees me standing there, half dressed.

"Vic . . . holy shit!"

I smile as I point my finger for a second. "I'm sorry, that's Justin. I need to see if he's okay. Give me a minute." I offer him a smile and answer the phone. "Hey, kiddo, what's going on?" I ask as I stand there staring at Dillon, who is looking at me with nothing short of desire. He's walking toward me when I suddenly hear the other person talking and realize it isn't Justin.

"Is this Victoria Bennett?"

"Yes it is, who is this please? Why do you have my son's phone?"

"Mrs. Bennett, my name is Janice Hughes, I'm a nurse at . . ."

That's about all I remember from the call. Well, except where Nurse Janice told me my son was injured in a fall and I was needed at the hospital. She wouldn't tell me anything else other than where to go. I know the moment Dillon realizes something is wrong by the concerned look on his face.

"Everything okay? What's wrong?" he asked as I started sobbing.

"It . . . it . . . it's Justin. He's been hurt. I have to get to the hospital. I'm sorry." I can't even get the words all out without wailing. My baby boy is hurt and I need to get to him. Dillon suddenly has me wrapped in his arms and pulls me to the couch to sit me in his lap.

"Shh, it's okay. I'll just blow out these candles and we'll go straight away. Do you need me to help you change?" I shake my head no while I continue to sob. "I'll close up down here while you change."

I sniffle and quietly request, "Can you help me upstairs while I change?" Without another word Dillon has my hand and is walking me upstairs and stops dead in the doorway to my bedroom.

"I had a plan," is all I manage to say before he leans down and kisses my forehead.

"Thank you. It's beautiful. Let's get you changed and to your boy." That's all he has to say and I'm heading into the bathroom to change while Dillon puts out the thirty-six candles I have set up on my bedroom. Yes, thirty-six. It was forty but I ran out of room.

Once I'm changed, we head out to his truck and he lets me in the passenger side and grabs my face in his hands. "Hey, it is going to be okay. I'm here." He gives me a simple kiss to the forehead and I've never been so grateful to have someone by my side as I am right now. I feel like he will keep me grounded when I face whatever it is that waits for me at the hospital.

"Dillon," I whisper through sobs as he starts the truck and turns to me. "I can't lose him. He's all I have."

Dillon grabs my hand and interlocks our fingers as he brings my hand to his lips. "You have me too, Victoria. It will be okay."

I hope he's right. I can't take another loss. It will break me.

Chapter Twenty-Five

THE ENTIRE DRIVE to the hospital I alternate between sobbing, sniffling, and staring out the window. So many thoughts run through my mind at once - sadness, worry, frustration, fear. Just so many different emotions that I can't get a handle on them. I am also extremely grateful - for Dillon and him being here for me. He hasn't let go of my hand since we got in the truck and I cannot imagine having to go through all of this alone.

"Dillon?" I squeak out as he looks at me. My heart is so filled with emotion in that moment. I think I love him. I am fairly certain that I have fallen in love with Dillon. Wow. This is really not the time for this kind of realization. "Thank you for being here," is all I manage to get out before I start crying again.

As we pull up to the hospital, I don't even give him an opportunity to put the truck in park before I'm flying out of it and headed for the doors. I can hear Dillon running to catch up with me and grab my hand as we head into the Emergency Department. Once I give my information to the nurse at the desk we are asked to wait for someone to call me back. It feels like an eternity, but Dillon assures me it has only been four minutes.

"Mrs. Bennett?" A kind-looking woman walks toward me and introduces herself as Nurse Janice. Once we've exchanged pleasantries, I begin to get a little antsy. Dillon interrupts Janice and politely asks if I can see Justin. I watch a lot of television. I love a great hospital drama, so this delay tactic is not lost on me. Obviously something is very wrong or Janice would have already brought me to Justin. I can't hold it in anymore and begin crying again.

"Oh my word, Mrs. Bennett, are you okay? Do you need to sit down?" No, lady, I need to see my son. Of course this is in my head and not aloud because that would be rude.

"Please just tell me what is wrong! I can't take this anymore. Where is my son?!" I'm becoming hysterical at this point and Justin is somewhere alone and needs me.

"Oh, I am so sorry. Justin is just fine. He's with his friends and I just wanted to make sure they had a moment to clear out before I took you back. Let's go see your son," Nurse Janice says as she motions for me to follow her. "Again, I am so very sorry for scaring you. Your boy will be just fine. He's a little stubborn, that one. I have two boys myself and know a lot of that attitude is his age and probably a little peacocking for the ladies," Nurse Janice is rambling at this point and I feel bad for yelling at her. Well, not really, I mean does she not watch TV? How can she not know that you never use the stall tactics?

As we head back and Dillon puts his arm around my shoulder, pressing a kiss to my temple, I stop in my tracks when I see Sara coming out of Justin's room. What in the hell is going on around here?

"Sara?" I ask at the same time as Dillon. Obviously he has no idea what is going on either. "Oh my goodness, Sara!" I exclaim as

I grab her into a hug. Nurse Janice excuses herself and I mouth a "thank you" to her as I pull Sara out of my hug. "What are you doing here? Oh my, are you dating Justin? Thank goodness. I knew you two would hit it off. No wonder he wouldn't let me set you up. Why didn't you tell me? Where is he? Is he okay?" I'm like a fountain with a broken mechanism because I can't seem to stop. I feel Dillon come up behind me and chuckle. Really? He finds this humorous?

"Hi, Victoria. Umm, first Justin is fine. I think he messed up his leg pretty good, which is totally going to suck for the Lacrosse team but otherwise he will be fine. Well, not fine, I mean he did fall down a mountain." I'm beginning to think Sara may not be the girl for Justin. Who cares about la-freaking-crosse?

"Sara, you didn't answer Mrs. Bennett. Hello, Dillon," a girl with beautiful brown hair says as she walks up and puts her arm around Sara's waist. They really are a friendly pair.

"Oh sorry. Victoria. This is Lila. My girlfriend." Oh.

"We were all out hiking and Justin slipped a little and down he went. We had to call for help to get him down the mountain but I swear he didn't hurt his head or anything, just his leg. Sophie is in with him now. I know he wants to see you." I realize I'm just standing here in the hallway of a hospital finding out a lot about the young people in my life. Who the hell is Sophie? Dillon must sense my confusion because he walks up and grabs my hand.

"Honey, why don't we go in and see Justin? Sara, we'll see you later," Dillon comments as we walk toward Justin's door. I open the door and walk in to see a woman sitting next to Dillon holding his hand. My poor baby.

"Oh Justin!" I cry as I walk over to his bedside. "Are you okay? What happened? Well, I know what happened because I talked to Sara. What did the doctor say? Are you here for the night? I'm sorry, I'm Victoria Bennett," I say as I extend my hand to the woman sitting on the other side of Justin's bedside. Holding his hand.

"Mom, I'm fine. Relax. I'm sorry they called you. It's not a big deal. I mean, it is because coach is going to have my ass for getting hurt. It's just that Sophie and I love to take hikes and I didn't think it would be a big deal. I guess I was wrong. Oh sorry, Mom this is Sophie. My girlfriend." No. No. No. This *woman* is not my son's girlfriend.

"I'm sorry, girlfriend? What about Sara?" I ask. Yes, I know. Sara has a girlfriend. I'm a little confused here. Girlfriend? I suppose this explains a lot of cancelled mandatory dinners of late.

"Well, I'm assuming Sara and Lila are still here if you're asking. Sophie is Lila's sister. That's how we met. Didn't Sara tell you that her and Lila are together? You do know that means Sara isn't interested in me and thank goodness for that because I don't think Soph would like that," Justin says as he continues to hold this harlot's hand. What is she, thirty? She is Mrs. Robinson, oh good grief. I look from their joined hands to his leg to the machine he's hooked up to. Okay, it's not a machine it's an IV but that is neither here nor there. Dillon nudges me and when I look at him he gives me a "pay attention" nod to Justin. Right.

"I told you I was seeing someone. This isn't the way I wanted you to meet but, well, here you are." My son looks so much like the little boy I used to tuck in at night right in this moment. He's snuggled up in a bed with a blanket up to his chest. Justin is eighteen years old. He should be dating a girl his age, not some woman who probably has a teenage son herself somewhere.

"I don't understand. This is a lot to process. How old are you, Sophie? And how long has this been going on?" I ask while I am pretty sure I am squeezing the feeling out of Dillon's hand.

"Mrs. Bennett," Sophie says before I cut her off.

"Victoria, please. I mean we are practically peers from what I can tell. Let's not be so formal." Yes, it's snarky. Yes, a little bitchy. I don't really care.

"Victoria it is, then. I doubt we are close to peers. I mean, yes you are young, but I'm only twenty-four. Justin and I met a few months ago and I really care for your son. I'm sorry we've met under these circumstances. We planned on setting something up in the next few weeks," she says offering me a smile. She really does have a nice smile. "Justin, I'm going to head home. I'll talk to you in the morning when you are ready to be released," the hussy says as she leans in and kisses my baby. Oh for heaven's sake. I wait for Sophie to leave the room before I turn to Justin.

"Justin, are you out of your mind?! That *woman* cannot be who you are dating. She is six years older than you! Are you on drugs? That must be it. You cannot be serious!" I frustratingly tell him.

"Victoria, maybe you should wait until we hear what Justin has to say and gets out of the hospital before you start in on this," Mr. Voice of Reason aka Dillon says. I hate when he is rational.

"Fine, but, Justin, we will discuss this. Now tell me about this leg. You'll obviously come home with me. I'll set up the den for you so you don't have to worry about the stairs," I declare.

"No, Mom, I'm not. I'm stuck here overnight but then I'm going home. I still have school and while it's going to be a pain in the ass to get around campus I still have to go. Plus, I'm not a child and I have my own place to live," Justin states matter-of-factly. Like I'm going to agree to any of that. "And, you need to apologize to Sophie. You were very rude and that hurt my feelings too. I know she's a little older but we are really good together and I need you to accept that." Again, as if I'm just accepting any of this.

"Dillon is right, we need to focus on your leg and what to expect with that. We'll table the Sophie issue for now but I don't appreciate the fact you kept all of this from me, Justin. It just tells me that you know it's wrong. She's twenty-four, Justin. Twenty-four."

After about twenty minutes of small talk that included Dillon and Justin talking about the hiking spot he fell and other crap I didn't care about, the doctor made an appearance. The doctor explained that Justin had suffered a plethora of tears and strains to his leg and would be in a brace for at least six weeks before starting physical therapy. I saw the color drain from his face when Justin realized he would be out the rest of the lacrosse season. I also saw the moment he realized his scholarship would be in jeopardy. I love my son, but hitting the books and putting his education above all other things college related hasn't exactly been a priority. I think that is about to change.

Once the doctor finished his examination, the nurse came in to give Justin some medication and let me know visiting hours were over. Dillon had to practically drag me out of the room after Justin asked me to go home and rest. He agreed, albeit reluctantly, to let me come back in the morning to take him home. He also agreed, okay was coerced, into staying with me at least for the first few days of his recovery. I figure if I can get him home and take care of him he'll realize he does need me to take care of him.

I must have fallen asleep on the ride back to my house because I awoke to Dillon scooping me out of the truck. I didn't even have the energy to argue as he grabbed my key, opened the door, and carried me upstairs to bed. I felt him tuck me in and kiss my forehead before he closed my door and I succumbed to dreams of nights of seduction gone wrong.

Chapter Twenty-Six

CARING FOR AN eighteen-year-old man is completely different than caring for a sweet, loving, and adoring little boy. This version of my sweet son is a little on the demonic side. I mean, I get it. He did fall off a mountain and destroy his leg. He is in pain and he is frustrated that I have to take care of him. I won't even touch on the topic of Sophie the Harlot. Obviously I don't call her that to his face, but come on, she is twenty-four. Justin has explained to me numerous times how they met and while it seems reasonable, I am still not okay with this.

From what Justin has told me, Sophie didn't start college until she was twenty-one. She was working and helping her mother with her younger siblings. I understand that and appreciate her commitment to her family. Justin seems to really care for this girl, err woman, and from his point of view she sounds lovely. She is, quite honestly, someone I would enjoy getting to know. Unfortunately for both Sophie and Justin I cannot accept this as a fulfilling and reasonable relationship to support.

"Mom, can we just please stop talking about this? I am with Sophie. I care about her a lot and honestly I don't need your permission to date her. I would like your blessing and willingness to get to know her, but I'm not going to stop seeing her just because you have a hang-up," he says as he tries to steady himself on his crutches. "Besides, how much older was Dad than you? Now, I'm going to go to my room and talk to my girlfriend on the phone. I promised you I'd stay here for the first week and I will, but if you continue to bash Sophie I may not talk to you." With that comment he heads to his temporary bedroom and I am left alone on the couch.

Yes he got me with the age difference of his father and I. And, yes he's about to turn nineteen. Perhaps it's not so much Sophie as it is Justin growing up that I'm struggling with.

Dillon has tried to come over and spend time with us over these first few days. I think he wants to work as a little bit of a buffer for Justin and me. That pisses me off. I don't need a buffer for my son. I need someone to talk some sense into him and Dillon refuses. Simply put, he feels I should let this relationship ride itself out. He thinks that if I continue to force the issue it will only push Justin closer to Sophie and farther from me. The fact that he has a point is infuriating.

I'm heading into the kitchen to start dinner when the doorbell rings. I head to the front door and am immediately overwhelmed with what is before me. A magnificent array of flowers is floating around my porch. Well, it's not floating; I'm sure someone is holding it but I can't see the person past the amazing colors that overwhelm me.

"Victoria Bennett?" the flowers ask me. I finally find the delivery person holding the flowers and have him carry them into the house for me. Once I show him back out, I head back to the flowers, almost floating as I do. The first thing I notice is that the card isn't one of those mini cards with a typed "Have a nice day" comments. It's an actual card that is handwritten. As I begin to read the words, my heart swells and my breath catches.

Victoria,

I know you are dealing with a lot right now and I wanted to make sure you know I am always on your side. Give Justin time and he'll come around. You are a wonderful mother. I chose these flowers because they remind me of you – vibrant, full of life and perfect. I will miss you this week and am always a phone call away.

Love,

Dillon

Well, there you have it. The official moment I no longer question whether I love Dillon Laughlin. How could I not? I have spent an entire day arguing with my son, questioning how I have raised him, and with only a few words I feel reassured and know that I am doing something right. Dillon is right and I know I need to back off the Sophie situation and let the situation play itself out. I'm smiling like a fool when Justin hobbles back down the hall.

"I'm sorry, Mom," he says as he attempts to hug me with his crutches in the way. I let out a little giggle and hug him back.

"I'm sorry too. Let's call a truce, shall we? How about some good old comfort food for dinner? Grilled cheese and soup?" He nods and follows me into the kitchen.

"So those are some flowers you have there. Are they from Dillon?" he asks me as I begin pulling items from the refrigerator.

I nod and smile and notice he looks oddly serious. "Yes, they are. We haven't talked about this, have we? How do you feel about me dating Dillon?" I know that as much as I care for Dillon, if Justin didn't approve it would be a problem for me. I can only assume this is how he's been feeling about Sophie and my lack of support. I really feel like a jerk right now.

"He's cool. I just . . . I guess I just don't know how I feel. When Dad got sick I was young and I kind of assumed you'd just be alone for the rest of your life. Not able to move on and stuff, ya know?" Wow, he assumed I would always be alone. Like some sort of spinster-type lady?

"Actually, no I don't," I say, shaking my head and trying to focus on the task of making some soup and sandwiches. "Why would you think I would stay alone? I don't mean that I was looking to date someone when your dad was sick but, I'm just now forty, Justin. I want to have a partner in life. I want to have passion and feel loved. Don't look at me like that. You have a girlfriend. You have to understand what I'm saying, you aren't a child." He isn't, and I know that this is a huge conversation.

"I know that now, but when Dad was sick and I was what, fifteen? I couldn't imagine you being with someone. Honestly, when you were doing the online dating I didn't have a problem with it because I knew nothing would come of it. Those guys were all a bunch of weirdos!" We start laughing and I told him it wasn't funny but continued to laugh along with him. They aren't weirdos; they may be a little weird but they are all good guys. I explained this to Justin and how much each of them has helped me with P&Q and truly in my relationship with Dillon.

"Do you love him, Mom?" Such a loaded question from the most important person in my life. I'm just realizing the depth of my feelings for Dillon and I suppose I expected to have this conversation with him before anyone else. Surely before I had the conversation with Justin.

"How would you feel about it if I said yes?" I ask him. I know, a cop out, but come on, how do you answer that?

"Hmmmm . . . First, did he teach you how to make this grilled cheese? It's the bomb! So if that's the case I say whatever happens you have him teach you to make more kick-ass food!"

Oh for goodness sake! Okay, yes, he did teach me, but I'm not telling Justin that. "Well, as long as my relationship keeps you fed I suppose I'll sacrifice my feelings for you!" I tease. Bite the bullet, Victoria, tell him. "Yes, Justin, I do love him. You are the first person other than myself that I have said that to. I need to know how you feel about this though because if you aren't okay with it then I will reconsider seeing him." Please don't be against it, please!

"What? Why would you do that? That's ridiculous. No, I like Dillon. I like that he makes you smile and he treats you good. I can tell you're happy with him and I'm just glad you said yes because otherwise Dad would be pissed at me," he says as he reaches for his third sandwich. They really are that good. Garlic butter is the answer.

"Why would your father be upset? I mean, I believe he watches over us but I don't think he is haunting us or anything. Explain." He holds up his finger and inhales his sandwich before speaking. It feels like the longest three minutes of my life.

"Haunting? Yeah I don't think Dad is haunting us either. I guess he watches over us but I really hope it's not when I'm doing private things cause that's just gross!" I agree and hope that we don't talk about his "private things" anymore. "No, I got a letter too. Anna said that we all got letters and she had to give them to us when the time was right. A few weeks ago she came by my house and dropped it off. She said she was headed here to give you the letter Dad left for you." Oh my goodness. My heart just dropped. I knew there was a letter, but I suppose in some way I was in denial about the content.

"Did you want to talk about your letter, Justin?" I'm torn on what I hope his answer is. Of course I want to know, I'm a woman.

182

I'm curious. I'm also scared to death to know what it says. I notice Justin is laughing a little.

"Dad said you'd be curious. He actually started it with 'Justin, your mother is going to want to know what I am saying in this letter. I leave it to you to decide but you know you'll have to tell her something.'" Oh that man. He knew me well, damn it.

"Anyway, I'm not going to tell you all of what he said but I will say that it was to be read when you fell in love again. Basically Dad wanted me to know that he wanted you to find love again. That all he ever wanted in life was for you to smile, laugh, and be happy. He made it clear I was to not be an asshole to whoever you chose and that I should support you and trust you to know what is best for you," he tells me as he suddenly seems sad, and then he continues.

"It really made me miss him. Miss our family, ya know? I also realized how lucky I was to have him for my dad. He was awesome." Yes, he was. "Anyway, I like Dillon. He's a cool dude and I know he loves you. He makes you happy and I think you do the same for him. I just wanted to make sure. I kind of felt bad thinking that I read the letter for the wrong guy, but when you came to the hospital the other day, I knew. I'm glad you have him."

"Thank you, Justin. That means the world to me. Yes, your father was awesome and he was an amazing man. I was blessed to have him as my husband and nobody will ever replace him. You know that, right?" He nods. "I am ready to move forward with the next phase of my life. This isn't the story I planned but I think it is the one I'm meant to have. I think that your dad would want me to be kinder to Sophie and support your decisions as an adult. I will try, okay?" We hug and Justin heads to his room.

Alone with my thoughts, I realize that I didn't cry when we talked about Patrick. For the first time I was able to talk about our life, our loss, and our future without crying. Knowing that Justin approves and accepts Dillon as part of my life and sees the changes he has made in my world is more than I can ask. Now if said man would get his East Coast business finalized maybe we could actually take this relationship to the next level. I suppose that means I will have to share my feelings too. I can only hope everyone is right and he feels the same way. I decide to send him a quick text before I settle in for a little time with my book.

Thank you for the beautiful flowers! They are perfect and the delivery was very timely.

I meant what I said. You are perfect and I'm glad you like them. How's Justin?

Ornery and stubborn! I have no idea where he gets it from ;-) He sees the doctor tomorrow and I think he'll go home after that. How's NYC?

Hmmm, stubborn you say? Weird! NYC is hot. Summer here is not my favorite. I am enjoying spending time with Liam and finalizing some business. I am a bit worried about him.

Not to rub it in but the weather here is a little wonderful this week! I'm glad you are spending time with your brother. Why are you worried?

Liam and his fiancé split a few months back and I don't think he's over it. He's talking about taking a long vacation before his move which is unlike him. I'm probably being overprotective.

No, you're being a brother. When do you come home? I need some kisses!!

Muah! There's a big kiss for now. I'm hoping to be home Sunday. I'll keep you posted. And yes, I'm being a brother and he hates it. I better get some rest. Let me know how things go with the doctor?

Of course. Sleep well.

Goodnight.

Night.

My fingers hovered over the keypad while I realized I almost typed "I love you." That would have been a little awkward for the first time, to say the least. I have four days to figure out how to say those words in person. Four days. I can handle that.

Chapter Twenty-Seven

NOW THAT JUSTIN has returned to his place and is preparing to start classes I'm once again home alone. I thought about having the girls over for a girl's night but ultimately decided to get some work done around the house. I wasn't exaggerating when I told Dillon our weather was wonderful. It has been sunny and a perfect 75 the last few days. I've decided to spend this beautiful Saturday cleaning and gardening. I get that seems silly to some people, but a beautiful day, the windows open, my secret playlist blaring through the house, and the smell of cleanliness is like heaven to me.

Anna suggested I hire a cleaning service now that I'm opening my home up to strangers and running a business. I just couldn't do that. I enjoy the control a little too much, I think. Okay, I know I do. Plus I feel a sense of accomplishment when I'm all done. We're still a little less than a month from the big event in September but I'm pretty booked until then. I did have to reschedule a few things this week after Justin's injury but everyone was very understanding.

I can't help but to laugh as I'm cleaning the downstairs bathroom. The smell of lemon is overwhelming and reminds me of one of my last online dates. I had stepped a little out of my comfort zone and agreed to meet a man named Ford at an indoor go-kart track for some lighthearted fun. The date was actually a lot of fun and I laughed so much. Of course, I was in my own go-kart for about an hour of the date so I was having fun alone, but regardless it was a great time. Then it came time for us to grab a bite to eat.

It turns out that Ford, while a lot of fun and easy to talk to, also had a very prevalent germ phobia. Not your usual "I need to wipe down the cart before grocery shopping" germ issue. Nope, this was "I own stock in hand sanitizer companies because I use so much of it" germ issue. I carry a small travel-size hand sanitizer in my purse. I get that you want to be prepared when it is necessary. I don't think pulling out an industrial-size bottle of lemon zest hand sanitizer from your backpack – let's skip right by the fact that he was carrying a backpack, shall we - and insist that we not only use some on our hands but all the way to our elbows. I ended the date smelling like a freaking bottle of lemons and not in a refreshing way, more like a clinical way. I also woke up the next morning with some sort of rash and really dry skin. I don't even need to tell you that there was no date number two for Ford.

After I finish the bathrooms and the kitchen, it's time for some gardening. Now this is where the super-secret playlist comes in. Anyone who knows me well knows that I like all types of music. In general I am like a random playlist - a little Kool & the Gang, some Maroon 5, quite a bit of country, some 90's alternative, and so on. Nothing all that unexpected. But my gardening playlist? I keep that to myself because I see how people judge and laugh when they see how much I love old-school hip-hop. Yes, of course I mean some Beastie Boys, Run DMC, Rob Base, and Salt-N-Pepa but I also mean some N.W.A., Ice Cube after N.W.A. split, and of course Tupac and

Biggie. What? I'm eclectic.

Since I'm headed outside, I turn on the outside speakers, which I'm sure if I had neighbors nearby they would just love. That's sarcasm for those who don't realize. Tilly loves when we are outside together and she can run and play while I toss her a ball or bone. She's easy to please and I'm grateful. I can only imagine what I look like in my cut-off shorts and tank top, hair piled on my head, dirt all over my legs and face. Hot mess is probably an accurate description, but nothing feels as good as the sun shining on my face and the earth's soil beneath my hands.

I'm so engrossed in the planting and, yes, the ass shaking I'm doing, that I don't realize Tilly is hopping around like a damn rabbit. I swear she acts so strange but usually only when someone is here . . . shit. I slowly turn to look over my shoulder and see a very entertained (and sexy) Irishman standing in my yard. I wasn't prepared to see Dillon, obviously, and this is not more evident than when I scream and fall flat on my previously shaking ass.

"Shit! Damn it to hell!" I squeal as I get up and try to wipe the dirt off my hands. I grab a bottle of water I had and pour it on my hands as I walk toward him. I've got to be a sight, with dirt everywhere, my hair all willy nilly, and my ass practically hanging out of my shorts. "What are you doing here? I didn't think you were coming home until tomorrow?" I ask him. I cannot believe he just walked up on me shaking my ass to freaking Notorious B.I.G. If the earth could just open and swallow me up, that would be super.

No words. Dillon offers me no words. He just puts his hands on either side of my face, and the look in his eyes, it's like he's burning up. I can see the passion in his eyes and I hiccup a little breath before his lips consume mine. The kiss is tentative and sweet to begin with, almost as if he is making a memory.

Before I can appreciate that moment, he parts my lips and I'm a goner. He slowly runs his hands down my sides ever so gently, grazing my breasts. All the while I find my hands instantly in his hair, oh my goodness. I can feel my heart beating outside of my chest and it's like I am an observer to this entire scene. Once his hands find my waist, he hoists me up so that we are eye level and I can't help but wrap my arms around his neck like my life depends on it.

He offers me a soft moan of appreciation and that's all I need before I wrap my legs around his waist and put everything I have into this kiss. Desire fills me instantly and he must be on the same page. As his lips leave mine and start dropping kisses to my neck, I feel him carrying me up the steps of the deck and to the double chaise. Holy hell, this is happening. We haven't even said hello and we're devouring each other. This isn't what I had planned. This is not the romantic and perfect night I envisioned. There aren't any candles, there is no soft music - well there is some Warren G playing, which is kind of mellow right now. I have to stop him and make this perfect. Oh, but his lips are on my neck.

As he runs his hand up and down my bare thigh I can't help but let out a slight moan. How can he bring me so close to the edge with just simple touches and his kisses? I feel like I am moments from exploding and he starts to pull away from my neck, cupping my face. "I want you, Victoria. More than I can express."

"Dillon, oh God. . ." I can't even put a thought together while he's kissing my neck. "This isn't . . . It's not what I planned. I'm, oh my . . . I need a shower, I look horrible. . ."

Before I can finish what I hope sounds like a coherent thought he's kissing me again and this time his hand is up my shirt and I'm melting. This is like nothing I have ever felt before. I don't care that we are outside. I don't care that I am covered in dirt or that I probably smell like sunscreen. All I care about at this moment is getting this man undressed and letting him take me over the edge of whatever cliff I'm hovering.

"Oh my God, Victoria. You are so beautiful. Please tell me you want this too," he's practically begging as he's trying to pull my shirt over my head and I'm tugging at his.

"So much, I want it so much," I say, but I know I'll regret doing this anywhere but in my bed. I'm just that girl. "Do you mind if we take this to my room though?" I ask, and before I can even fathom what is happening Dillon has scooped me up and tossed me over his shoulder caveman style. Of course, because we are civilized adults, he manages to turn off the music just as some R. Kelly's *Bump N' Grind* starts playing. I can't help but let out a squeal and a giggle as he sprints up the stairs.

Once we reach my room it's like my clothes are on fire and I am tossing the shirt and shorts to the side as I watch him slowly undress and toss a foil packet on the bed. Oh wow. I knew I was a lucky girl, but seeing Dillon before me in nothing but boxer briefs and his perfect body, I feel like I've won the Lottery. I walk up to him and can't help but take a moment to run my hands over his body. I mean, the man has a complete twelve-pack of abs. Lord in Heaven, thank you.

As Dillon begins kissing me again, I take the steps backward to the bed. He gently lays me down and looks me in the eye before anything else, and I see it there in that moment. The look of love. I know right then that this is forever. The love I have for this man, the way he makes me feel, and how free I know I can be. These are the feelings you wish for and never think will happen. He continues to kiss me, to caress me, to make me *feel* everything before he does it. It is as if our bodies are speaking to one another before either of us are conscious of what is happening.

His touch is gentle yet demanding at the same time. He is in control, managing to give me everything I need and desire through the way my body reacts. Whimpers escape me. There are no words to express how absolutely amazing this man makes me feel. The way he is pushing my body to the edge without pushing *me* to the edge. My heart is so full of love and emotion. My body is on the brink, the fullness I feel in my heart, my soul, and my body - it all comes to an explosive finish as I let out a cry and he cries out my name.

After savoring that moment just a little longer, I'm delirious and overcome with emotion. I close my eyes so tight, trying to hold back the tears that threaten to escape as he pulls me into him in a spooning position. I can't help but smile and blink away the tears – tears of overwhelming emotion – as he moves the hair from my ear and I can tell by his breathing that he's exhausted. He lays a gentle kiss and with the faintest of whispers I hear him. At least, I hear the words that my heart feels: "I love you, honey."

I want so much to say it back. I love him too. So very much in this moment. Then I hear the faintest of snores and realize he's asleep. If I've learned anything these last few years, it is that there may not be a tomorrow and that forever isn't a given. Before I can even begin to figure out how to handle this, I succumb to sleep myself.

How in the fresh Hell did a damn elephant get in my room and why is it smothering me and trying to sweat me out? Oh shit, that's not an elephant, that's Dillon. Oh sweet mother, we had sex. We had sex and I'm still covered in dirt - sexy. I need to get out from under his arm before I overheat; goodness, he's like an electric blanket on high. I'm going to just slither out from under his arm ever so . . . oh wow, his hands are big. Poor guy, he's obviously exhausted. It's either that or he has swallowed a freight train because snoring is putting that sound mildly. It's sweet in its own way, and how this man manages to look so damn sexy while he sleeps is beyond me.

I manage to untangle myself from his hold without waking him and head for the bathroom. One look in the mirror and I am *very* grateful I didn't make this pit stop before the sexy time. I look like a cross between a coal miner and Medusa. As I reach in and start the shower, the words I heard Dillon whisper come back to me like a flash of lightning, *"I love you, honey."* Shit on a stick. I've always been told people speak the most truth in two scenarios - when they are drunk and when they are in a light sleep. I doubt there is actual scientific proof of this, but if that's the case, and he *does* call me honey, could he really love me?

I ponder this while I scrape the mud that is caked on my legs like a seven-layer dip and use half a bottle of my favorite citrus shower gel. He said it, maybe he even means it. I do find some joy in the fact that I didn't say it first, but then again he didn't *actually* say it *to* me consciously. I consider all my options while I deep condition my hair and ultimately decide I'm not going to say anything to him. I want him to say it again, but this time to me while looking in my eyes. I have to know this is real.

Once I finish my shower and confirm it's not too late, I decide to let Dillon sleep and head downstairs to make us something to eat. I can't help but let out a little laugh as I make it to the kitchen. Thank goodness nobody was here when Dillon decided to go caveman style and toss me over his shoulder. I would have died of humiliation!

As I throw together a salad and put some pasta on to cook, the hairs on the back of my neck stand up and I turn to see Dillon leaning on the doorway. He's put his shorts back on but chose to leave the shirt elsewhere. He's standing there like some sort of Greek - okay Irish - god. Good Lord in Heaven. I know there's probably no way he has an actual twelve-pack of abs, but there is some serious effort to have them.

"Hey," I say shyly. The realization of the step we took today suddenly hits me and I find myself almost embarrassed. He gives me that panty-melting smile and, embarrassed or not, I could turn this pasta off and have a do-over. Dillon walks toward me with what is now more of a smirk.

"Hey, yourself," he says as he places his hands on my hips and leans in for a sweet and tender kiss. There go the toes curling up into their self; the butterflies are in rare form as they take over my tummy, and my mind turns to mush. I let out a sigh as Dillon slowly pulls me to him and I wrap my hands around him, lightly brushing my fingers along the nape of his neck. "I suppose I didn't so much as say hello before, did I?" he asks me as he leans in for another kiss.

"I don't know about that. I personally enjoyed your greeting," I reply as I lay a gentle kiss on his lips and pull away from his embrace. I've managed to go from shy to bold in a nano-second. This is what this man does to me. "Did you sleep okay? I probably need to change the sheets if the dirt on my legs was any indication. I'm sure they are a mess." I try so hard to seem casual. I know he can tell this is awkward and new for me because he grabs my hand and leans over to turn the burner off. He slowly leads me into the den and pulls me to his lap as he sits on the couch.

"Are you okay? Was I too rough? I'm sorry, I don't know what came over me." Oh no, I can't believe he thinks he hurt me. That couldn't be further from the truth.

I try to convey this by snuggling into him and looking into his eyes as I reply, "Dillon, you were perfect. It was perfect. I just . . . it's just been a while and I don't quite know what to do here. I had this plan, as you know, and this . . . it was beyond my dreams, my plan. Don't worry about me." I hope he can feel my sincerity because I kind of hope that once we finish dinner we'll be back in bed.

He lets out a breath and smiles that smile of his that sets my soul on fire as he leans in for a kiss that gradually deepens. I can't help but let out a slight moan as I run my hands down his chest. "I'm so glad, honey," he says between kisses. There it is, *honey;* maybe he'll say it again.

As I consider this he continues, "How about some dinner then we light those thirty-six candles you bought a few weeks ago and spend a little more time *catching up?*" He begins nibbling at my neck and suddenly I'm at a loss for words and can only sigh and lean into his nibbles as I nod yes.

Chapter Twenty-Eight

OVER THE NEXT two weeks Dillon and I spend more time together than apart. He's spent most nights at my house and I can safely say that if I doubted my love for him, it is no longer in question. He hasn't said those three words again and I am holding strong while I wait to only say them in return and not first, but it's getting more difficult. It turns out I'm vocal in bed and have had to literally bite my tongue to keep from saying them.

I feel bad that I haven't seen Anna or Charlotte in a few weeks and have only managed a few phone calls and text messages. Of course they know that we've taken our relationship to the next level and I did tell Anna about Dillon's sleepy declaration. I decided it was time to stop being some unleashed sex kitten and put my best friend and big sister cap on. I told Dillon I needed a few nights with the girls and he completely understood. Again, proving that he is as close to perfect as anyone can get.

Tonight Anna is coming over to help me with some P&Q work

for the upcoming D.L. Cardwell event and indulge in some wine. When we made plans and I asked for her help she gave me so much grief as to why she has to work when I pay Elaine. That was when I knew something was up with her and I felt like a crap friend. Just as I'm pulling the Chinese takeout from the bags I hear Anna walking up to the back door.

"Party's here!" she shouts as she flings the door open. I can't help but laugh as I roll my eyes at her.

"Well, I didn't know I invited Snooki circa 2009 to have a girl's night but come on in!" She just rolls her eyes right back at me and flips me off. Oh, this is going to be a fun night. I pour her a glass of wine before she can even ask and I get a smile of gratitude.

"Oh shut up, you know you've missed me while you've been screwing your brains out!" She's got a point.

"You shut up! I haven't been screwing my brains out!" I manage to say while I hold back a smile and take a drink of my wine.

"Oh puh-lease, you and Dillon are probably going at it like damn bunnies. Have you managed to get through the *entire* book of *Kama Sutra*?" she tosses out as she heads upstairs with her bag.

I decide to have a little fun and shout as she makes it about halfway up the stairs "The *entire Kama Sutra*? Not entirely, but I did pull out my yoga and Pilates DVDs to help with my flexibility!" I can hear her laughing as she heads to my room. My phone chimes and I know without a doubt who it is.

I'm already missing you.

I will never get tired of receiving a text message like this. With a smile and typing as fast as my fingers will allow before Anna makes it back downstairs, I shoot off a reply.

I miss you too. I'm a little spoiled and don't think Anna will appreciate cuddling :)

Well I'm only a quick phone call away should you need an experienced cuddler.

Haha. Noted. Have a good night and I'll talk to you tomorrow.
Night. Sweet dreams.

I stash my phone in what I think to be a stealthy manner, and, of course, I am wrong. "The man can't be away from you one night? I swear I need to have a conversation with Dillon and explain that girl's night does not mean a text-a-thon."

I know she is teasing, but I can't help feeling a little guilty. "Oh hush now. We're in puppy-dog stage, give me some credit. He'll tire of me soon enough." I hope he doesn't, but that simple comment seems to appease Anna.

For the next few hours we fall back into our routine and over indulge in Chinese food and wine while we put together some swag packs for the event. "Vic, explain to me again why I'm here helping you when you have an employee? I mean, we could be doing anything and we're here, on a Friday night no less, folding and stapling something about an author that can't even put her damn picture on her books. What's that about anyway? Ridiculous!"

I stop what I'm doing as Anna rants and can't help myself when I ask, "Anna, have you been reading *romance novels*?"

She simply huffs and says, "Oh please, you know I don't buy into all that crap." Yeah right.

"Well, then tell me how you knew that the author doesn't put her photo on her books!" Busted. I can tell by the look on her face.

"Fine, I read one, maybe two of them. I'm unemployed and bored out of my mind and figured if I am going to be here to support you in a few days I should know what the hell is going on. "

"Wow, you did that for me? You hate romance and happily ever afters." She really does. She thinks romance novels are so ridiculous that she'd rather read a book about basket weaving than anything remotely close to romance.

"Yeah well, they actually weren't too bad. I did like the guy and all the sex. This lady must have sex ten times a day the way she gets into detail. No wonder you've been so sexually frustrated these last few years." I wouldn't call myself sexually frustrated, I'd call it more sexually paused. Like the DVR - on pause.

"I wasn't sexually frustrated, I was just waiting for the right person is all. And let me tell you, thank goodness I did. It is so worth it." I know the smile on my face is probably annoying and I promised myself I wouldn't just talk about Dillon tonight, so I try to change the subject. "How's the top-secret, run-from-your-problems vacation plan coming along?"

Whoops, I may worded that poorly. I watch as a wave of emotion skirts Anna's face before she seems to gather herself. "I'm not running. I'm *escaping* for some peace and quiet. I don't appreciate you making fun of me either. That's kind of an asshole move."

Shit. "I'm sorry, Anna, you're right. That was kind of an asshole comment. It's just that this is so unlike you. You face everything head on, like a bull at battle. I'm worried about you, that's all. Do you want to punch me? You totally can. I deserve it. I mean, I *am* having a lot of sex." That's all it takes before we're in hysterics and the topic of her running from her problems is on the back burner.

"Okay," Anna says to me with a serious expression on her face. "Truth time. How is the sex? And don't leave anything out."

I decide we can work on this P&Q stuff later. "PJs and pillow talk?" I ask and she nods in agreement. We close up the downstairs and head up to my room to snuggle in for girl talk. Once we're settled in my bed I notice Anna is sniffing the pillow, kind of like a dog. "What are you doing, you nut?"

Sniff, "I'm. . ." sniff sniff, "I'm trying to see if this pillow smells like Dillon or if you're being a creepy girlfriend and snuggling with his . . ." She leans over and sniffs my pillow. "Oh my God, Victoria! You are that girlfriend; you're sleeping with his pillow tonight, aren't you?! You are totally that girl now! I love it!"

"Okay, relax. I'm right here, you don't have to shout. Yes, I'm sleeping with his pillow. Sorry, babe, I love you, but you are not sleeping with my man's pillow." I fluff the pillow that smells like rain and vanilla, that smells like Dillon. We both start laughing and I realize how much I miss this and her. It's been awhile since I've seen her so relaxed. That entire Dick fiasco has really done a number on her.

"I get it, really, I do. If Dillon was my man I wouldn't share him either. So dish, I want to know what I've missed while you've been all consumed with your sexy-as-hell Irishman."

"Well, he is sexy, that's for sure. I told you about the first time. Gosh I was so mortified at first, but the look in his eyes, I can't describe it. It was so . . ." I find myself at a loss for words to describe that moment.

"Carnal? Primal? Fuckable?" Anna suggests, and the look on my face must be amusing because she's laughing.

"Yes, all of that. And passion filled. It's hard to explain. There really were no words exchanged, it was all unspoken. So amazing. All of it. Except for when we fell asleep. He hasn't said it again," I say, defeated. I told Anna the basics and she supports my resolve to not mention his declaration. Part of me worries that if I say something to Dillon about saying *those* words, it will create tension if he didn't mean them *or* force him to say them with the off chance he didn't mean them.

Anna must sense where my thoughts head because she grabs my hands and gives it a reassuring squeeze. "He will. He loves you, Victoria, there is no doubt in my mind. I just think that he isn't ready for that big declaration, ya know."

I do. "Yeah, I know. Now let's talk about something less dramatic. Where are you going on your trip? Bora Bora? Tahiti? Rome? Greece? Come on, give me a hint!" Anna just smiles at my inquisition and does the whole "lock it up with a key and toss the damn key" gesture. We continue on talking about everything, including a few sex pointers from Anna, before we finally fall asleep shortly before dawn.

I've grown accustomed to Dillon's early alarm and only manage to get in a few hours' sleep before I stumble down to make some coffee. I am not surprised to find Charlotte in the kitchen when my feet hit the tile floor.

"Morning, sis. I let myself in. You look like shit," my lovable little sister so kindly tells me.

"Umm, thanks? Coffee ready?" I ask as she smiles and hands me a mug of heaven. I love my little sister and feel overcome with emotions suddenly as I grab her for a huge hug. "I love you, Char Char." She squeezes me back and suddenly I feel her tears. "Charlotte, what's wrong?"

She pulls away and waves her hands to shoo me away as she reaches for a towel that is now officially a handkerchief. "Nothing. Everything. Hell, I don't know. I had lunch with Mom last week and now I feel all cruddy. I know I act like she doesn't get to me but I swear she oozes disappointment when she looks at me."

Our mother. I should have guessed. Marian Williams is a force to be reckoned with and a domineering one at that. She's like a hurricane you can't predict. "What happened, Char? Let's sit." We sit down at the table with our cups and I can already tell this is going to piss me off.

"Nothing really happened and she didn't actually say anything. That's the point, it's what she *doesn't* say. I get it, I quit college a semester before graduation. I know how much money they put into my education for me to ultimately choose a career as a fitness instructor. I just don't see why they want me to be something I'm not. I am not going to be a woman that sits behind a desk in an office staring out a window wishing I was outside. I want to be the woman that *is* outside. I think Dad finally accepted I wasn't going to get a business degree just for the sake of having it. Mom, of course, doesn't understand how I could do this to her. To her. Can you believe that?"

Yes, I can. We had the same conversation when I withdrew from school to become a full-time mom.

"Charlotte, you know I completely understand because I've had this conversation with Mom too. I think the only reason she didn't disown me was because of Justin. She loves us, Char, she's just not the best at articulating that. Patrick used to try to convince me to give her the room to be her and just take what she said for what it was and drop it. I never could, but I think I can now. Mom wants us to have what she didn't. She never went to college and never did more than volunteer at charity events and be Dad's number one cheerleader. I think what she needs to do is go back to college herself and let us be who we are."

Charlotte offers me a smile that is more evil than good. I've seen this look many times in the past. Of course, Charlotte was a teenager and she was usually concocting some sort of plan.

"Hmmm, I suppose you are right. Wouldn't it be wonderful to tell her that?" my lovely sister says as she taps her chin, pretending to be in thought as she widens her eyes in excitement. "You should, Vic! You're the big sister, you should be the one. Let's do it. You tell her and I'll be here to support you when you do. Next week."

Say what now? "Excuse me? What did you say?"

"I. Uh . . . well, kind of mentioned the author event to Mom and she plans on being here. Don't be mad." Shit on a stick. I do not need nor do I want my mother here. We've unofficially taken a break from each other. Mostly I've taken a break from feeling judged and stopped making an effort. Marian, on the other hand, has not taken the hint.

"Don't be mad? Are you kidding? I don't want her here. She's going to be all judgmental and . . . and . . . *Marian*. I'm likely to have a panic attack or something. I haven't even introduced them to Dillon! Thankfully he's not going to be here but, Charlotte, really? You invited *Mom!*"

"Hurricane Marian is coming here?" Anna asks from the doorway.

"Morning, sunshine. Yes, apparently my asshole sister decided she should be included in the single most important day of my life in recent years." I'm not angry, but I am slightly perturbed. I cannot believe she did this.

"Oh suck it up, Victoria, it's your mother not the mafia. I highly doubt Charlotte called up Marian and invited her. Did you, Char Char?"

"That's what I've been trying to say. I was cornered, Vic. She was just badgering me with questions. Am I dating? Am I putting myself out there? Have I considered getting a job that is a little more dependable? I had enough so I told her that I was sick and tired of being ashamed of who I am. That she has no idea who I am anymore and what makes me happy. I told her that she should be proud of us for all that we have done and how happy we are. I was in the *zone*, Vic! The zone. I couldn't stop, it was like everything I ever thought to say was coming out of my mouth."

I have no reaction to this other than awe. I'm watching Charlotte pace the kitchen and wave her hands around frantically as she tells us and I feel a solid moment of complete happiness for Charlotte. This is huge for her. She's always played the good girl and never spoken up and told our parents how she felt. When she left college I was really worried, but she insisted she was fine. I've always wondered how much of a front she put on, and in this moment I can see what a strong woman she has become.

I know I've missed part of what she said as she continues, "And that's when I just told her that you were making something wonderful here with P&Q and that she should be supportive and quit being so damn negative. I told her that you were doing what you love and mentioned that your favorite author was going to be here." Damnit. Now I feel shitty and selfish being angry. I know Charlotte would never do anything to hurt me or create more drama with our mother.

"I'm sorry, Charlotte. I really am. I guess even when she's not standing in front of me she can still push all my buttons. Tell me how you know she plans on being here."

"Well, after I kind of blew my lid and she sat there staring at me for a good five minutes, she just said, 'You are right. I will go to this event of your sister's and see what the hoopla is.'" Hoopla. She's such a bitch sometimes.

"Well then, that's done. Marian is coming and she'll eat crow and it will be fabulous. I, for one, cannot wait. Now, let's get some breakfast. I'm starving and we've got some shopping to do ladies!" Anna declares. We all clink our coffee cups in solidarity, yet I can't help feeling like the dark cloud of doom is heading my way. I fear that dark cloud is coming in the form of Marian Williams, my mother.

Chapter Twenty-Nine

THREE DAYS. I have three days until "Pages & Quiet presents an afternoon with D.L.Cardwell," also known as, three days until I have the biggest panic attack of my life. What the hell was I thinking starting this business and who thought it was a good idea to invite D. freaking L. Cardwell? Oh yeah, that was me. Excellent plan, Victoria. Cue a little meltdown and freak out. I can sit in the bathtub and eat an entire bag of Lindor truffles - the assorted pack obviously - and drink a bottle of wine. No, I'm not bothering with the glass. This is a serious meltdown status.

Thankfully, none of this happened. In fact, according to my checklists, I am ready. I have everything set, including my outfit, first backup outfit, and emergency backup outfit. The swag packs are ready, the food is ordered, the chairs and tables are even sitting patiently on the deck. I have seventy-five confirmed guests plus Hurricane Marian, Justin, and Sophie. Yes, Sophie. Much to my chagrin, I like her. Well, that's not fair, I suppose. I never disliked her, per se,

I just don't like my son dating her. I am, perhaps reluctantly, taking Dillon's advice and letting this play out. Hence, the invitation. Plus I need as many people here to run interference with my mother as possible. I have enough to worry about, such as the likelihood I will make a complete ass out of myself and this will all be a bust.

Instead of dwelling on all of this I'm going to enjoy these delicious truffles in the bath and the even more delicious wine. I wonder what Dillon is doing today. He has spent the last few nights at his place and was on a conference call this morning when I went into Irish Coffee. I close my eyes as I think of the last time he was here when suddenly I feel a wash cloth on my arm.

"Holy shit!" I scream as I grip the wine bottle with both hands because, let's be honest, I'm not wasting the wine. "Dillon! Are you kidding me?!" I'm shouting as Dillon is sitting there soaked and laughing hysterically.

"Sorry, I couldn't help myself. You had this array of emotions playing across your face. Tell me what you were thinking of when I walked in? And don't cover yourself, let me help you wash your back."

Oh goodness, this has turned into the best bath in the last 2.3 seconds. When he said he was going to wash my back I didn't expect him to get *in the tub!* I scoot forward and he lowers himself in behind me. I take a rather large sip of my wine as he grabs the body wash and begins lathering his hands. "So tell me, what were you thinking about? You went from what looked like distress to happy in just a period of less than two minutes."

How do I explain myself without sounding like a crazy person?

"First, I've had some wine. Want some?" I ask as I point the bottle toward his mouth and he opens. Oh those lips. Focus, Victoria. "I was feeling all of that. I'm scared, Dillon. What if this P&Q thing was a bad idea. What if none of the seventy-five people show up on Saturday? What if it rains? What if I spill red wine on myself? What if D.L. Cardwell hates me? I wish you were going to be here. Do you have to leave town? Can't the mafia or your family give you up for one day?" I attempt to joke, but I'm kind of serious. I need him here and he's going to be with someone else.

I'm momentarily distracted as his hands knead my shoulders and his hand makes its way down my spine ever so gently, sending a shiver up my spine and a warmth everywhere else. I place the bottle of wine on the side of the bathtub as Dillon gently kisses at my neck and gives a little tug at my earlobe with his teeth. I'm not sure which one of us does it first, but we both let out a sigh and perhaps there's a slight moan. That moan was me.

"Honey, I told you I have a prior commitment I can't get out of, but this is it. After this I have no reason to go out of town. Liam will be moving here in a few weeks and all of my East Coast commitments will be satisfied as of Saturday evening. And, again with the mafia and family? Haven't I shown you that you are my family? There is no place I'd rather be." Oh yeah, the words again. Family. That's only one word and not those three, but it is equally as swoon-worthy. "Plus, none of that tells me what made you happy before I scared the shit out of you," he says with a chuckle.

"Oh . . . that," I say as I find myself leaning back against him, knowing where this bath is headed. "I was thinking of you, of course." That's all it takes before Dillon has me turned around and I have my legs on either side of his lap, leaning into him as I brush my hands through his hair. I am looking directly into his eyes when I have to bite my lip to keep from professing my love to him. My unconditional and all-encompassing love.

I don't have but those few seconds to think that before his mouth is on mine and his hands are gripping my hips and I feel all of the tension leave my body. I can feel every emotion he hasn't expressed in the way he kisses me. The way his hands touch me in places that send me to the edge of the cliff.

I arch my back and close my eyes in time to see the kaleidoscope of colors as I fall over the edge. As I come down from the place he has taken me to, he grabs my face with both hands and just looks me in the eye. Every feeling, every emotion, every ounce of love is shared between us in this moment.

Dillon stands and steps out of the tub, holding one of my bath towels for me to step into as he wraps one around his waist and we make our way to the bed. Suddenly every doubt I had, every insecurity about what I am doing with P&Q or my life in general, is insignificant. This moment, the connection I have with Dillon, the level of emotion and love I feel for him and I know in my soul he has for me, that is what matters. None of the other stuff is important as long as this never ends.

I realize that no words have been spoken as we approach the bed. I stop and guide him and gently nudge him to sit down. I stand between his legs and as he reaches for my towel I grab his hand. "Dillon, let me." With those three words I express to him over the rest of the afternoon how much what I meant to say was, "I love you."

Chapter Thirty

WHEN THEY SAY starting a new business is like having a newborn baby, that's actually true. Well, for me it's true anyway. I haven't slept but a few hours a night since my afternoon with Dillon. He left for New York and I have been walking around with this knot in my stomach and a feeling that something bad is going to happen. I've quadruple checked every list I have, communicated with that Elizabeth Barnes woman, and Charlotte has been sending me weather updates at least five times a day. Still, I'm not feeling good about any of this. I don't dare voice any of this to anyone aloud. They will all tell me I'm being ridiculous and that I need to relax and enjoy the moment.

Yesterday, I took some time and visited Patrick. I suppose in some way I figured I could tell him everything that was scaring me or making me nervous and he couldn't judge me for it.

Hi, my love. Is it still okay to say that? I mean, I love you, and I will forever, but I've suddenly found Dillon. Thank you for him, I know you sent him to me. I don't even feel weird talking to you about Dillon. That's not true, there are certain things we won't talk about. I'm sorry for not visiting much the last few weeks. I need you to know that you are never far from my thoughts and are always in my heart.

Do you remember that first year we opened the office? What a shit show that was. If it wasn't for Mrs. Jennings and her overwhelming amount of questions and receipts we likely would have closed the doors. I miss that lady, she was so fun to have around. I stopped by there, you know? The office is still there and Charlie is really handling the business well, as I knew he would. Selling to him and Wendy was the best decision, they really remind me of us when we were just starting out.

Anyway, I have that feeling again with P&Q. Some days I sit there and wonder what I was thinking. Then, I remember that first year and how damn positive and sure of yourself you were. Where did you find all of that confidence? Couldn't you have left me some? I hear you. I hear you telling me to stop the whining and have faith in myself.

I spent the next few hours there with Patrick. I talked about Justin and told him that my mother was coming to the event. I could almost hear him laughing at my mother being in our house. In all the years we have lived here, my parents have been here maybe six times. Marian doesn't do the traditional family dinners. She prefers a waiter and bartender for her family dinners. Really, I think she just doesn't want to admit that she can't cook and refuses to wash a dish for the fear her hands will prune. My mother is a little high maintenance, what can I say?

As I glance at the clock and notice it is still dark out, the sun nowhere near gracing me with its presence. I will myself to do some meditation-style breathing and try to grab a few more hours of rest. This is going to be one hell of a day. I manage a few more hours of sleep, which is actually a restless nap but at least it's something. Once I'm up, I allow myself a long shower, hoping that it will help me wash away some of the gloom I feel.

I stare at the outfit I have hanging on my closet door and I'm not feeling it. Yes, a simple pair of capri pants and a cardigan set is perfectly acceptable, but who is that person? I look at the backup and emergency backup outfits and still no. Then it dawns on me. I go to the back of my closet and there in the dry cleaning bag is my favorite dress. It's been years since I've pulled this out. A simple cap-sleeve wrap dress in a beautiful plum color that makes me feel confident and a little sassy. I love the way it hugs my curves and makes the girls look marvelous. I pull out my leopard peep-toe shoes I haven't worn since my last online date and feel good about my choice. If I'm going to do this, I'm going to look my best and hell if these shoes don't do that.

It amazes me how every time I have an extra few hours to get things done, I manage to run late. I'm running around setting up chairs outside as Charlotte and Anna arrive to help. Justin and Sophie are supposed to be here too, but aren't. I've texted and called Justin and still haven't heard from him. When the doorbell rings I open it assuming it's going to be another delivery, but it's Justin.

"Justin, what are you doing ringing the bell? Where's Sophie and why are you holding those flowers? Come in here," I say as I step aside and let him in the door.

"Hey, Mom. I saw the delivery guy outside and offered to take these. I couldn't open the door so I rang the bell. Where do you want them?" I direct him to the entry table and grab the card as he sets them down. I don't need to read the card to know they are from Dillon.

Today will be great. I'm so very proud of you! Kick some ass! xo D

"Dillon?" Justin asks me and I just nod. "Must be with that puppy dog look on your face. Man, Mom, you really need to work on your poker face," he says as he walks past me.

"Hey, you didn't answer me. Where's Sophie?" I look at his eyes and they look so sad. Oh, this can't be good. I watch as my son shifts from foot to foot and puts his hands in his front pockets while he slowly looks me in the eyes and my heart breaks.

"We broke up. Well, no, she broke up. I got dumped."

I've admitted I didn't love this relationship, but I never wanted to see my baby hurt. Regardless if it's a skinned knee at seven years old, a broken arm at fifteen, or a broken heart at eighteen, it all sucks. I go to him and wrap him in my arms, which is no simple task since he's just about twice my size. As he steps back I see him casually wipe a tear away and my heart breaks. "I'm sorry, sweetie. I'm sure you'll work it out," I say when I know this is his first real breakup.

Justin kind of huffs and rolls his eyes before he answers me. "Yeah I doubt that. Sophie said she needs to be with someone that 'gets her needs on a more cerebral level,' whatever the hell that means. Plus she's decided to move to freaking Florida. I'm so done with chicks."

I don't even bother responding. I direct him to the back to help Anna and Charlotte. I'm about to confirm Elaine has everything set up in the den, which we've decided to use for the swag packs and display table, when the bell rings again. Seriously?

I open the door and the last person I expect to see is standing there. My mother.

"Mother." Give me a break. I didn't think she'd actually show up.

"Hello, dear. May I come in?" Manners, Victoria, you have them, might as well use them.

"Of course, sorry. I wasn't expecting you."

"No? Did Charlotte fail to tell you I would be here? I thought surely she would have told you straight away." Now, to the average person that would be a perfectly normal exchange. This is not a normal woman. That, was Marian Williams dropping the first dig. Fortunately for me, it is at the expense of my sister.

I watch as my mother walks in the door casually yet masterfully assessing everything within five feet of her. Impeccably dressed in what some women would call a "smart suit," she stops her assessment when she sees my flowers.

"What beautiful flowers."

Excuse me? "Um, thanks?"

My mother does something I've never seen: she smiles and laughs. No, it's not quite a laugh but more of a giggle or perhaps a chuckle. That is one thing, Marian Williams does not giggle and certainly she doesn't chuckle. "Don't sound so surprised, dear, they are beautiful. You must be very loved to receive such a lovely delivery. May I?" she asks me ask she motions toward the card. I can't even put together a sentence to respond, I simply nod. "Hmm. Tell me, Victoria, do you plan to 'kick ass' today? And who is D?"

Suddenly I feel like I did when I told my parents I was withdrawing from college: judgement and a disappointment. "Yes, actually, I do. And *Dillon* is my boyfriend." Obviously my mother is on medication because she just smiles and offers me a nod as she grabs my hand and squeezes. What the hell?

"Excellent. I expect nothing less from you. I'd like to meet this Dillon of yours. Will he be here soon?" I look down where she's holding my hand and then back up to her. I'm sure I look like I'm seeing a ghost, but really it is more like seeing a unicorn. Completely weird.

"Thank you," I reply as I take back my hand. "Dillon will not be here, he has business in New York today. Perhaps we can meet you and Daddy in the city for dinner one night." There I go again with the need to do the right thing. To do what is expected by the dutiful daughter. Regardless of how far apart we are, how much our relationship has had ups and downs, these are my parents.

"Oh don't be silly, we'll do dinner here in Abbott Falls. Now where is my handsome grandson? I suppose he'll put me to work." And with that my mother has blown through in true Hurricane Marian fashion. Except instead of a Category 4, this Marian was a confusing Category 2, okay maybe 1.

I stand there stunned at what has just happened and smile to myself. Perhaps a new career and new relationship aren't the only things changing in my life. It is quite possible that it is time for me to rekindle a relationship with my parents. I take a quick look at my flowers and put the card back on the arrangement before I too head to the back where all of the activity is. We have about three hours until the guests begin to arrive and I'm pleased to see we are right on schedule. Yes, schedule. Down to the quarter hour, you can't expect anything less at this point. I see Charlotte across the yard and we make eye contact. A slight nod of her head and I start toward her.

"Let's pretend to set up this spot while we try to figure out how Mom was invaded by body snatchers," Charlotte says in a rushed whisper.

"What did she say to *you*? Because she was like a Category Two with me, which is weird," I reply as I pretend to be moving a chaise around.

Taking a deep breath, Charlotte looks me in the eyes and confusingly replies, "Nothing. She said nothing. Well, not true, she did say, 'Hello, Char Char' . . . Vic, she's never called me that in my entire life. Then she said I looked lovely and offered to help me set up the last few chairs. Obviously she's sick. Someone is dying or something equally awful."

Normally I would agree with her, but this time I think our mother is finally just accepting us for who we are. "Char, you know that isn't true. Nobody is sick and nothing awful is going on. Maybe Mom just finally accepted her fate as a mother of two women that will do as they please." I actually believe the words as I say them.

After Patrick was diagnosed I completely distanced myself from everything and everyone, including my family. Of course, they were still around. I just didn't have it in me to deal with my mother and perhaps that distance actually made the difference in our relationship. The woman who was kind to me an hour ago is the woman I wished was my mother all of these years; I hope it lasts. Regardless of how old I am, how many children of my own I have, or had, I still long for a caring and supportive mother.

As we finish setting up the back with tables and chairs, I have been ordered to head inside to get ready. After a quick stop in the kitchen to check with the catering company, I decide a nice bath is just what I need. Just as I hit the first step to head upstairs, the bell rings and without a thought I grab the door to open it.

To my shock and delight there stands the man I have wished was here all along . . . I can't help but smile and let out a sigh and his name as almost a whisper, "Dillon." Then I notice the woman snuggled up next to him possessively with one arm looped through his and the other resting on his forearm. The forearm I watch as he whisks cream into frosting. The forearm I hold when he spoons me and we fall asleep together. The forearm that belongs to me. I can't even put a thought together before I hear, "Dahling, do you know this woman?"

Chapter Thirty-One

ARLING? FIRST AND foremost, who even says that any-more? Second, who is this woman and what is going on here. I'm blinking excessively, looking back and forth from Dillon to the woman to the forearm and back to Dillon. Someone needs to speak here and unfortunately for me, I seem to be rendered speech-less.

"Dillon, dahling, where are your manners? You must be Victoria, I am Elizabeth," someone says. I assume it is the woman but I am staring into the eyes of the man I have handed my heart to. The man I have shared myself with the past few months. The man I know loves me. And yet, there is a woman calling him darling and snuggled up to him. I look over to the source of the words just spoken and notice that this woman, quite beautiful and elegant in her own right, has extended her hand to me. I find myself extending my own hand as I give her a onceover. She's taller than I, a little on the thin side and, unfortunately for me, completely flawless.

"Honey," I hear that word, *my word,* and shoot my gaze to Dillon and pull my hand back. He has got to be kidding me. "Liz, can you give us a few minutes please?" Elizabeth/Liz nods and offers me a smile and a pat to *my* forearm as she walks by, leaving us standing there. I step aside and motion Dillon in. I have yet to say a single word and I am a little afraid of what will actually leave my lips when I finally do.

I head upstairs to my bedroom where I know we'll have privacy. As I open the door to my room, I have the slightest realization that the relaxing bath is out the window and the next few minutes may change my life. I sit down on my window seat as I watch him pace back and forth a few times. He's obviously upset and looks rather stressed. My heart wants to go to him, to offer him some sort of comfort for whatever is brewing in his mind. My head, however, is telling me to sit here and let him talk. I clear my throat in an effort to move this along. Regardless of what is happening in my personal life right now, I have a major author scheduled to arrive in the next ninety minutes and my home will soon be filled with people expecting a relaxing day. These people are not expecting the latest episode of a horrible reality show involving a baker, a book enthusiast, and her drama.

"I'd like to explain if I can; will you listen?" Will I listen? Do I have a damn choice? I suppose I do have a choice. I can either listen first or talk first. Talking seems to be the smarter option, in my opinion. I stand up from where I am sitting and stare Dillon in the eyes and then turn my back on him. I look out my window and see the people closest to me below coordinating and making this day happen. These people, those I trust most, are handling my business while I stand here possibly having my heart broken. I spin on my heel and look Dillon dead in the eye and my first reaction is that I love him, then I remember the *darling* woman and I am livid.

"Explain? Yes, *darling,* please do explain. Why don't you pick what you're going to explain because I'm all ears. Why don't I help you along with a few starting options?" I know I sound like a super bitch but I don't care. This was only one of a few possible reactions to this. I suppose the greatest defense is a strong offense. He did bring a woman to *my house*. He brought a beautiful woman who called him darling, damnit.

"Who is the woman? Why aren't you in New York? Who *is* that woman Dillon? I thought. . ." I pause halfway through my last thought before I look down. It seems that I may have used up all of that offense in one single rant. I want to shout, "You said you loved me!" but I don't. I can't. I just breathe and look at him waiting for something, anything to make this all make sense. Then it happens, the tears. I'm sobbing and find myself pulled against his chest; damn this man smells good. Why is he such a good hugger?

No. "No. Don't do that. Answer me." I'm not hysterical or anything. That all wasn't one huge, long sentence. Not me, the epitome of cool.

Clearing his throat, Dillon takes my hands in his and refuses to let go as I try to pull them away. "This is not how I saw this going. I am so sorry, Victoria. I swear, I tried to get here early so we could talk but my flights were delayed. I know that sounds like a cop-out but I would never hurt you. God, Victoria, I am so sorry. Nothing in my life hurt as much as seeing you standing there at the door. So obviously confused and hurt." I sit down again at the window as I let him still hold my hands. He kneels before me and lets go of a hand long enough to wipe away the tears running down my face.

"God, this has gotten so out of control. I told Liz this would happen. That stupid contract, I should have just told you anyway," he says as he stands up and starts pacing again. I have no idea what he is talking about and frankly I don't care what he told *Liz*.

"Dillon, I don't know what is going on but this is supposed to be my day. This is the event I've planned for months, the moment my business is a reality. I don't have time for this. I need you and that woman to leave." I stand and step away from him. I start to head toward my bathroom to do some damage control on the mess I've made of myself.

"No. I can't leave. I won't leave," he says just as I reach the door to the bathroom. The nerve.

"No? I'm sorry, but this is not negotiable. You need to leave and I need to pull myself together and go downstairs," I say as I walk to the sink and brush my teeth. Don't judge, I need something to do.

"That's what I'm saying, honey. I have to be here. Please, just five minutes. It will all make sense." He is so damn infuriating right now. But hell, what's another five minutes in this shit day.

"Fine," I spew as I spit in the sink, which I'm wishing was his face right now. "Five minutes."

"Thank you, come sit." Dillon motions for my window seat. Once I am sitting he takes the spot next to me and takes my hands again, gently laying a kiss to the palm. He takes a deep breath and looks me in the eye as he begins.

"Okay, first and foremost know that what I am about to say, what is the most important thing I will say, well, I planned to say it in much better circumstances. The irony of how unromantic this is, well, it's quite funny." I am not laughing but do raise an eyebrow to him encouraging him to move it along. "I love you, Victoria Bennett. With all I am, you are my happily ever after. Please believe me when I say I don't want to see you hurt."

Well, shit. "I know," I say and slightly smile. Because, regardless of what he says, I do know that he loves me. Perhaps this love isn't enough, but I don't question it.

"What do you mean, you know?" He seems quite confused at me knowing he loves me. I smile again.

"Dillon, you told me. I never said anything because you were asleep but you said it. And, you show me every time we are together that you love me." He smiles back at me and for a moment I think this is going to work out. Then he throws a curveball. Not even a curveball it's like a combination of every sports analogy rolled into one.

"The reason I'm here when I said I had business to attend to is because I am *here* for business. That woman at the door, Liz? That is Elizabeth Barnes. . ." I hear him still saying words but nothing is registering. "You've talked to her on the phone a dozen times the last few months. I can see you figuring it all out. Yes, that Elizabeth Barnes. The same woman you've talked to about today's event."

I just nod. I simply cannot think of another reaction to this. Is there an appropriate response to this? Well, there is one: "Your, your happily ever after?" So sue me, that's the most important thing he's said so far.

Gracing me with his beautiful smile and eyes full of love, "Yes, baby. My happily ever after. *Our* happily ever after. Now, shall I go on?" Dillon asks me as he kisses my palm again and I just nod. Yes, my head is likely to just bob right off my neck at this point from all the nodding.

"Oh boy, I've waited months to say this to you and really years to say it to anyone other than Liam. I am D.L. Cardwell."

Holy shit on a stick, I didn't see that coming.

"What?! That can't be. D.L. Cardwell is a woman!" I screech out, exasperated. "I mean, she must be. She writes romance." He just chuckles as he smiles that freaking smile again and I almost forget all of this is happening.

"Well, honey, I think we both know I am not a woman. It's true. I am an author, specifically a romance author. Cardwell is my mother's maiden name." I just sit there looking at this man, who, let's face it, is all man. He is brooding and sexy and my heart and soul flutter when he looks at me. I have read every book by D.L. Cardwell, admiring her writing and ability to pull me into stories and allowing me to forget my real life. He expects me to believe *he* is that same author?

This is so weird, cue the *Twilight Zone* music.

"I know you and I both have a big day and must get downstairs, but let me give you a shortened history and I'll answer any questions you have."

Oh you bet your sweet ass you'll answer my questions.

"I told you about how much I traveled when I was younger. Well, during those travels I kept a journal. At some point, I began incorporating stories I made up of the people and places I encountered. Those stories took on a life of their own and suddenly I had a book written. The only person I ever shared those stories with was Liam. Well, I didn't share as much as he found them and read them. To both of our surprise, he thought they were good and dared me to submit one to a publisher. The rest is history. They loved it, picked it up, and two grueling years and a dozen rewrites later my first novel was complete. The powers that be explained that while they felt confident in the story and my writing, they weren't certain a male romance writer would be accepted. Hence, the new name and lack of presence. When I was given the task to choose a pen name I wanted a name that mattered. My mother hasn't even made the connection." Wait, his mother doesn't know.

"Everyone has assumed D.L. Cardwell was a woman and I've allowed that. My contract with East Coast Publishing stated I must keep my identity a secret or I would be in breach of the agreement. When you and I started dating, I contacted my business manager, who coincidently is Liam, and asked that I be allowed to tell you. Unfortunately, the confidentiality clause is, or was, ironclad and I would have not only been sued but my ability to work with ECP in the future would have been impossible. Are you doing okay?"

Still no. Well, maybe I am more okay than not, but still very confused. "I'm okay, but this is a lot. Liam knew? Why couldn't you just tell me? I never would have said anything. I told you I needed honesty, Dillon. This is not honest."

"Victoria, I know. Every day I have struggled. You have been so open and honest with me about everything. I told Liam I was willing to lose it all if it meant I could be honest with you. We argued a lot about it but he convinced me that I needed to keep up my end of the contract."

So his brother encouraged him to lie to me. Wonderful. "Your brother wanted you to lie to me? I don't think Liam is my favorite person right now," I tell him frankly.

"I don't blame you. He wasn't my favorite person either. He was right though. I would have ruined everything I worked for and you not only would have been angry with me but your love of D.L. Cardwell would have been affected. The upside is that my contract was set to expire. My travels to the East Coast have been to finalize the transition from what is assumed to be a female romance writer into just me. Today is the first step of that."

Dillon is a romance writer. I suppose this explains his way with words and romantic tendencies. "Bastard." Yep, I said that out loud. "For the record, I mean both of you. You've lied to me this entire time. I feel like such a fool. I thought you were a coffee shop owner. No, you're a successful author. An author I have followed and loved for years. I'm such an idiot."

I feel so stupid. What do I do now? I have seventy-five people ready to take over my home, people waiting to meet D.L. Cardwell. Instead they are going to meet my boyfriend who makes a mean cup of java and bakes like a dream. I have to be down there.

I stand and brush the invisible lint off my shorts and put some distance between us before I speak, "Thank you for telling me this. Honestly I cannot deal with this right now. I have to be downstairs. I suppose we both do. I look like shit and need to get ready. Do you mind going down and checking in with Anna? She's going to need to take the lead with handling the author for today," I tell him.

Dillon looks at me for a long moment and then leans in to kiss me on the cheek. A part of me wants to turn my head to have those lips on mine. I want to feel the love I felt just days ago from him, the support I know he has had for me. I just can't.

"I know you are hurt, Victoria. Please believe that everything will be okay. I love you more than I ever thought I could love a person. You, baby, you are my forever. Please trust that. We'll talk after the event."

I nod in agreement and before he makes it to the door I call to him, "Dillon? I love you too."

Chapter Thirty-Two

ONCE I MANAGED to compartmentalize the bomb Dillon dropped on me, I made my way downstairs to play hostess. I was relieved to see that my team had everything ready to go and I was able to take a minute for myself. That is exactly what I had, a minute, before I was cornered and pulled into the pantry by Anna and Charlotte.

"Holy shit, Victoria! What the hell is going on? Dillon is a woman?"

Oh, for goodness sake. "No, Char, he isn't a woman, what the hell kind of question is that? I don't have time for this. I need to focus. But to clarify, Dillon is D.L. Cardwell, romance author extraordinaire. Now, we need to get back out there," I declare as I fling the door open and leave the two of them standing there.

Elizabeth, or Liz as she insisted I call her, and I spoke briefly where she apologized for any confusion. She confirmed what Dillon told me earlier, he tried to get to me to tell me everything. What she told me that he didn't, or perhaps I didn't let him, was that his confidentiality clause ended at midnight last night. That he tried to be here this morning to tell me the minute he could. Liz explained how hard he worked that last few months to get out of contract and essentially end the secrets. I understand what a tough place that put him in, I understand the frustration he must have felt but I still can't help feeling hurt. I can't help feeling that I don't really know him at all. How can I love someone who hasn't been completely honest with me? The bigger question is, can I simply move past this? Forgive him?

With only a few minor hiccups throughout the day, I can declare the first official author event of Pages & Quiet is a success. At first, I was worried about how the guests would react to D.L. Cardwell's true identity, but both my mother and Liz assured me everything would be fine. They were right; the guests - mostly women - loved the idea that there has been a mystery this entire time. Beyond the mystery, they were very pleased that such a "handsome and obviously in-love man was bringing them such amazing stories." Well, at least that's what they told me when they thanked me for allowing them to be the first to find out. I didn't have the heart to tell them I was the lucky number one and allowed them to bask in their glory as the first in the know.

I found myself conflicted throughout the day. I alternated between admiring Dillon and how much success he had found as an author, and brooding over how much the man hurt me. Watching his fans interact with him, I was so proud. Then the reality of what was happening and who he was would hit me and I was hurt again. I wanted one person at this event, other than me, to be outraged. Not even Anna was visibly pissed; that was confusing. I shouldn't say that. She was plenty angry and gave him a piece of her mind, but he was able to calm her down enough to offer an apology. Justin asked Dillon if he thought he could be a romance writer and have all the ladies pining for him. Thankfully, Dillon just laughed and told him he could be whatever he wanted.

As the late afternoon approached and the guests started leaving, I checked in with Elaine, who confirmed that the day was a success and she managed to book a few book club parties. Overall this has been a wonderful first full-scale event and I am proud of myself and my team. I should mark this day down as a point in history because you may never hear this again, thank goodness for my mother. She was definitely a force to be reckoned with and managed to keep everyone on task. I don't even bother thanking her as she ties things up with the caterer and decide to step outside for a minute to myself.

Once I'm in my private reading nook, I slip off my shoes - cute and empowering but really not a smart choice for being on your feet for hours - and settle in when a glass of wine appears in front of me. I don't even look to see the person handing it to me because I know it is Anna. Both Anna and Charlotte sit on the end of my chaise as I take my first sip.

"Thank you," I say.

I brace myself for a lecture from these two for my behavior today as Anna speaks first. "So, do we hate or love Dillon? I need to get my emotions on track before I leave."

I can't help but smile. She's really leaving today for destination unknown. I almost feel like inviting myself. "Honestly?" I ask them and they both nod in affirmation. "Both," I say with reservation. "Actually, that's not true. I don't hate him. I hate what he's made me feel and I am so damn pissed off at him and myself I want to cry." It's true, I don't hate him.

I keep talking, "I'm mostly embarrassed and feel like a fool. Then there are the other feelings. He loves me. He wants a happily ever after with me. I love him so much. I think that is why this hurts so badly. I'm just so confused. Is it all worth it? How do I get past the betrayal I feel?"

This is the moment I expect Anna to invoke her wisdom, but instead it's my sister who speaks. "Maybe you don't. Maybe you just accept that he did this because there was no way out of it. Quite frankly I don't see it as betrayal. I know honesty is a huge thing for you. I know that you needed him to tell you what was happening but I heard him talking to Mom. Who, by the way, really seems smitten with Dillon herself." I raise an eyebrow to this and Charlotte simply shrugs. Really, who can blame any woman for being slightly smitten with Dillon. "Anyway, Mom was a little hard on him at first for springing all of this on you. Dillon was very apologetic to her, well to all of us, and he explained to her the confidentiality clause. Vic, he could have lost everything."

I know all of this, but it's still frustrating and then I remember confidentiality didn't include everyone. "Did he tell Mom or either of you that his brother knew? That Liam was the one that convinced him to lie to me. Not just keep a secret, but to intentionally lie. Every time he went to New York or had to be on a conference call, he was lying. I'm not sure I can forgive that."

I take another sip, okay large sip, of my wine when Anna finally blurts out, "What an asshole."

I choke a little on my wine as I look at her, a little confused, and Charlotte smacks her. "Ouch! Damn, Charlotte, that hurt. I'm sure there was some sort of loophole. He could have called me for some legal advice. Then at least one of us would have known this big secret." She's completely serious. I look at her with a raised brow to remind her this is not about her. "Right, not about me."

I smile and ask her, "Do you think I should forgive him? You seem to be dancing around the subject and that's not you."

Anna looks at me and I can see her searching for the words to convey what she means to say while not hurting me anymore than I already am. "I knew. And truly I don't think there's anything to forgive. He didn't lie, he didn't cheat, and he didn't intend to hurt you.

This is more about you than it is about his secret."

I hear her say the words, but they don't compute. "What do you mean, you knew. You knew he was a romance author? And, for the record I know he didn't outright lie and I truly believe he would never intentionally hurt me."

Anna laughs and shakes her head. "No, silly. I didn't know that he was a romance author. Who would guess *that*?" she asks and we all start laughing; that feels good. "I knew he loved you as much as he's saying. Look, I have to leave for the airport, but I want you to know that I think you should forgive him. You've been given a gift, Victoria. Love doesn't come around for everyone and you've had two wonderful men love you with all that they are. Don't let that go."

I look at Charlotte, waiting for her to chime in. "I agree. I think you have a great guy that loves you and wants to be with you. He screwed up. He's not perfect, Vic. Let him love you."

Anna scoots over and gives me a hug as she says, "I love you very much. I want you to live life and let Dillon love you. He is your forever. I may never have that; perhaps I don't even deserve it. But you do. You really do."

I sit and contemplate what both Anna and Charlotte have said as I watch them walk back toward the house. Anna is leaving for someplace in this world for an undetermined length of time and, as I watch her walk toward the door, I feel like I'm watching a part of me walk away. I know it's not forever, but everything is changing and there is so much I need her for. I hope she finds what she needs on this trip and that she comes back whole.

I continue to lay in this spot that brings me so much peace and contemplate all that has happened today when I look up to see my mother walking toward me. She's smiling. That's a new expression.

She motions toward the end of the chaise as she begins talking. "May I?" I nod in agreement as she sits down. "So this has been an eventful day. How are you holding up?" How am I holding up? That's a loaded question. "This chaise is plenty big for two, scoot over and let your mother next to you," she says. For some reason, I do.

"Your home is beautiful, Victoria. And that grandson of mine? Amazing. I'm sorry I've missed so much with you. I've been terribly selfish all these years. I hope you can forgive me."

After all this time being somewhat estranged from my parents, well my mother specifically, I have never been more grateful to have her nearby. It's true, no matter how old you are, how many children of your own you have and how much you go through in life, your family just gets you.

"I suppose talking about all I've missed is a conversation for another time. You have enough on your plate today." Now if that isn't the understatement of the year. I don't even know how to process this new Marian so I'm just going to table it for another time.

"Thank you, Mom. Justin is pretty spectacular. I'm very proud of him," I tell her. We sit there in silence for a few minutes before I speak again. "And thank you for today. You really saved my ass. I suppose I didn't kick as much ass today as I had planned." I know I sound defeated, but truly, I don't feel much like I did the ass kicking as opposed to having my own ass kicked.

"Oh dear, I think that is where you are wrong. You kicked major ass today. I am very proud of you. I don't think many people would have handled so much chaos and emotion with such grace and professionalism. No, I would say you kicked today's ass," she says matter-of-factly.

My mother is obviously confused about what happened today. I might as well ask her the million-dollar question. "What are your thoughts on this Dillon situation?" She smiles as I look off to the other side of the yard. My eyes immediate find the man himself. He's so at ease talking to a few lingering guests who seem thrilled for the attention. I have to admit, he's just about perfect.

"He's quite handsome, isn't he?" my mother asks me. I can't do anything but nod in agreement and smile.

"You asked me about my thoughts. I am far from qualified to offer an opinion on your life but I do have one. Dillon loves you. I don't say that because he told me, which he did. Repeatedly. No, I am saying that because I can see it in everything he does. The way he is with your sister and Anna, how he was with Justin today, and what he said to the guests about you and P&Q. He was right. What you've done here, what you've accomplished? It's wonderful. I also know he couldn't tell you about who he was even though he wanted to. I think you should accept his apology and let that man love you for the rest of your life. "

Right on cue, my cellphone chimes a text message.

I just wanted to tell you I love You. Always.

I look at the text and feel my eyes fill with tears as I blink them away. Always. For the rest of my life. It seems so simple, but can I just let it all go? The level of betrayal I feel? Then my mother says it: "Patrick would want you to forgive him and to be happy."

Damn her, she pulled out the big guns. She's right. "Mom, this isn't the life I planned. All of this heartache and drama. I just wanted to be happy and be loved," I tell her, defeated.

As my mother grabs my hand in hers, she lets out a little sigh. "I suppose it isn't the life you planned. Truly, who has a life that is planned? How boring would that be? Besides, life is full of unexpected twists but it is also full of gifts. I didn't plan on having a second child but I wouldn't give up having your sister. She is the best twist in my life. Instead of worrying about the life you planned, love the life you have. This is your life, Victoria, your life rewritten."

Life rewritten, how fitting. I have to agree with her; it is true.

"I am going to leave now. I believe you owe that man a conversation. I will call you in a few days to check in and schedule that dinner. Let him love you, honey; you deserve it." In true Marian Williams fashion, she is up and making her way across the yard as quickly as she appeared. I watch as she stops and talks to Dillon in the yard before heading into the house.

Dillon begins walking toward me, albeit a little cautiously. As he approaches, I don't move and he motions for the spot my mother just vacated. I motion back for him to take the spot. An olive branch.

"Today was amazing. You did a wonderful job. I'm proud of you." I can't even respond to this because I'm not sure I can keep from crying or throwing myself at him. "Have you decided if you hate or love me yet?"

I smile, remembering Anna asking me the same question. I have decided but I don't know that I have it in me for this conversation. "Hmm, well that is the million-dollar question isn't it? Honestly?" I ask him and he nods. "I think I have but I also know that we need to have a long conversation and that I need a little time. Do you think you can give me that? Let me decompress and process?"

"I understand, I'll just head home and give you some time. You'll call me when you are ready to talk?" He is so sincere and while my instinct is to wrap my arms around his neck and tell him I love him. I need this time. I agree to call him when I'm ready and walk with him to the door. I notice as we go that everything is almost back in order and everyone has left.

When we reach the front door, Dillon turns back to me. "I love you, just remember that." I nod and let him pull me into a hug and kiss the top of my head.

Chapter Thirty-Three

ONCE DILLON LEAVES, I begin locking up the house. I grab a movie, bottle of wine, and a few snacks before I make my way to my room and that bath I promised myself hours ago. As I soak in the tub and enjoy the wine, I remember the time Dillon surprised me, the hours that followed, the complete happiness I felt. Why am I being such a jerk about all of this? If a friend came to me with this situation I would encourage her to look past the secret and look at all the positive. I would tell her to allow herself happiness instead of trying to convince herself she doesn't deserve it. I do deserve it. I want it. I have it. I have a second chance at a wonderful love.

I've settled into my comfy pajamas and put in the only kind of movie I can handle at this point – horror. I can't even fathom a romantic comedy or even an action movie. It's likely the action movie will have some sort of hero setting out to save the day and I could do without that. No, in a funk like this where I need to decompress only one movie is the answer – *Scream*. Nothing could be further from where I am in my life than a story of a pissed-off serial killer picking off teenagers in a small town while wearing some sort of Halloween costume.

Something my mother said to me earlier is really bothering me. She mentioned Patrick and that he would want me to forgive Dillon. I know that Patrick was a forgiving man and always looked to the good in everyone. He also was very sure of himself and us. I can't help but remember our first date.

I went into our first date so completely convinced I would get the date over with and never have to see the infuriating man again. I spent almost an entire semester dodging him and figured accepting his invitation was the only way to put an end to it. Patrick picked me up in his immaculately detailed car, dressed casual but as if he did put some effort into it and attempted to woo me. I was determined not to be wooed.

"You know I don't plan for this to go past dinner, right?" I snarkily asked him as I buckled my seat belt and turned to look at him.

"Oh, I know you *think* you don't plan for this to go past diner. I, on the other hand know better. Just you wait, Victoria, this night is going to change your life," he confidently told me as he pulled away from the curb. Damn if he wasn't right. We spent the entire evening laughing and talking. I had dated a bit up until that point but it wasn't ever anything I took seriously. I was twenty years old and a plan was in place for me. A plan I had accepted and was committed to. Finish college, find a teaching job, eventually find a man to marry, live a comfortable and predictable life and give my parents grandchildren.

All of that seemed like the perfect plan until I met Patrick Bennett. The first thing he told me on that date, other than my life would change, was that he was always Patrick and never Pat because that was his granddad. Once he had established his name, he simply let me be me and took the time to know me.

"Victoria, what is it you want in life? You've told me this plan that has been told to you by your parents but I just don't feel like that is what you want." I had never given it much thought up until that point but it was right.

"Honestly?" I asked him. He nodded between bites of his pizza and wiggled his eyebrows to encourage me to keep talking. "I want to be a mom. I know that is part of the plan but I want to be a full-time mom. My mother, well, she wasn't really hands on when I was little. She is more involved with my younger sister which is great, for her, but I want it to be different with my kids." Saying it aloud was freeing in some way. I continued, "My mother spent my childhood supporting my father and his career. My father was always the priority and I never felt anything more than second best to that, until my sister was born. Then I felt like a distant last in the scheme of things. I know my mother loves me but the childhood I had, it wasn't what I want for my children."

I half expected Patrick to run for the hills at that revelation. Instead he surprised me, "Well, then that's what we'll do."

I looked at him, confused, while choking a little on my pizza before stammering out a response, "Excuse me? We? Aren't you jumping the gun a little there, pal? Let's get through dinner before you start planning our wedding."

This memory brings a smile to my face and reminds me that we did have a good life. An excellent life. I'm fully engrossed in the movie while Tilly snores lightly on the floor next to my bed when I swear I hear something outside. I assume it is just my mind playing tricks, I mean I am watching a horror movie after all. It is when I hear a scratching noise for the third time I figure it is time to investigate. This is when I wish I had taken those self-defense classes with Charlotte. Or the gun classes with Anna. My guard dog? Still sleeping. She's of no help, that's for sure. I grab the only thing remotely close to a weapon – a pair of stilettos.

As I descend the stairs toward the first floor I notice that it's gotten quite windy out and a storm is obviously coming. That probably explains the noise. I feel silly as I look at my "weapons" of choice. I set the weapons down on the entry table next to the beautiful flowers that Dillon sent this morning and head into the kitchen for some rocky road. I mean I am down here, might as well make it worthwhile. I'm pulling out the container of ice cream when I hear another noise outside. I should make sure it isn't a flying chair or something and head to the back door. Just as I reach for the handle I see a man's face and scream for my life.

I flip the light on as I reach for the phone to call the police. As I'm about to pick up the receiver I notice the face belongs to Dillon. What the hell? I fling the door open. "You scared the shit out of me! What the hell are you doing?" While I'm yelling I notice it is now raining and he is soaked. I step aside and motion him in as I go to the laundry room to grab a towel. When I get close enough, I throw it at him as I cross my arms over my chest in frustration.

"Thanks and sorry for scaring you," he says as he uses the towel to dry his hair and then he begins to peel off his shirt. Seriously? With the abs?

"Well, it's my own fault. I'm watching Scream. But really, what are you doing out there? And when did it start storming?" I ask him as I put the ice cream back in the freezer and reach for the kettle. It looks like Dillon could use some tea instead.

"The rain just started when you came in the kitchen," he tells me as he sits down on a barstool. "Not that I was spying. I wasn't, I swear. I said I would give you your space and I meant it. I just . . . I, uh, realized I dropped something earlier and needed to get it."

"What could be so important that you had to come here in the makings of a storm? You know anything left would be safe. You had your phone when you left so what was it?" I ask him as I ready our mugs for tea. I can see him contemplating whether or not to tell me what he came here for.

"It was just something important. I should be going. Call me when you're ready," Dillon says as he gets up, grabs his shirt, and heads toward the front door.

"Wait," I say before he gets too far. Shit. I'm afraid if I let him go this will hurt us. I need to address this now, before I thought I would but when I need to.

He stops and turns around and smiles. "Are you sure? We don't have to do this. I told you I would wait and I will." That is why we have to do this; he is the person I need, no want, in my life.

"Come sit with me. I've decided," I tell him as I take a seat on the couch, crossed-legged and facing him when he sits down.

He turns to me with a slightly confused look on his face. "Decided?"

I smile. "Yes, decided. You asked me earlier if I decided if I hated or loved you. I never answered you."

"Before you tell me, can I just remind you that I love you. I suspect I started falling in love with you from the first day we talked in Irish Coffee. I knew you were going to forever be part of my heart that day you burned a pan of chocolate. I believe in moments, moments that matter and change the course of your path. You are my moment, Victoria."

I smile at the memory of that burned chocolate and all the memories since then. He continues as he gently rubs circles on the top of my hand, "I am so sorry for keeping such a huge part of me from you. I suffered like you can't believe. Victoria, you are the air I breathe. I want us to be together. I want to write books and I want to watch you grow your business. I want to take walks with you and Tilly. I want to watch Justin graduate and hold your hand while you sob uncontrollably because you are just that mom. I want to be the last man you ever go on a first date with. I want to be the reason there are no more first dates for you. Please tell me you love me and we can have all of that."

"First, you are really going to have to scale back on all the perfect words. You make me feel so inferior," I tease as I lean in and lay a simple kiss to his lips and feel his grip on my hands tighten. "I won't lie, I was very hurt. I felt betrayed and lied to. I know, you didn't technically lie and you had no choice but to keep this from me. In my head I know that. In my heart I even know that. It was my initial reaction, but now? I'm really okay. I mean, I don't know how I feel about my favorite romance author being my boyfriend but I'm sure I'll get used to that. I have a really long list of questions on characters and storylines. I mean, really, why in *Undeniable Secrets* did Tucker disappear all those months? You never explained that and. . ."

I'm still talking when he takes my face and kisses me. Not the kind of kiss like I gave him just minutes ago. No, this is a kiss of promises and unsaid words. "Stop," he says as he releases my face and grabs my hands again. "I love you, but I am not going to talk about my books right now. We can save that for morning." I let out a little laugh in response and then I notice he is no longer holding my hands and is now he's on the ground. What in the world?

It takes me a few seconds to realize what he's doing. I blink rapidly, as I see he is holding a small square box in his hands. "This is why I came back. I've been carrying this with me for days. I had plans. I had a plan to get here to you this morning, to wake you up, to love you and make love to you. To tell you everything and then I screwed it up. I love you, honey," he says as he opens the box and a beautiful diamond stares at me. Holy shit, this has escalated quickly.

"Dillon," I barely whisper because I'm crying. Not 'beautiful my boyfriend is proposing to me' crying, no 'I am ugly snotty' crying. A Hallmark moment this isn't. "Dillon, I love you. So very much. I'm sorry I freaked out earlier. This is just . . . it's just not the life I thought I'd have." I watch as his face falls and by the expression I realize how my words sounded. "No, no. I don't mean it like that!" I exclaim as I shift to my knees so that I'm facing him. "You are an amazing man. I love you more than is even possible in a normal life. Ask me. Please."

I can't believe this is happening. Dillon smiles at me as he removes the ring from its little velvet home and holds it up to me with his perfect smile. The smile meant only for me. This moment is completely overwhelming. When I sat down in Irish Coffee with a business plan and a slight crush on a handsome coffee shop owner, I never expected this moment to happen. The connection we share is undeniable; I know this is our happily ever after.

"Victoria Bennett, I love you more than the sun and the moon combined. You came into my life at a time that I thought I was destined to be alone forever and changed my world. I have never been as happy as I am when we are together. Please make me the happiest man in the world, and say you'll be mine forever, be my happily ever after."

The best part of loving a writer? The words.

"Dillon, I love you so much. You make my days better and I see forever when I look at you. I would love nothing more than to be your happily ever after," I say as he places the ring on my finger and kisses me so passionately I can feel my pulse racing and my heart beating out of my chest.

One kiss to turns to another and suddenly we're both without our clothes, on the couch, kissing, caressing, touching, loving. We are just together, exactly as it should be. Exactly as it is meant to be. After giving me what may possibly be the best orgasm of my life, he pulls me to him so I'm slightly resting on him, my leg over his, and covers us with the blanket on the couch. I take this time to catch my breath and admire my ring. Crap on a cracker, this is a hell of a rock! I am simply in awe. Of this moment, this ring, and mostly this man. My mother was right, again. Okay, twice in one day, mark that down.

I deserve this. I snuggle into Dillon's side as he puts his arm around me and kisses the top of my head.

"Baby, what did you mean earlier when you said this wasn't the life you planned?" Dillon asks me.

I lift myself up so I'm looking at him, laying a hand to his cheek before I answer. "Dillon, I didn't mean it like it sounded. I've always thought I needed plan. A way of keeping things organized in my life. Plans require lists and you know I love a good list." I say with a sincere smile and nothing but love in my words. "Those lists? They have never prepared me for actual life. No, all those lists have done is set me up for disappointment. The life I have today? It was never planned, it was never on my list. This life, the life we are building together? This is my life. The life I want. The life I deserve. It is our life, Dillon. It's *our life rewritten.*"

From the author

When I started this process I had no plan and no expectation. Today, I have a slight plan and perhaps wishes but still no expectations. This journey has been somewhat of an adventure and has changed the person I am and the person I want to be. Through the words on these pages, through these emotions, and through these characters I have found that life isn't about plans or expectations. Life, this journey we are all on, is about moments and the people we share them with.

If you take nothing away from this story, take the idea that you should embrace the today you have because you never know what tomorrow will bring. Never allow an opportunity to pass you by simply because you are too afraid of not having a plan or meeting your expectations. Within each moment is the chance that amazing things are happening.

Your life is a book and you have the ability to write the story, make it count.

Acknowledgements

First and foremost, thank you to every single person that has read Victoria's story. Without you, none of this would be possible. It should be noted that I have written this section no less than a dozen times. I am forever humbled by the number of people in my life that have supported me. Thank you.

Immeasurable gratitude to those that have made this possible: my editor, Kristina Cireclli, for your patience and guidance; Stacey Blake, your formatting is on point and I appreciate you; and Jada D'Lee, I am continuously in awe of your talent and for creating a cover beyond my wildest dreams; my web designer and photographer, Andrea of Stuck in North Idaho, thank you for your beautiful work and for managing to make my chaotic and unhelpful ideas a reality; and my publicist, Erin Spencer and the team at Southern Belle Promotions, you have made this process possible.

An extremely heartfelt thank you to Heather Lyons. Heather, your unconditional friendship and support has been instrumental in this entire process. There will never be a word or series of words to convey my level of gratitude. You inspire me.

Suzie, through your words and my epic stalking skills came one of the greatest treasures of my life. You, my friend, are a gem. Thank you for telling me I can do this and for answering the most ridiculous questions imaginable.

Casey, thank you for never letting me psych myself out, for always being there, and for encouraging me. Your honesty was pivotal in my process and I am forever grateful. You inspire me every day to enjoy this journey.

Christine, I don't know if I can even express the level of love I have for you. The fact that you listened to me (read me) almost daily for a year while I chugged a cup of self-doubt and never cut me off is phenomenal. Thank you for loving Victoria and Dillon (almost) as much as me.

Stephanie, thank you for telling me every day that I deserve this. Your patience with my insecurities has never gone unappreciated. Your friendship means the world to me.

Tricia, I love you. Your passion for reading and writing is a force. You gave me the extra push every single day and without you there would be no book. Thank you for stepping outside of your comfort zone and falling a little in love with Victoria and Dillon.

Deanna, Nanci, Jessica, JoAnn, Amanda & Sandi - Each of you has encouraged me when I needed it most. You have told me I deserve this and supported every word I have written. Your friendships are limitless and I am grateful for that and you every day.

Amy, Jennifer and Tracy - thank you for spending time with Victoria and Dillon. Your insight, care, eagle eyes, and willingness to support this endeavor is forever appreciated.

For every author, blogger, and fellow book lover that I have "met". *Thank you*. I have found a tribe through the love of words and without all of you I would never be in this moment.

IWYLM community and page admin family, without any of you I would never have had the courage to write.

Aunt Christy- Thank you for reading the earliest draft of Life Rewritten (when it had a different name) and liking it enough to keep me going. You took a chance on me and were honest - I can never repay you for that.

Family and friends- Thank you for supporting ME without question. When I said I was writing a book you stepped up to offer kindness and encouragement and I am so completely bewildered by that and forever grateful.

My boys, thank you for inspiring me every day. I am so damn proud of both of you and the young men you are. This book is proof that if you believe in yourself enough you can accomplish anything. It's never too late to follow your dreams. I love you both to the moon and back.

My husband and soul mate - Thank you for loving me unconditionally and for encouraging me to follow my dream. You are my happily ever after and I am forever grateful for our moments.

About the Author

Andrea Johnston spent her childhood with her nose in a book and a pen to paper. An avid people watcher, her mind is full of stories that yearn to be told. A fan of angsty romance with a happy ending, super sexy erotica and a good mystery, Andrea can always be found with her Kindle nearby fully charged.

Andrea lives in Idaho with her family and two dogs. When she isn't spending time with her partner in crime aka her husband, she can be found binge watching all things Bravo and enjoying a cocktail. Nothing makes her happier than the laughter of her children, a good book, her feet in the water, and cocktail in hand all at the same time.

Connect:

Website: www.andreajohnstonauthor.com

Facebook: www.facebook.com/andreajohnstonauthor

Goodreads: https://www.goodreads.com/author/show/14151380.
Andrea_Johnston

Twitter: https://twitter.com/AndreaJ1313